THE GRAND CONSPIRACY

What the corporatist system is telling us in various ways is that the democratic system is no longer appropriate. This attitude involves the active or passive agreement of large parts of our elite.--John Ralston Saul.

THE GRAND CONSPIRACY

A NEW YORK LIBRARY MYSTERY

by

David Beasley

SIMCOE
DAVUS PUBLISHING
BUFFALO

DAVUS SUM/ NON OEDIPUS

Any similarity of any character or any situation in this novel with real persons or actual situations is purely coincidental.

copyright 1997, David R. Beasley

My thanks to Gladys Todd and Violet Beasley for suggesting improvements in the manuscript.

Beasley, David, 1931-
    The grand conspiracy: A New York library mystery

ISBN 0-915317-06-0

I. Title.

PS8553.E14G73 1996   C813'.54   C96-900671-3
PR9199.3B3762G73 1996

DAVUS PUBLISHING

CANADIAN ORDERS TO
150 Norfolk St. S.,
Simcoe, On N3Y 2W2

AMERICAN ORDERS TO
P O Box 1101
Buffalo, N.Y. 14213-7101

ONE

When I walked into my office at the New York Public Research Libraries, my wide-hipped secretary handed me a note with a concerned look. "I took the message about ten minutes ago."
"Is that word 'help'?" I asked, frowning.
She took the note back and read with dramatic urgency. "I'm in trouble. Please help me, Arbie."
I smiled appreciatively. "Where is she?"
"At her Local Headquarters."
"Call her, will you, please."
I went into my office, took off my coat, and stood for a moment to let the air-conditioning cool the hot perspiration off my back. It was another scorching August day in New York City. My phone rang.
"Hello, Arbuthnott?"
"Oh Rudy! Thank God you called! I've just heard something that frightens the be-jesus out of me."
"Calm down, then tell me what's wrong," I said slowly.
She took a deep breath. "The man who runs the messenger service on the floor below me here, you know, the one about my size with the dirty blond hair like mine? He was just knifed eleven times in the waist."
"Just this morning?"
"No, no, last night about eight o'clock, when he was locking up."
"Where were you?" I asked, alarmed.
"Upstairs, getting the ballots ready for mailing on the thirty-hour work week." Arbie paused, sensing my relief, and brought her voice down to a lower register. "A fireman next door told me. One of the girls downstairs heard a commotion, saw a black guy dash down the stairs and the manager sprawled on the landing. The firemen rushed him to the hospital."
"Didn't you hear anything?"
"Nothing," she admitted, "but I'm at the back, and we've got an iron door. I came down about nine o'clock, and the only thing I noticed was, when I passed the open door where the girls are, one of them, sitting on a chair, saw me and looked scared shitless."
"Yeah," I said. "Well, it's over with now. They got their man. They won't be back."
"No, Rudy, they did not get their man," Arbie said, echoing my matter-of-fact tone. "I was their man."
"You!" I cried, amused. "How do you know that?"
"Because I figured it out. Are you coming over?"
I looked at my watch. "As soon as I check out the building."
I found it incredible that anyone would want to kill Arbuthnott Vine, President of the Library Union. True, she was fighting the City to stop the lay-offs and making enemies in high places. I had told her to cool her stance, play the game for the time being, but she was not the compromising kind. She did everything with directness and great

energy. In fact, that was how she made love. I felt a sudden satisfaction as I picked up my coat and set forth to tour the Central Building.

"Everything okay?" my secretary asked, her eyebrows sprung high.

"For the time being," I said. I rather liked this secretary. Within ten steps I began to sweat. A guard stood like an ebony statue at the Fifth Avenue entrance. In the heat the guards signaled readers with their eyes to open their cases and purses for inspection. I climbed the marble stairway to the second floor, ambled along the corridor to the Business Office, stuck my head in the door and felt the cool air-conditioning.

"Nothing today," Bugofsky's secretary said vaguely, "except maybe this." She held out a legal size letter. "Something from the union."

"Could be important," I smiled, pocketing it. "Hear anything from Sharkey?"

"A post card from the Bahamas," she said, picking it up and waving it at me.

I took it, glanced at yachts in a harbor, and read the greetings-- "In a sunny land with great bars" from Sharkey Bugofsky.

"Trust him to find the bars," his secretary giggled.

"He's having a good time." I returned the card. "I'll call in later."

Actually, I was having a good time, free of that petty carping and drunken fury which characterized the business manager. I checked with the guard on the second floor.

"Had trouble in Economics with one guy, Rudy," the guard said. "A flasher-- you know, the old guy, Rubinowitz."

"Back again!"

"He flashed two dolls. I heard 'em screamin' all the way down here like someone bein' murdered. Then I bumped into our little friend tryin' to get out the door. We gave 'im to the cops." The guard, a tall young man, smiled. "He kept laughin' away to hisself, like it was a big joke."

"What happened to the women?" I frowned.

"They went out for a drink."

On the third floor, I checked the stone benches set before the wall frescoes of naked men and women of olden days. A Puerto Rican had hung out on these benches after killing two young women in a much-publicized case. Today, I recognized a resident playwright, brooding, and a woman tourist, carrying a camera and studying the frescoes on the ceiling.

I stopped by the guard at the entrance to the reading halls. Bugofsky, alarmed by the number of books being stolen, had replaced the benign Irishmen with fierce-looking Asians.

"No problem today, sir." The guard spoke in a South Indian sing-song.

In the South Hall, I surveyed the readers hunched over their books. The librarian, a thoughtful-looking young man with thick glasses, looked up expectantly.

"How's everything?" I asked. I made it a point to be friendly with the library staff, who had a tendency to regard me with suspicion and, on occasion, with disdain. They tolerated the guards as fixtures, like necessary furniture, but the library detective seemed to symbolize disruption.

"Everything's just fine," the librarian mumbled with an undertone of sarcasm.

Noticing the playwright glide past on his way to the Wertheim Study walled off in one corner of the South Hall, I asked, "Everything all right in the Wertheim Study?"

"Why shouldn't it be," said the librarian, "despite the weirdoes."

I watched dumbwaiters bring up books from the stacks while I waited for the freight elevator. My thoughts returned to Arbuthnott Vine and her fear that someone wanted to kill her. Arbie had a finely developed sixth sense, which was why she held onto the union presidency despite management's attempts to unseat her with its staff candidates. This thought reminded me of the letter from the union to Bugofsky which I now took out of my pocket. It was from Hector Bratwurst, the Executive Director of the Union Council, whom Arbie referred to as the Big Blast Himself. It began, "Dear Sharkey." Arbie said that Hector never communicated directly with the Local presidents he represented but remained on the chummiest of terms with their bosses, those directors and business managers whom Arbie called "The Enemy."

I stepped into the freight elevator, dented, and blackened by book trucks, which had banged its walls for decades, and read the letter under the solitary light bulb.

> This is to confirm our agreement by phone. You give us agency shop, we give you management responsibilities, etc.
> Yours, Hector

I smiled. There was not a Local in New York that had agency shop. It was a big deal when the union could get management to agree to make everyone on its staff pay union dues whether or not he or she was a union member. I wondered what was the union giving up in return? "Management responsibilities" could mean almost anything.

The ranges on the first stack were crammed to the point where volumes had to be piled on the floor. Turning through the Jewish Division and nodding at the guards at the 42nd Street exit, I passed into the street, cut across at a break in traffic, went through the hallway of the building opposite, and came to Arbie's small building wedged between the fire station and a mammoth block of offices. A white-haired, easy-going Jewish guy from Brooklyn had run the coffee shop on the first floor and rented the back half of the fourth and top floor to the Library Local for token money, then sold the building and joined the exodus to the suburbs. Before he left, Arbie asked him who was fixing up the second floor with what looked like little offices. "A university study group," he had said without batting an eye. The next week, girls in bathing suits sat by the door and waited for customers who were lured up the steps by scruffy men with leaflets. Arbie knew that organized crime had persuaded the owner to move to the suburbs. But when the massage parlor called itself "The Library" and billed its girls as "librarians," she sensed that her Library Guild, two floors above, was being targeted. But by whom? and why?

As I climbed the stairs by the massage parlor, a buxom, dark-skinned lady in a skimpy red swimsuit and high heels swung her hips at me from the doorway. I smiled appreciatively. The messenger service was the only business on the third floor. As I turned up the stairs to the fourth, I stood for a moment. From here I could see the door to the messenger service on the third floor and the door to the Library Guild's office on the fourth floor. Neither door was marked. The messenger office was used only by its own messengers while the Library Guild's sign had come unstuck and been lost. The knifer could have picked this spot because he wasn't sure which door belonged to the Library Guild. Luckily for Arbie, it was the manager of the messenger service who closed up first. Arbie had good reason to suspect that she had been the real target. It was unlikely that a disgruntled messenger boy had decided to wipe out the manager of the messenger service.

I continued up the stairs and rapped hard on the steel door to the Library Guild's office .

"Who's there?" Arbie's husky voice demanded.

"Rudyard Mack, library detective, at your service."

The bolt shot back, and the door opened to the pretty face, high breasts, and lithe hips of the girl I had been sleeping with for the past year.

"Oh, Rudy, I'm glad you've come at last." She kissed my face and lips, then pulled away. "Ever since I heard about the poor man downstairs, I've been scared stiff. Do you know the killer missed his vital organs by a fraction of an inch?"

"He took eleven strokes and didn't get one vital organ!" I cocked an eyebrow. "He must have been a circus performer, or a rank incompetent."

"He was a rank incompetent," Arbie said, leading the way through the outer room with its long meeting table and chairs to her inner office. "And I'm glad it wasn't me he was incompetent with."

She flopped down on the leather chair behind the huge desk she had bought second-hand as I unfolded a metal chair. The three large windows in Arbie's office remained shuttered because they looked out on the cement backs of other buildings and Arbie was afraid they might be left open by mistake. The Guild had little of value worth stealing other than the lives of its officers. That is why there were three iron bars across all windows save one where there was an air conditioner, which was distant enough from the fire escape for one to believe that an intruder could not reach it without slipping and falling to his death on the cement below.

"Tell me why you think," I said carefully, "that you were the intended victim."

"Let's look at the options," Arbie said, holding up her fingers like a union negotiator and grasping them one by one. "One, the killer is a psychotic who hates women and was waiting to ice one of the massage dames. Two, he hated the messenger service because it wouldn't pay him for delivering a week of messages. Three, some newspapers are beginning to highlight me as the most democratic union leader in town because I'm the liberal threat to the bankers and their union allies who want to shut down the City, hence I'm seen in some high places as a little punk getting too big for her britches."

"Any more?"

"Four, I'm starting a coalition of liberal and left wing forces which could upset the bankers' plans, so I have to be eliminated before I get big enough in the news where my death by mugging might raise questions."

"That's pretty close to number three," I said.

"If you weren't so indulgent," Arbie said, "you might think seriously about what I'm saying."

I laughed. "I think I like number one. The killer was a psychotic."

"Ah, Rudy, honey, come on. I need you?" Arbie pouted. "I'm all alone against these bastards."

"How about your executive board?" I asked with a note of sympathy.

She patted the air as if bouncing away an unwanted ball. "Most of them don't know what's happening and never will. They think the District Council is like a Knight Crusader when it talks for us with the ugly politicians. I've got three who are tied up with those sleazy Democratic Party clubs which are playing ball with the bankers. Only one guy's a Socialist and has a real clue as to what it's all about. I mean, he sees the Big Picture. But," she raised her arms in a hopeless gesture, "he's a Trotskyite: I can never tell whose side he's on in any one question."

"You think he's for you, though."

"He calls me a 'progressive,'" she raised her eyebrows, "which means I'm so tolerant I can be used for any left wing program they got on their minds."

"You don't trust him then?" I asked, exasperation beginning to creep into my voice.

"I have to trust him!" Arbie cried. "He's the only guy I've got who's neither a political innocent nor a would-be capitalist on the make. Look, Rudy, you're glued into the Conservative mass. You don't know what it's like trying to present an opposite view to this monolithic business machine called America."

"You're teaching me," I said. "I'm picking up a few things. All I know is that if someone is trying to wipe you out, that's not real politics. That comes into the field of human motivation."

"Rudy, you're sweet," Arbie smiled. "Anyone who can divorce politics from human motivation is sweet."

"Don't get smart if you want my help," I said, pretending to be insulted. "You and your little library guild can be knocked over in the political field like straw in a wind. Maybe there is an order out to do you in, and someone interpreted it with all the deep-seated hatred he's built up for you over the years."

"Maybe you're right," Arbie said, widening her eyes.

"You have to pretend you don't know it," I warned.

"I'm ahead of you there." She held up a letter. "I just typed this to our landlord, calling his attention to the stabbing, and the fact that librarians are mostly women and need protection devices in this building like mirrors to see around corners and an intercom at the door. It's clear from this that I think the man is a rapist."

"That's good," I said. "It'll throw them off-guard. I don't think you'll get those protection devices, though."

"You're right there," Arbie glowered. "This building is strictly for prostitution."

"That's where I begin," I said firmly. "With the massage parlor. We should've looked into it when it first moved in here."

"Well," Arbie said, "we New Yorkers don't mess with our neighbors."

"Even if they do call themselves librarians and perform sexual acts in a range of little cubicles," I added testily.

"Uh, uh," Arbie said, "don't let your conservative principles overrule your better judgment which tells you that real librarians perform strange sexual acts in little places."

"Not for money and not for organized crime," I replied sharply. "Now, tell me, have you met your landlord?"

"When I said landlord," Arbie explained, "I meant his real estate agents. Tenants in this kind of building never know their landlord." She took a card from a drawer in her desk and handed it to me. "Slidsky and Benbow. They came here once to look the place over. Two guys in their thirties, one with a mustache and pockmarks, the other cherubic, a sort of grown-up choir boy."

I noted the address on Times Square and pocketed the card. "By the way, sweetheart, how goes negotiations on working conditions?"

"One more issue and we're done, after almost a year of bickering," Arbie said with a sigh of relief. "We're waiting for Sharkey to come back from vacation. That drunken sod has caused us a lot of trouble."

"Over agency shop?" I asked innocently.

"I can't believe it," Arbie said, "but I think the screwball library's going for it. And I don't know what they want from us. The whole thing's fishy."

"There's an option we forgot about," I said with a smile. "Management might want to do you in."

"For sure!" Arbie stood and came round the table. "But those stupid bastards wouldn't know one end of the knife from the other."

I stood and embraced her. "See you tonight, sweetheart, after I call in on Benbow and Slidsky and get this case rolling."

"You think I'm safe, Rudy?"

"You're okay for the time being, but maybe you should carry a sharp knife."

"No!" Arbie put her hand up. "Definitely not. I depend on my fleetness of foot."

I moved to the door. "Get out of here, though. Go down to your Council office where there are people around."

"Among whom might be my killer," she grimaced.

"And don't get paranoid," I warned.

"And you be careful of Benbow and Slidsky," she warned. "They're tougher than they look."

I went down the stairway, encountered a couple of messenger boys, saw a half-dozen ladies of pleasure loafing in the massage parlor, and plunged into the throngs in the street in mid-morning. I remembered the newspaper editorial praising the president of the Library Guild for being democratic. No local president had ever been written about with praise; only the big boys like Hector Bratwurst made the news. It was enough to provoke Arbie's downtown unionists to pull out their knives with envy.

TWO

I found the address off Broadway a block south of Times Square--a new office building. The realtors were on the 14th floor which in superstitious New York meant the 13th. The shiny new wood of the office door with its gold-lettered plaque gave the firm a distinguished look. I walked in and asked the receptionist, a platinum blonde, for either Mr. Benbow or Mr. Slidsky.

"Looking for office space?" she asked cheerfully.

"Thinking of removing my firm from Houston to New York," I said. "Need a lot of space."

She spoke over the intercom and looked up with a broad smile. "Mr. Benbow's available. Just take the first door on your left down the hallway."

The thick blue carpet showed little wear. I gathered that the firm could not have been in business long. Benbow, with cherubic

features and an expectant look, jumped to his feet and came out from behind his desk when I entered.
"What business are you in, Mr. Mack?" Benbow asked pleasantly when we were seated.
"Communications," I said. "I know the kind of space I need. Something on three or four levels."
Benbow looked slightly surprised. "Businesses may be leaving the City, but that doesn't mean rents are coming down. A floor covers a lot of space!"
"I don't mean one of these modern office buildings," I said, looking at the pennants on the wall, a framed realtor's license, and photographs of the Rocky Mountains. "I've got my eye on a small building on 43rd Street, which, I understand, you represent."
Benbow cleared his throat. "You want that old dump?"
"Without the librarians," I said sarcastically.
Benbow chuckled, pretending to be amused. "One of our biggest clients just bought the place. He doesn't want to sell. You wouldn't want it anyway."
"Just the right accommodation I need," I insisted. "Where do I contact your client, Mr. Benbow?"
"I can't give you his name. Sorry. And call me Tom, will you? You know how it is, Rudyard. He doesn't want his name connected with the librarians."
"That's understandable, Tom," I said. "But I'm kind of set on having it." I could see him thinking behind his eyes, wondering just who he was up against.
"Leave me your card, Rudyard, and I'll see if he won't get in touch with you."
"Don't try to brush me off, Tom," I said sternly. "I want that building."
Benbow's cherubic features looked hurt. "But I can't help, Rudyard. Not till I talk to him. Leave me a number where I can reach you."
"I'll call you tomorrow," I said and stood up to go. "Everyone has his price."
"If he won't sell, I can't make him, can I, Rudyard?" Benbow said helplessly. "But I can find you a place like it. Leave it to me."
"We'll be in touch," I said and strode out.
The platinum blonde gave me a big smile as I left.
I knew that it was useless to check the records in the Municipal Building. I'd find only the names of Benbow and Slidsky. But I'd seen vertical files behind the secretary's desk. She must file the records from the firm and presumably knew what they contained. The owner's name couldn't have been that big of a secret. If he was one of Benbow's biggest clients, that set him in a league of half a dozen who owned large slices of the City, all of whom had houses of prostitution under their control.
I stopped at a public telephone in the lobby and dialed Detective Buckle's number. The police had regarded me as little better than a

doorman until I solved a case or two. Now Buckle grudgingly gave me respect.

"So it's you, Mack! You got trouble in those halls of ivy?" he asked humorously.

"We may have trouble in the Local Union HQ on West 43rd," I said. "Do you know about the manager of the messenger service?"

"He'll live," Buckle said. "But he didn't get a good look at the guy who hit him. We're not wasting our time on it."

"Who owns the massage parlor on the first floor?" I asked.

"You see a connection?" Buckle was amused. "I'd stay away from it, Mack. Stick to your librarians."

"Nevertheless," I said patiently.

"If you won't take the advice of the experienced," Buckle said, "you'd better know that Wallenberg and Lanzetta have the territory on the West Side from Thirtieth to Fiftieth Streets. Further, you should know, they're what the types in your library refer to as the 'rich and the powerful.' Understand?"

"I understand why you leave them alone," I said.

"Ha, ha," Buckle said. "Why are you interested?"

"I think they were trying to ace the Local union president," I said blandly, expecting a hoot from Buckle.

But Buckle paused. "If you're right, that's bad," he said seriously. "Somebody's got his signals crossed."

"Thanks for the information, detective." I hung up more certain that Arbie's life was in danger.

It was half past twelve. I guessed that Benbow's secretary would be coming down for lunch. She didn't look like the kind who ate at her desk. I picked up a newspaper from the lobby vendor and perused it while keeping an eye on the banks of elevators. Within ten minutes she came trotting out and aiming for the swing doors. I followed her down the street to a Brew and Burger, which she entered and went to a stall in the back. I stood beside her table and gestured at the seat opposite.

"May I?" I asked charmingly.

She looked surprised. "I'm expecting a friend," she said.

"Just for a moment." I sat. "You struck me as a good woman. Someone who can help me with your boss."

She looked wary. Her long face went as pale as her hair.

"I want to get in touch with his clients, Wallenberg and Lanzetta, and swing a deal."

She became interested as if the names were familiar to her.

"How much pull does he have with them?" I asked.

She didn't seem to understand.

"Does he do enough business with them to really be helpful to me?" I asked sharply. "Or am I wasting my time?"

"On no, Mr. Mack, you're not wasting your time. We do a lot of real estate deals for them. Mr. Benbow often calls them." She was trying to reassure me. "They depend on us a lot."

"Good!" I smiled. "Then you're sure I'm doing the right thing working through Benbow?"

"Oh yes." Her face radiated with her receptionist charm. "Here comes my date."

I stood up and left the restaurant as a woman came to the table.

Now came the hard part. I had to beard Wallenberg and Lanzetta in their den right away. I was sure they were the kind who sent out for their lunch.

I knew from various exposes of these realtors in the newspapers that they owned the Chrysler Building and kept their offices on one of the top floors, from where they could survey all they owned. I knew, too, that I would never be admitted to their offices. I decided on a strategy. I walked over to Lexington and 42nd, looked at the address board in the lobby, and took the elevator to the thirtieth floor. I stepped into a large, richly-furnished receiving room. There were three men in dark suits sitting at desks. Each of them looked as if they carried a sidearm. The man at the middle desk was heavy-set and scowling.

"I'm from the Library," I said to him, proffering my card. "And I want to see either Wallenberg or Lanzetta."

The man glanced at my card and slipped it into a corner of his desk blotter. "What about?"

"I'm registering a complaint."

"What about?"

"His massage parlor called 'The Library'."

The man's face tightened. "We don't have anything to do with massage parlors," he said scornfully.

"That's not what Mr. Benbow told me," I said, trying to match his scorn.

The man looked uncertain. The two other men raised their heads and stared at me. There was an awkward pause.

"Hold on a moment," the man in the center said, his scowl becoming more pronounced. "Do you say Benbow sent you?"

"In a way."

He picked up his telephone and said, "There's a guy from the public library wanting to complain about massage parlors. Benbow sent him." He pointed a beefy finger at a corner of the room. "See that elevator? Take it up one flight."

The elevator doors opened immediately. The three men watched me push the second of three buttons. When the doors closed, I felt I was going into a trap with my eyes wide open.

The elevator opened into a richly-furnished room. A tall lumbering man in a dark suit ambled toward me and leered. "You a friend of Tommy Benbow?"

"This has nothing to do with Benbow," I said irritatedly. "I want to see either Wallenberg or Lanzetta."

"Hey, hey, pal," the big man said, reaching out to punch me lightly on the shoulder. "Let's look at your problem first. Come on over and sit down." He led the way to a number of easy chairs in a semi-circle near a floor-to-ceiling window overlooking the East River and the United Nations Secretariat Building.

"We're all for scholarship, education, books and stuff," the man said. "By the way, my name's Dean. You gotta card or something?"

I gave him my card.

"Library investigator," Dean nodded impressively.

"The West 43rd Street massage parlor is in your building," I said.

"Wait a minute, Rudyard, my man." Dean stood up and lumbered over to his desk. He flipped through a ledger, found a number which he mumbled to himself, went to a vertical file near-by, and looked in a folder in the second drawer. "Yeah, there's a massage parlor called "The Library" on West 43rd. I don't know what we can do about it. Want us to change the name? Offends the Library, does it?"

"You bet," I said angrily.

"We're ready to oblige a big institution like the Public Library. Mr. Lanzetta is on record as getting his education in a branch in the Bronx," Dean said. "He's a regular contributor to your library fund."

"Then maybe he'll close the parlor down to oblige the trustees," I replied grimly.

"Your trustees!" Dean looked surprised. "Well, we can get them to change the name, but it's gonna be hard to get them to move, 'cause they got a lease, you know."

"Let me talk to Lanzetta," I said impatiently.

"Wait, hold your horses," Dean smiled lazily. "Let's see what I can do." He picked up a phone on his desk and dialed. He asked to speak to Lanzetta. He waited for over two minutes. "He's a busy man," he said apologetically.

I watched the traffic in the streets below. I decided I had pushed my luck as far as it could go. I heard Dean quickly telling Lanzetta my complaint. It was the most respectful rendering of a complaint I had heard.

"I didn't know that," Dean said quietly. "Yes sir, I'll tell him. Yes sir. I'm sorry, sir."

Dean set down the receiver carefully. The niceness left his personality. He came over to me with a tinge of embarrassment still in his face. "Listen, bud. Are you here representing the Library or the Library Guild?"

I stood up. "I represent the Library."

"Is that so?" Dean sneered. "You're either lying or you've got it wrong. Who sent you here?"

"The business manager."

Dean wrinkled up his nose as if he'd encountered a bad smell. "Tell him to get his facts straight. The way we've heard it, the Library is pleased that there's a massage parlor on West 43rd Street calling itself 'the Library.'"

I pretended to look surprised. Actually, I was surprised. "Why? Because the Library union's in the same building?"

Dean shrugged. "How should I know anything about Union-Management relations? We don't let our staff unionize." He pointed at the elevator. "Now Rudyard, hurry along. I got work to do."

I gestured good-bye, stepped to the elevator, and glanced back at Dean, who was glaring down at the papers on his desk as if trying to remember where he had left off. I took the elevator one flight down; then, with the three male receptionists watching me like hawks, I took the main elevator, and began breathing more easily when I stepped into the street.

I stopped at a street telephone and called the Library Guild Headquarters. The line was busy. Arbie was still there. Relieved, I walked over to the Guild Headquarters, dodging pedestrians, and occasionally catching sight of good-looking women. I figured that Lanzetta's contact with the Library was higher than Bugofsky-- probably higher than Anders, the Director. There were about thirty trustees, any one of whom could have been involved. Some I could rule out right away such as the Cardinal, the NBC president, the stock brokers, although all of them were directors of a variety of companies and institutions and one never knew what they might be up to. But I had a hunch that since their little game seemed directed at the Library Guild, I could narrow the field down to those trustees involved in City politics, that is, those who were extremely concerned about City affairs during the fiscal crisis the City was in. This meant the bankers, and, as every observer of financial institutions knew, when it came to unions, the bankers elected to set the strategy were Rockefeller men. The President of the Rockefeller Foundation had a permanent seat on the Library Board of Trustees.

The heat had gotten to me by the time I reached Arbie's building. Sweat stood out on my face as I climbed the wooden stairs. The door to the massage parlor was closed to keep out the hot air from the hallway, but I passed the parlor's "guardian" as he was coming from the toilet behind the stairs. He looked as if he had worked out in gymnasiums and gave me a hard, indifferent look.

Arbie shouted from behind her office door and, assured it was me, let me in.

"Glad you're still here," I said.

Arbie smiled, pleased that I looked concerned. "Can't do my telephoning at the Council without the characters down there listening in. Come into the inner office where it's cooler."

I found a large, fat, black woman sitting at the side of Arbie's desk and ticking off names on a sheet of paper. She was Petula Simon Clarkson, library clerk and Guild secretary. She didn't look up until she came to the end of the list, then she smiled warmly from a round face. Her eyes didn't smile, though; they betrayed the anger smoldering deep down inside her.

"Fancy Mack bein' here," she said. "You ain't got enough to do in your end of the Library?"

"I'm doing extra duty," I said.

Petula looked over at Arbie with a smirk. "What you got that attracts this cat, Vine? What you got that I ain't got?"

"Right now I got trouble," Arbie said. "What did you find out, Rudy?"

"First, that the slumlords, Wallenberg and Lanzetta, own this building." I slumped into one of the large chairs with wooden arms that Arbie had bought from the Salvation Army. "Second, that the Library wants them to call the massage parlor 'the Library.'"

Petula let out a cackle. "Someone's got a weird sense 'a humor."

"Someone's trying to drive us out of here," Arbie frowned. "Hector would love to get us down at the Council where he could watch our every move."

"He sure would," Petula agreed. "'Specially since we're organizing this march on City Hall. You coming?" she asked me.

"Not my affair," I said.

"You sound just like Bratwurst. Don't he sound like Bratwurst?" she asked Arbie. "It ain't the union's affair. Here the Mayor's layin' off hospital workers, parks workers, city planners and even librarians, and Big Hector lies back in his big chair, and he say it don't concern him."

"He's made his deal," Arbie said. "What concerns me is how big a deal it is."

"Does it include knocking you off?" I asked. "When's the last time you had a confrontation with Bratwurst?"

"Confrontation!" Arbie threw back her head and laughed. "Hector doesn't have confrontations unless there's lights and cameras, and then he's shouting from the far side of a wide table at City negotiators who've been clued as to what he's going to say. I've never been able to get close enough to him for a confrontation. He hides in his office. The only time I saw him was when our chief of the professional division arranged for a quick meeting once, and I could hardly get a word in."

"No sign of bad blood between you? Nothing?" I looked disappointed.

"I ran for the Executive Board at the Council last year," Arbie said. "I sent out position papers about the crisis I saw coming up, saying what I thought the union should do, you know, what one does in a democracy." She smiled wearily at Petula. "Tell him what happened?"

"We's all set to vote at the delegates' meetin'," Petula said, widening her eyes for dramatic effect, "and the Board secretary says they don't have the correct voting count for the Locals. They gotta put the election off for a month. We go ready to vote next month, and the Council puts up this Local president who just come from the hospital recoverin' from a heart attack. He gets all the votes." She sniggered. "They called it 'sympathy vote'."

"It was overkill," Arbie said, shaking her head with amusement. "The guy who won didn't serve on the Board anyway. The next month, the Council hired him to look after their data processing. The big thing for the Council, though, was that me and my big ideas didn't cause Bratwurst any trouble. He fooled the delegates, and now he's got the workers accepting cutbacks in working conditions, no pay raises, and he's teaching them to look the other way as our members are laid off--not just in the tens and twenties, but in the thousands."

"He's a real Pied Piper," I said. "How does he get away with it?"

"Simple," Arbie said, leaning forward as if to illustrate a difficult problem with her hands. "You got two main groups in municipal employment: blacks who can see nothing but better deals for blacks, that's health plans, dental plans, pension plans, and like Petula here, they play along with the crooks who run the Democratic Party so they can get more benefits on the side."

Petula looked darkly at her, but Arbie continued. "The other group is conservative and cowed. The union is the only thing they've got. They believed in it from the good days in the sixties when Bratwurst made the political deals that got them good benefits. They don't want to see who pulls the strings to make him dance."

"You sound more disillusioned than I've ever heard you," I said with a smile, though I felt the deep disappointment that underlay her matter-of-fact manner.

"Sometimes I wonder if it's worth it," Arbie sighed dejectedly. "Why don't I just play the game like Hector, get a big salary, and hob-nob with the bankers? Who the hell cares?"

"You do," I smiled.

Our eyes met, and I saw the moisture in her eyes.

"Probably I'm nuts," Arbie said, "but we're wasting time. What's the next number, Petula?"

"Is the Council marching with you?" I asked before Petula could answer.

"Hector told the Locals they couldn't march," Arbie said flatly. "Not officially, of course, but he warned them. It's pitiful. Here was Hector year after year flexing his muscles as if he were Mussolini, and when it comes to war, he grins like a kitten."

"You'd better get a big showing," I warned.

"There are tens of thousands--old folks, boy scouts, dozens of groups protesting cuts, but all marching on different days. If we could get them together, we could make it mean something." Arbie picked up the phone. "Let's go, Petula, next number."

I got up to leave.

"Do us a favor, Rudy, and find out who stabbed that poor bastard downstairs. We'd all breathe easier."

"That's right, get back to duty, Mack," Petula laughed. "I sure don't want to have to worry about bein' stuck full 'a holes."

"He wouldn't be so bold," I joked.

Arbie ran after me to bolt the door behind me, and sneaked a quick kiss as I stepped into the hall. "Thanks, mister," she said. "I appreciate it."

"I'd appreciate it if I could get off square one," I said. "Maybe I should try the massage parlor."

"Don't you dare!" Arbie glowered and slammed the door.

I sensed then how much Arbie meant to me, how important she was in my life, and how proud I was of her dedication to trying to make life better for everyone. Her life seemed to me more important than anything, and the fact that it was threatened made me determined to do anything to erase that threat.

As I passed the massage parlor, the door opened and a blonde woman in a blouse and skirt rushed into the hall and descended the stairs in front of me. I recognized her as one of the hostesses and figured she was coming off her shift.

"Hey, neighbor," I called out to her. "Let me take you for a drink."

She looked back and shook her head with a tired look. "Not tonight. I'm bushed."

"No, on the level," I said. "I want to talk. Anywhere you want to go."

She brought her hand to the side of her face. "Do I smell a cop?"

"No, no," I assured her, "on the level."

She shrugged. "Take me to the Plaza then, honey. I like their daiquiris."

THREE

When we were seated at a table in the foyer of the Plaza Hotel, and the drinks were in front of us, and we had exchanged our first names, I broached the subject of the knifing in the hallway.

"Yes, wasn't it terrible!" she said, eyeing the people around her.

"Did you see the guy who did it?"

"I wasn't there," she said off-handedly. "I work another place, you know. Pays better than 'the Library.' We get a better class from the Wall Street area." Her eyes followed a couple of good-looking young men who were walking to the door, and then, seeing me turn to follow her gaze, she made a face. "Gays."

"Did anyone see the guy?" I insisted. "He was black, wasn't he?"

"I thought you wasn't police!" she said, glaring at me.

"I'm with the Library Guild upstairs, Annie," I explained. "The real librarians are scared."

She nodded. Her placid face showed the first signs of aging under the eyes and in the line of jaw. She could no longer be a call-girl of the first rank, I thought; she had fallen to the level of massage parlor work; soon, too soon for her, she would be forced to work the streets. "I know some guys talk about that Library Guild. They come in from the District Council downtown, where I work."

I leaned forward with interest. "Who are they?"

She gave me a smug look. "We're not supposed to give our customers' names," she said.

I pulled out my wallet and gave her five dollars. She crumpled it in her hand. "One of them's a son-of-a-bitch, if you know what I mean. He makes me work real hard. Name is Harold Poppin. He's always telling his friend about the Library Guild and a dame called Arbuthnott somethin'. Says he wants to bust her balls."

"They discuss their business in front of you?" I asked, amused at the picture I was getting of these union bosses.

"Oh, they treat us like animals, as if we don't exist, and talk over our heads while we work at them." She looked disgusted. "I try to avoid him, but he asks for me."

"Tell me if they talk about the knifing, will you, Annie?"

I handed her my card and watched her slip it into her purse. "You did say somebody saw the knifer?"

"One girl. Didn't see much." Annie swallowed the rest of her drink. "He was middle height, muscular, coffee skin, sort of a broad face, in his twenties, maybe."

"Want another drink?" I motioned to call the waiter.

"No, I gotta go." Annie stood. She was tall, her figure was still good. "I gotta cook dinner. Thanks for the drink. And listen, will you. Don't tell anybody I talked to you. I only did it 'cause I admire dames who organize a union. I like their guts."

I watched her walk away through the tables toward the doors, took out my expense book, and entered the taxi fare and the drinks. I entered the name Harold Poppin, then went to a telephone in the lobby. Arbie was still in her office.

"Library Union," she said sweetly.

"Honey, who's Harold Poppin?"

"He's head of our section, professional and white collar," she said. "What's he done?"

"How do you get along with him?"

"Okay, I guess. He's not very helpful, though. Just like most of them down there."

"When the Library deals with the Union, it probably works through him, right?"

"Him or the Council negotiator. What's up?"

"I'm just trying to get off square one. When is your next union meeting with the Council?"

"There's a delegates meeting tonight," Arbie laughed. "Why the sudden interest, Rudy? You want to come?"

"Take me in as a delegate from your Local, can you?"

"I can, sure. Security down there is next to non-existent. Meet me at the Council entrance, sweetie. Seven o'clock, okay?"

When I hung up, I went to a coffee shop and ate a good dinner before becoming a trade unionist.

Arbie was waiting outside the door to the Council building, which was next door to the State government offices in the Trade

Center and a ten minute walk from City Hall. The Council had raised union dues for a Defense Fund, a euphemism for Strike Fund, but since the Fund was illegal (which Arbie claimed that the Union had known all the time), it put the money as down payment on its new building. Then the Council raised the members' dues again to pay off the mortgage. Arbie remembered that Hector Bratwurst was particularly skilled in increasing the dues paid by the Locals to the District Council, and, thereby, increasing his domination over them. Arbie had told me many interesting stories about Bratwurst and his background as an agent working out of the U.S. State Department in Third World countries. Taking her socialist bias into account, I was intrigued by her suspicions that he was a government plant in the union movement, which helped to explain his success in negotiations in the good old days of the sixties. I looked forward to seeing in the flesh the tall, big-framed man with the square jaw, round black eyes, and rugged handsomeness, who appeared aggressively from time to time in television newscasts.

"Just on time," Arbie said impatiently, one hand on the door. "We're allowed six delegates from our Local," she told me as we entered the hallway and proceeded to a carpeted hall, off which there were many rooms. The carpet was worn and blackened into pathways. A man in a white shirt, looking over the delegates as they entered, motioned at me, but, seeing that I was with Arbie, waved me through. "Three of them aren't coming. That leaves Petula, me, and our resident radical whom you haven't met."

I winced. Radicals made me feel uncomfortable.

Throngs of delegates were gathered in the large room into which Arbie led me. Some stood talking and gesticulating, and some sat and stared ahead at the podium. Black-and-white, brown and olive, the delegates from each Local sat together. I thought I could discern their vocations by the look in their faces and the lines of their bodies: heavy-set and some skinny hospital workers; parks and sewer workers with large hands and rough-hewn faces; City planners and computer operators, many wearing glasses, looked about sharply at their brother and sister unionists, and huddled in private discussions, their thin white faces tense with conspiracy; delegates from the quasi-public Locals: the zoos, the museums, the libraries sat quietly observing and perhaps bewildered by the noise made by the larger Locals such as the great mass of black delegates from the large clerical Local, colorful in dress, handsome women with blonde or orange hair here and there, all confident in their majority power at the Council, which they readily relinquished to Hector Bratwurst as long as he pushed successfully for black power in the halls of government.

Hector himself was sitting on the podium and talking with his right-hand man, a thin black with owlish eyes and large slim hands named Alexander Mackart. Hector had brought him from a union in Chicago and expected him to guide him delicately in his relations with blacks. Hector, who was Jewish, relied on his co-religionists to fill most of the management positions at the Council. Their common allegiance assured him of their loyalty. His other lieutenant was a round-faced, happy-looking Irishman, Ted McConnell, who administered the building and supervised the preparations for rallies, such as hiring buses and manufacturing placards and leaflets. McConnell approached the microphone as we sat down beside Petula Simon Clarkson. Petula looked round peremptorily, declined to recognize me, and turned her attention to the podium.

McConnell commented on a dance recently hosted by a Local, which brought hoots of laughter from a section of the audience who knew what he was talking about. I perceived his role as the union wiseacre whose job was to make the delegates think they were part of a large family. Uncle Ted was always available for party functions, he seemed to say. He was followed at the microphone by the Council President, who as a president of the small elevator workers' Local, was chosen by the Council delegates for the position.

Executive Director Bratwurst, however, undercut the man's authority; the Council President was little better than a rubber stamp. Arbie told me that the President had reached the point where his most notable function was to introduce the Executive Director, who, as he liked to say, needed no introduction.

When Hector looked with a stunned half-smile at the delegates, there was silence. He began with some asides about the Mayor, a few negative comments about the Governor, and threats to unseat some State senators if they didn't start behaving. The delegates were transformed from their menial jobs washing bedpans or laying sewer pipe to the corridors of political power in which legislators were on a first-name basis. Bratwurst grew serious, his voice strident as he warned the workers of the dangers of the fiscal crisis. The small investors in City bonds would lose their savings, and the City could not pay its employees if it went bankrupt. Hector spoke as if pestilence and flood were about to sweep over Manhattan Island.

"He bullshits with conviction," Arbie said. "Look around you, Rudy. They're like lost sheep. They know the voice of the shepherd, but they suspect he's leading them over a cliff. They don't know where else to go."

The huge audience riveted its attention on Bratwurst as if anxious not to miss a word. Hector warned them of attempts by the Mayor to cut back on working conditions, freeze wages, and so on.

"It's all in *Capital*, Volume One," Arbie whispered to me. "Hector is telling them what the bankers would tell them if they were in Hector's shoes. What a creep!"

I smiled and watched an untidy young man with windblown, curly brown hair, and an expression of determination stamped all over him come up to us. "Hey, Arb!" He pushed himself between us. "Why didn't you get up and answer that shit?" he demanded. "We can't let him get away with that. If we want to hear that we can get Vice-President Rockefeller to give us a fire-side chat."

"Not now, Alf," Arbie placed a restraining hand on his sleeve. "Let him ramble."

"But I can't stand this crap! He's gotta be opposed. These people gotta be shown an alternative!" Alf's voice rose with emotion. "I'm gonna say somethin' about our march on City Hall."

"Okay," Arbie shrugged and turned her attention back to Hector who was taking questions from the floor on the fiscal crisis.

"Use the mike!" Ted McConnell shouted at a woman delegate who could not be heard.

A pugnacious-looking, white woman of burly form and florid complexion moved to the microphone standing in the center aisle. Alf Landy, who, as Arbie informed me, was the name of her radical colleague, stood behind her to ask a question.

"We've heard a rumor, Hector," the woman began.

"Name and Local number," McConnell shouted at her, and the secretary, taking notes, shouted the same thing.

The woman looked flustered, gave her name and Local, seized the microphone as if strangling it, and continued, "It's not true, is it, Hector, that you're putting all our pension money into City bonds?"

Bratwurst grinned sheepishly at his cronies on the podium with him and said, "One of you guys tell me it's not true." He laughed with them, and then spoke in a soft, conciliatory voice into the microphone. "It's been suggested that you could play the biggest role in saving the City." Hector's Brooklynite "r" made "role" sound like "wole," which made him sound as guileless as pigs and bunny rabbits in an animated cartoon. "You would wun a wisk, that's wery twue, but if the City goes under, you and your pensions go under with it. If we save the City, we save the Union. They owe us something. So we're givin' it thought." Hector looked over her shoulder at Alfie, and grinned with a look of mockery in his eyes. "Let's hear it from the librarians." He looked down at the maintenance workers who sat up front, and his face reflected their thought that all male librarians were pansies.

"The son of a bitch does it every time," Arbie said. "Alfie's half his age and screwed more skirts than Hector has dreamed of, though Hector tries, God knows!"

Alf Landy gave his name and Local, stood back, looked round at his audience like a boy at his classmates, and said into the microphone, "Well, yeah, we've been listenin' to ya tell us how much we can help keep certain banks from goin' bust, how we can give up things we've worked hard for, things which are our hard-won rights, and which we won't get back again if we let them go. I'm here to talk about fight back." His voice rose and hovered on that note of alarm close to hysteria and reminiscent of untold generations of Irish barroom orators seeking rebellion. "We're marchin' on the City Hall. We say, 'Stop the lay-offs!' We're tellin' the Mayor, we're tellin' the bankers, we're telling the U. S. President, we're tellin' 'em all. 'Stop the friggin' lay-offs.' And all of you join us. Make it a big howl! That's the only way we're gonna win. Be there, a week Saturday morning at Union Square."

"Okay, Alfie, you've had your time," Hector cut in. "This Council is not marching on any City Hall. Get that! No Locals march with the librarians."

"You made deals, Hector, that's it, isn't it?" Alf Landy shouted. "You've been kissin' bankers' ass."

Bratwurst's charming manner evaporated. He was transformed into an angry bear, clawing at the air, and rasping. "I'm not taking that fuckin' crap from a shit-head commie like you. Get out of here!"

Two heavily-built men in sweatshirts from the parks maintenance Local moved down the aisle towards Alfie Landy.

"Get out of my sight!" Hector was screaming now, beside himself with rage. "You want to start a revolution, you ass hole. Go to Russia! Get out!"

Alfie, pushed back roughly by Hector's "mafia," and unnerved by Hector's fury, retreated to his seat. The Council President quickly called for new business, and, hearing none, adjourned the meeting. The members got to their feet talking up a minor storm.

"Alf hit Hector's funny-bone," Petula laughed. "He's still jumpin'."

"Arbuthnott," a voice called mildly. "Who's your new delegate?"

"Oh," Arbie said. "Hi, Harold."

A broad-framed man of middle-height, late middle-age, with a small gray mustache spoke between his teeth in an apparent relaxed fashion. But he seemed to conceal a tenseness like a coil waiting to be released. "Who's your good-looking friend?" he asked, smiling mildly at me.

Arbie introduced us. I pretended to be a librarian. "I'm just an alternate, Mr. Poppin," I said apologetically. "It was really interesting."

"Stick around," Poppin said with a superior smile. "We'll show you radical bookworms what real life is."

"Like those refugees from gangland around Bratwurst?" I asked. "Is that what you mean by real life?"

"You're a little new to start insinuating anything." Poppin's jaw hardened. "Tell your friend to be careful what he says, Arbuthnott. He could upset some people." Poppin moved away with a surly look back at me.

"You don't have to stay around to talk business, do you?" I looked pleadingly at Arbie. "I just want to be reminded as quickly as possible that there are some trade unionists who are soft and tender."

Arbie laughed. "Okay, honey. We'll settle for a taxi direct to your place. But are you satisfied now that you met Poppin?"

"I'm satisfied that you were the target," I said grimly, taking her arm and heading for the hot outdoors. "And I think you still are the target." When she looked at me questioningly, I added, "I'll know more after I check through Sharkey Bugofsky's files tomorrow morning."

FOUR

The heat dissipated during the night. Rain fell. When Arbie and I left my apartment house near Gramercy Park to go our respective ways, the temperature was in the low eighties. I walked to work at the Library. I liked coming upon this two-block-long Beaux-Arts building of white marble low amidst the skyscrapers--an oasis of learning in the deserts of commerce. It gave me a feeling of preserving the intelligible amidst the rush and chaos of the mindless. I checked for messages with my wide-hipped secretary, whose sexiness came out in the way she shook her head and pursed her red lips in a "no."

I went directly to Bugofsky's office and made the excuse to his secretary that I had to go through the correspondence in order to answer a problem that had arisen in the Director's Office. As guardian of the files, she suggested that she do the searching, but I brushed past her with a warm smile and a confident look, as if to say this was really important business.

Bugofsky's room was neat when he was on vacation. The absence of whisky bottles in the desk drawers misrepresented him as someone meticulous and efficient. I feared the files were truer to form, and they were. I had trouble locating correspondence with the District Council. There was little of it. A few notes from the negotiator for the Union, memoranda that Sharkey wrote to himself, but nothing along the line that I was looking for.

I glanced through the other folders, which were in no order that I could discern, and was about to give up the search when I noticed an unmarked folder at the back of the bottom drawer. It was crammed with scraps of paper with addresses, telephone numbers, brief messages, either passed to him during negotiations or taken over the telephone by his secretary. I unfolded a green Library memorandum form. It was from Library Director Anders, re: "30-hour work week."

> J.T.R. informs us plan is to trim wages to shorter week. Essential we encourage Local in that direction. Will form staff groups to challenge Local leadership on question.

I re-read it as if it were a revelation. The memo was dated mid-June, over two months ago. The 30-hour-work week issue surfaced in late July. The *Times* and the *Post* ran articles about it as a demand made by Library workers. Arbie had been mystified by it and the publicity it brought her. She had been surprised by the vociferousness on the subject by a sizable group of library workers, largely Library Technical Assistants in the Central Building. They were led by Bradley Tone, an angry young man, who had worked part-time with the Library Branch system while attending college and had recently been employed full-time. Arbie called him a full-time provocateur. With this memo the mystery was beginning to clear, but it was

"J.T.R." whom I had to look for. I pocketed the memorandum, and, fishing in my pocket for the letter from Bratwurst to Sharkey about agency shop, I placed it in the folder marked "District Council."

Bugofsky's secretary came into the office looking suspicious. "Finding what you want?" she asked. Bugofsky chose his secretaries for their form rather than for their intelligence.

"Not yet," I sighed. "I'll be back when I have more time." I stood up and yawned.

"If you tell me what it is," she said archly. "I can find it."

I shook my head. "Special investigation," I said softly.

"Oh, sorry," she said, her face suddenly contrite.

I held the door for her to precede me out of the office.

Back in my office on the first floor, I studied the List of Trustees in the Library's annual report. None of them in the present year had the initials "J.T.R." The Trustees appointed themselves to serve every three years by consigning themselves to three "classes." I found the complete list of Trustees in my desk drawer and alighted upon Joshua T. Raikes in class II. Class III was now in office, which meant that class II would not return for two years. But Joshua T. Raikes could be chairing one of the Trustees' sub-committees where the real action took place--possibly a committee on the 30-hour-work-week issue? I felt uncomfortable. I wanted to shy away from problems which involved trustees. After all, I was supposed to be working for them. I was prepared to overlook the common meannesses and staff troubles which the management inflicted upon Arbie and her Local, but not murder. Right now, I had to admit that I was far from knowing who was behind the knifing. But at least, I had found pieces of the puzzle which I could try fitting together. My problem was that I was working against time.

My phone rang. It was Anders' secretary. Would I come to the Director's office right away? I climbed the stairs and wondered if there had been a complaint about security. Had purses been stolen? someone raped or beaten in the Library washrooms? a rare book stolen? I never knew what to expect.

Serious complaints were never made to the Chief of Security as they should have been. They went to the Director or the President who then threatened the Security staff to do a better job or else find another. I had learned to keep it from bothering me because Bugofsky, as head of Security, had to accept most of the blame unless he could pin it on me. But now that I was acting in Bugofsky's place, I felt more vulnerable.

"Go right in," the secretary said without expression.

I sensed a coolness in the air which did not come from the air-conditioning.

Anders, a lanky man in his mid-sixties, came from behind his desk and directed me to sit at the long table in the room at which he normally conducted meetings. His hair was gray and his hand trembled nervously as he looked down to study some papers. He sat at the head of the table and frowned.

"I've had a report that you were at a union meeting last night," Anders said with a questioning ring.

I swallowed. "Yes."

Anders cocked his head. "Why was that?"

I thought fast. "I'm keepin an eye on some radical staff members."

Anders paused, wondering whether to believe me. "You know our rules. Never associate with unionized staff."

"I had to test the climate in the Council," I explained. "We in the Library have not had bomb threats for months, but the underground is at work."

"Assuredly, it is. But you shouldn't be doing that sort of thing without touching bases with me first," Anders said breezily. "Remember that next time, Rudy."

"Yes sir." I stood as Anders got up to return to his desk.

Anders stopped and turned back to look at me. "No complaints about security in the building? Everything running smoothly?"

"Very smoothly," I assured him.

"Keep your nose clean, Rudy. The Library doesn't want to lose a good man through a silly mistake. Ah," Anders smiled suddenly as if amused at his forgetting to inform me, "a trustee, Mr. Raikes, has been appointed to fill the chair of the Sub-committee on Library Security. He'll be getting in touch with you soon."

"Mr. Raikes?" I queried, then made a moue, and mumbled, "Thanks."

"Not to your liking?" Anders asked with a half smile.

"Well, he's a publisher," I said. "What does he know about security?"

Anders put his head back and laughed shortly, his prominent teeth showing like a chipmunk's. "Not many people know this, and don't let it go any further, but Joshua Raikes helped organize the C.I.A. after the Second World War. There is not much that he doesn't know about security."

"I'm glad to know that," I said, impressed.

Nevertheless, I left Anders' office with a sense of unease. Had Raikes' new responsibility been planned for some time or was it because of the bungled knifing at the Local headquarters? And who had reported me as present at the union delegates' meeting? I decided that I had to move more carefully. I went to General Reference on the third floor and began looking through the indexes to the *New York Times* for the name of Raikes as a first step to informing myself about this mysterious figure.

It was four in the afternoon before I rose from my research at the microfilm reader and went back to my office to read through the notes I had taken. My secretary handed me a pink slip with a telephone number.

"He wouldn't leave his name, Rudy," she said, "but he wanted you to call as soon as you came in."

I asked her to call for a hamburger and a coke, dialed the number, and heard the voice of Tom Benbow.
"Mack here. You called, I believe."
There was a pregnant pause. "You got me in deep trouble with Lanzetta, Rudyard. Why? I didn't do anything to you," Benbow said in a sulk.
"Needed information, Tom. You wouldn't provide it."
"What's your game anyway?" Benbow's voice rose in challenge. "Let me warn you, Rudyard," he continued before I could speak. "You can get hurt playin' with fire. I'm warning you to forget about West 43rd Street. That's not just me talking, that's Wallenberg and Lanzetta."
"You received a letter from the Local president to provide security for the building," I said. "Are you doing it?"
"Are you kidding me?" Benbow snarled. "She doesn't like it, she can move out. Nobody is stoppin' her."
"There was an attempted murder in that building two nights ago," I barked. "Behave like a responsible landlord."
"Stuff it!" Benbow said and hung up.
I slowly replaced the receiver. By nature I was even-tempered, but, at the moment, I felt my temples throbbing. I sat back in my chair and tried to relax. The more I thought of it, the more sure I was that Arbie was on collision courses with Bratwurst and Poppin on one side and Benbow and his henchmen on the other. Should the two of them be connected somehow, she was in for one hell of a collision. She was up to her neck in problems, and, at the same time, she was taking on City Hall and the consortium of bankers, who were gradually usurping the chair of government with Economic Control Councils and other low profile, final-say committees. As library detective, I had no business being involved, but, since I was involved with Arbie, I had to find out who was behind the knifing before someone struck again. I sat listening to the low hum of the window air conditioner and waited for inspiration. It came in the form of a telephone call.
"Hello Mack," said the deep, breezy voice of a woman. "It's Petula. I got some information for you."
"About what?" I asked, aware that Petula Clarkson often came up with thoughts irrelevant to the issue at hand.
"'Bout the stabbin' at our Headquarters." She paused to lend significance to what she was going to say. "Friend of mine at the Democratic Club heard it was planned to get Vine."
I sat up straight. "How does she know?"
"She wouldn't tell me. She just say I should clear away from protestin' the cutbacks," Petula said worriedly.
"What's your friend's name?" I demanded.
"What you gonna do?" Petula asked in alarm. "You ain't gonna get her in any trouble?"

"I just want to talk to her," I said soothingly. "It's important for your sake as well as Arbie's that I find who's behind this dirty business."

"Okay, Mack, but don't forget, make her understand it's confidential." Petula paused to look up her friend's telephone number and street address on the Grand Concourse. "Her name's Barb Janes. I'll call her and tell her you'll see her at seven-thirty. Okay?"

"Will she be home tonight?"

"Who goes out up there? Stupid!"

I strapped on my gun holster and hurried to call by on Bradley Tone, the radical conservative in the Preparations Division, before I quit for the day.

Tone was a fresh-faced kid, the only son of a widowed mother who worked in the library system. I thought he had been spoiled from the cradle.

"Hello Bradley." I stood beside his desk over which were scattered cataloguing planning sheets. "Do you have time to talk?"

Tone looked up at the wall clock and made a face of resignation. "I got to leave in a few minutes."

"I just want to know how your 30-hour-work-week campaign is going," I said. "I saw your handouts, the ones that say, 'Tone will make a progressive president.'"

"Oh yeah," Tone smiled, "we're doin' okay. Want to join us?" His smile grew sarcastic.

"Maybe," I said seriously. "I want to know if you can really get us a 30-hour-work week. Management hadn't been receptive to the idea ever since Arbuthnott Vine raised it years ago."

"Vine!" Tone dismissed her with a distasteful look. "It'll be different when I get in. This time we'll drop salaries by five hours. Management will go for that."

"You can't sell the membership on it. The staff can't afford to have a reduction in wages in the best of times," I argued.

"The alternative is lay-offs," Tone smirked. "You should see the number of guys supportin' me. All those staff who've got pink slips effective the end of the month. Boy! They're scared."

"How do you know management will listen?" I asked. "It'll set a precedent for workers in the whole city."

"I know," Tone said, as if he had a secret. "I've got contacts."

"Mr. Joshua Raikes is one of them," I said, smiling knowingly in my turn.

Tone's face fell. "How did you know?"

"He's taking charge of the Library's business operations. I may have to work with you." I leaned closer to Tone. "We have to keep this quiet."

"I know," Tone whispered. "Is he going to use you as a go-between?"

"We'll see." I straightened up, glanced at the wall clock, and added, "It's after five. We'll be in touch." I winked and walked away from Tone, who sat watching me go, surprise still registering in his face.

I was satisfied with this addition to the foundation of the motive I was gradually building. If the Local was forced to negotiate a 30-hour-work week with management, the District Council would come under pressure to do the same for all the city workers. With the lowering of wages there would be pro-rated savings to the City on fringe benefits and pension contributions, which, according to the bankers, could almost solve the fiscal crisis alone. Arbie stood in the way of this solution.

Young blacks stood at the entrance to Bryant Park behind the Library and called aggressively at me as I passed. "Smoke, smoke, smoke." I watched a young white man and his girlfriend slip bills to one of them in return for a packet. That was no smoke, smoke, I thought, that was sniff, sniff.

The heat had sharpened people's tempers. A jam of cars at 6th Avenue and 42nd Street set car horns honking and bleating. The news vendors stared hostilely from their wooden huts. Pedestrians were in a hurry to get off the sidewalk into an air-conditioned building or a bus. The peep-shows, the x-rated cinemas, the girl and boy prostitutes standing in front of the fast-food joints, the shoe and liquor stores, the old men, black and white, lying on the sidewalks asleep or begging, how many hundreds of times had I passed them with an inner calm as if they hadn't existed? But this time, in the humidity and the heat, they affronted me with their salacious ugliness. At the 7th Avenue subway entrance, there was a black Muslim dressed in white, his back to the railing, a card table before him, on which were copies of the Koran and Islamic literature and slow burning sticks of punk in a jar. This missionary to the dregs of Times Square was playing a tape recording of a deep-voiced fanatic reading in Arabic and paraphrasing the meaning in English. The sound was turned high to overcome the noise of the traffic. I listened to the heavy rhythm of the voice as I descended the stairs to the subway. It was selling! Just as surely as every thing, every person loitering on the Square, was for sale.

The hot, stagnant air of the subway hung upon me like a wet sheet. The IRT Uptown when it came was crowded with angry, frustrated passengers who glared at the mobs who tried to force their way through the doors and into the densely-packed cars. I was wedged between a short woman and a tall man, and, thus, had to ride leaning over the woman, one arm stretched to touch a window to maintain my balance. Only when the subway moved through the tunnel did the hot air rushing through the opened windows bring some relief. This was the city that Arbie claimed the bankers were trying to rip off.

The soothing, swinging, sticky, smelling ride took me painfully, stop after stop, into the Bronx until I was able to push and slide off bodies onto the dirty platform, and walk under the blackened girders past the soot, the vomit, and the upset garbage-cans up the crowded stairs, patiently out the gate to the slight breeze and sunshine of the outdoors. I had witnessed no robberies and no murders, but that may have been because the trains were too crowded. Certainly conditions in the City were abrasive enough to provoke New Yorkers to commit murder.

I found Barb Janes's apartment house on the Grand Concourse. It had been a mansion in better days. Now it was a run-down rabbit warren. I pushed the buzzer next to her name at the door, but there was no inter-com to speak through, and the door could not be locked. I watched the passers-by, some looking furtively about them, others street-wise, and old people moving slowly with heads down and arms dragging carts of groceries. I rang again. My face was bathed in sweat. I felt drops trickle down my back. My hair was wet and clotted. Finally a buzzer answered. I went through the lobby, its tiles broken, dirt swept to the sides, elevator broken. I walked to the third floor and looked at the doors down the narrow hallway, its floor covered by a worn brown carpet. At the end I came to the number I wanted. I rang again. I sensed someone looking at me through the eye hole.

"Who is it?" a woman's voice demanded peremptorily.

"Rudyard Mack from the Library," I shouted. "Friend of Petula's."

"Wait a minute," the voice answered.

I stood sweltering in the hallway. In the early days of summer, the thick walls of these old houses kept the indoors cool, but, by August, they became hot houses. After a full minute, I heard a chain being lifted off, locks being unlocked. and, then, when the door swung open, I saw a tall, voluptuous brown woman in a red silky dressing gown standing in the doorway.

"Okay," she said huskily. "I'm Barb. Come in."

A sheet of cool air caught me as I stepped forward.

"I didn't know when you were coming," Barb Janes said, as she shut and bolted the door. "I was having a shower and almost didn't hear you buzz." Her dressing gown fell open as she turned revealing light blue panties and a slim brassiere on a beautifully shaped body. She quickly closed it and tied the sash. "Sit down and I'll get you a drink," she said. "You like red wine?"

"Fine," I said, somewhat stimulated. I sat in a soft-cushioned sofa and looked at the polished tables, comfortable, chintz-covered armchairs, the Persian rugs, the small windowed bookcase holding leather-bound volumes, African implements such as blow-pipes, bows, head-dresses, whatever, on the wall across the room. Behind me were framed photographs of Barb. She was dressed as a fan dancer in one, as a belly dancer in another, others were portraits, obviously career resume photos. I figured she was about thirty-five. The air conditioner in the window was almost soundless.

She came back from the kitchen carrying a tray with a bottle of Beaujolais, two wine glasses, and a glass dish filled with mixed nuts. "Pour, will you, Mr. Detective," she smiled from full red lips. "I can go for a tall glass right now." Her brown eyes appraised me approvingly.

I poured the wine. "You don't expect us to finish this?" I said jocularly.

"Don't see why not," Barb said, as if insulted. "I got nothing else on tonight." She sat across the coffee table from me.

I handed her a glass and ticked it with mine. "To a good friendship," I said.

Barb smiled impishly and took a big swallow.

"Been living in New York long?" I asked.

"Twelve years," Barb said with a grimace. "I came from South Carolina. Came to dance. Ended up as a nurse's aide."

"You got a nice place," I said, looking round.

"Not bad," she pouted. "But it took me a long time to get it lookin' like this, believe me, Rudyard. When I was workin' days and dancin' in the nights, I was just payin' the rent. It wasn't till I got into this union racket that I began saving some money."

"Petula said you're a big wheel with the Democrats."

"You're getting to the subject pretty fast, aren't you? What's 'a matter, do I bore ya or somethin'?" Barb frowned at me, her eyes menacing.

I held up my hands. "No, I like you, Barb. It's just that this friend of Petula's and mine was almost killed. I'm sort of anxious to find out who's behind it before she really gets knocked off."

Barb took a long swallow of wine and held out her glass for more. "Keep me company or I won't tell you nothing," she said.

I poured her a glass and, draining mine, filled it up again. "I'm with you, Barb," I smiled warmly.

"You look wet," she said, suddenly. "You want to take a shower and get clean?" She said it as more of an order than a question.

I put my hand through my hair and felt its wetness. "Okay, good suggestion," I said.

"The bathroom's in there," she pointed archly with her arm to the other end of the apartment. "Take the yellow towel." She stood up. "I'll fix us something to eat in the meantime. I'm starvin'."

I enjoyed the shower. The City grime fell away from me, the sticky heat was of the distant past. I hummed a tune, feeling rejuvenated, when I heard someone poking around in the bathroom. I looked out of the shower curtains to see Barb hanging up my clothes and putting my revolver on a shelf. She looked at me crossly. "Your clothes are soakin'. I'm drying them. You wear that blue dressin' gown on the hook there." She pointed to the back of the door. "Do you hear me, now?"

I did not mind her domineering tone because she seemed to be concerned for my welfare. "Okay, Barb. I'll be with you in a moment."

When she left the bathroom, I dried myself, found my underpants, put them on, put on the dressing gown and slippers she had left in the center of the room, and walked back to the living room in a new-found feeling of intimacy.

Barb had refilled our wine glasses. Refreshed, I drank with gusto. There was a sound of frying from the kitchen. Barb came into the room. Her eyes glowed excitedly.

"I hope you're hungry," she said. "I got us yams and spare ribs."

"Beautiful," I cried. "Beautiful."

"Petula told me you were good-looking," Barb said watching me. "But you're looking better than I thought."

"I feel better than I thought I would," I said glibly and took a drink of wine. "But I'm still interested in what you know about union politics."

She snorted and threw back her handsome head like a wild antelope on the African plain. "I'm in it only for the perks, Rudyard. The Club supports the District Council, and old Bratwurst supports our Democratic candidates. I get invited to lots of dinners, lunches, parties. We get free tickets to Broadway shows, and I get pocket money on the side. It's a good deal, Rudyard. You should get active in politics if you aren't."

"What about our Local president and the attempt to kill her," I reminded her.

"You got one thing goin' for you, Rudyard." Barb looked kindly at me. "Persistence."

"What do you know about it?" I insisted.

She laughed. "The word went out that Vine was gettin' too much publicity; Bratwurst didn't like it. Only him's got to be the Big Cheese. All the Local presidents don't exist 'cept when he wants to piss on somethin'. Then they can be got out."

"Like a pot," I laughed. "But Arbie Vine's no pisspot."

"Exactly!" Barb snapped her fingers and pointed her arm full length at me. "She's not playin' ball with the nice set-up he's got with the banks around here."

"Aren't they all Republicans--those bank presidents?" I frowned.

"Bullshit!" she said. "They're whatever suits them, Rudyard baby. You see Bratwurst hollerin' away on TV about the lay-offs, then he's havin' dinner at one of the homes of the Big Boys, black tie and all that, and they sit around and smoke and plan how many cuts they're gonna make next. The Mayor's there. He's a Democrat. Look, Rudyard, it's all these Jews got their money in city bonds and livin' it up in Florida. The Mayor's got to protect them to protect his job. Bratwurst is Jewish; he's got to protect them for the sake of the synagogue, and if you don't think the big institutions in this City don't have Jews owning them and the banks, you think again. They're not goin' to allow the City to default. Bratwurst is like Solomon. He'd sell every one of his workers into slavery before he'd let the Jewish middle class lose their money."

"Simplistic," I said, amused by her reasoning, "but what's that got to do with murdering Arbie Vine?"

"She's leading a march on City Hall!" Barb exclaimed. "They're nervous as hell. But I think they're gonna undercut her. They're gonna play the radical game. Red-bait her," she smiled. "Wait and see."

"Do you have proof that they planned to kill her?" I asked earnestly.

She looked at me slyly and shook her head with amusement. "Drink up, Rudyard baby. Our dinner's ready." She got up, and walked on long, lithe legs into the kitchen. I smelt the whiff of enticing perfume she left in the air. I could not be sure if she really knew what she was talking about or was playing a game with me. Beyond the dance photos on the wall, there were pictures of her a little older and surrounded by stout men with cigars, whom I recognized as local politicians who appeared in the newspapers whenever there were political scandals.

She re-entered with our dinner on plates which she placed in front of me. She took cutlery and paper napkins from the pocket of her dressing gown and handed them to me. "The Democrats got a candidate to run against Vine in her next union election. She can't win when the Democratic Party is against her."

"The Democratic Party is interested in controlling a library Local!" I cried, amazed.

"Oh yeah, we're gettin' rid of Vine. She's a pain in the ass. They got a candidate who's workin' as a children's librarian and active in the woman's liberation movement."

I laughed. "You don't know Library workers. You can't beat Arbie Vine that way."

Barb put a forkful of sweet potato into her mouth and continued talking. "They're smarter than you're givin' them credit for, baby. Petula's gonna run to get the black vote away from Vine."

I put down my fork and stared at her. "So they're splitting the Local all ways. Poor Arbie!"

"Don't fret over her," Barb said with indifference. "It's better bein' dumped as president than bein' dumped in the East River. Come on, Rudyard. You like my cookin'?"

"It's good," I said, eating the spare rib. "It's really good." I knew she wasn't going to tell me any more for the moment. We talked about other things, whatever entered Barb Janes's head, until we finished eating.

I helped her take the plates into the kitchen and wash them. We finished the wine, and I felt that my speech was slurring. Barb dried her hands on the towel behind the door, came to me as I dried the last dish, and put her arms around me. I sensed the magnetism of her body, and when she brought her lips to mine, I felt the passion flow into me. I kissed her strongly and, reaching around to pull off her dressing gown and undo her brassiere, I felt the strong full brown breasts and slipped my hands down around her waist. She took off my dressing gown and pull down my underpants, then, holding my balls firmly in her right hand, she threw her left arm about my neck.

"You haven't seen my bedroom," she said softly. "Want to come?"

"I'm in no position to refuse," I said. "You've been the most hospitable hostess I've met." I sensed I was a bit drunk.

Barb laughed, a full-throated, lovely laugh and led me away. Her bedroom could have been a Hollywood set for a film in the thirties. It was all boudoir. The soft rugs had long threads, the bureau backed by a beautiful oval mirror had silver and gold bottles of perfume and toilet water, hand mirrors, brushes, and other knickknacks. The window was draped in heavy velvet. The bed was immense, a veritable playground. Barb fell with me onto the bed and we made love with great energy.

In the morning, I rose from a deep sleep and looked round me at the plushness of the bedroom. Barb, her beautiful nude body curled beside me, had a smile on her face as if she were enjoying a dream. I watched the sunlight against the curtains and tried to remember why I had come to see Barb Janes. Oh yes, on account of Arbie. I felt a slight twinge of conscience. I caressed Barb's shoulder and back until she awoke and stretched straight out.

"Barb, do me a big favor," I asked. "Who told you that Arbie Vine was going to be wiped out?"

Barb opened her eyes wide, looked at me and grinned. "God, you're persistent," she said. "You deserve a reward! It was a guy name of Martin Slidsky. He contributes to our Democratic Club. He's in real estate--a vicious little rat, Rudyard. You take care." Her eyes fell on the small clock by her bed. "Jeez! I'm goin' to be late for work!" She sprung out of bed, and, with her figure rising like an Amazon Queen over me, she cried down, "Let's move it! Fast!"

FIVE

"A vicious little rat," Barb Janes called Slidsky. Probably his partner Benbow was the nice guy in the firm who worked the "up front" side of the business. All the dirty work was left to Slidsky.

I saw Barb on to a cross-town bus to the hospital where she worked. I telephoned my secretary to tell her I was investigating a book-theft suspect in case Director Anders checked up on me. Barb had given me Slidsky's home address in Riverdale, a richer area in the north of the city. I got a compact car for the day from a nearby car rental and noted the rental in my expense book. In half an hour I was parked outside Slidsky's modern apartment house, which had a round front like the stern of a ship and little trees planted in the front patio. If Slidsky had been foolish enough to talk openly of "wiping out" Arbie, he'd be careless enough to leave clues about how it was to be done. It was amazing, I thought, how these petty gangsters were so confident of the absolute support of their political colleagues--possibly because everyone knew they would not be prosecuted.

It was after ten. I used a telephone on the corner to call Slidsky's real estate office to see if he was at work. "Who shall I tell him is calling?" asked the secretary. I hung up. There was a doorman at the front door so I skirted the building to the back door which led to the street behind the building. I waited only a moment before a young lady opened the door on her way out after a night in one of the apartments. I seized it before it locked and went in. I went alone on the elevator to the tenth floor and was unseen as I picked the lock on Slidsky's apartment door.

The apartment was plush. There were a couple of abstract paintings on the wall--a Miro, a Still. I passed through the bedroom with its unmade bed, left, no doubt, for a maid who would do the cleaning later in the day. A study beyond the bedroom had a large window overlooking the front street. Before it was a long desk upon which were scattered scraps and sheaves of papers. I began going through them. They were telephone messages, calling cards, names, and telephone numbers, all the bits Slidsky collected in his pockets during the day and dumped here at night with a view of sorting through them some time. I opened a drawer. There were a pistol and computer print-outs of building addresses and their owners' names. In another drawer there was a photograph of Slidsky with his blonde wife and two boys, no doubt maintained in style in some fashionable community outside the City. Buried under some papers, I found a notebook with the names Wallenberg and Lanzetta sketched in pencil across the cover. The entries were dated, covering the past five years, and beginning with "Arranged for..." or "Achieved..." The entries themselves were brief, of little meaning except to the man who wrote them. I flipped through to August to the day of the knifing. "Arranged for the settlement with Local president." That, I thought, was, on the surface, an innocuous statement. It was followed by the words: "To pay Gabriel $2,000." In the entry for the following day were the words: "Arranged for the non-payment to Gabriel." There seemed to be no further reference. To the description of the knifer given by the girl from the massage parlor I could add the name "Gabriel." I replaced everything exactly as I had found it and hastily retreated to the door, which I opened with caution. There was no one in the corridor. I stepped out, closed the door quietly, and went to the elevator, which, as I reached it, stopped in front of me. A tall, heavy-set woman with stern features stepped off and walked to Slidsky's apartment. Waiting for the down elevator, I watched her enter. I became impatient for the elevator to arrive, and, when it did, I rode down with a great feeling of relief.

When I called my office, my secretary told me that I had a mysterious message from a girl named "Annie." She had left word to meet her at the Algonquin Hotel lounge at 12 noon. I called Arbie at her Headquarters.

"Library Guild," she said sweetly.

"Hi, sweetheart."

"Rudy, where have you been? I called you several times last night and there was no answer."

"I didn't get home until late," I lied. "Had anymore trouble?"

"I haven't been attacked if that's what you mean," she cried. "But I'm having a fuck of a time with my Local membership. They left all the organizing of our march on City Hall to me, and I've got grievances galore to handle."

"What about Alf Landy! Isn't he helping?"

"Oh sure, Alfie's got his Workers' Party to pitch in. All these young socialists come down here and telephone organizations and arrange preliminary meetings. They're goddamn wonders. If it weren't for them, there'd be no march. But my trouble is, darling, since you asked, is that they call themselves Socialists, and I wonder if that's not causing more problems than they're solving."

"Can't you tell them to forget the socialist bit?" I asked.

"Like asking a leopard to change his spots. They've got a mission and it shows in their eyes."

I coughed. "Well, honey, you're committed now."

"At least I'm offering an alternative to Bratwurst and his asskissers. If workers don't want to defend their jobs, that's their funeral. And that bloody Hector! He's spreading rumors that we're communist and want to take over the Government. What do you think about him as a trade unionist?"

"Typical," I said. "I'm glad you're beginning to see the light."

"Rudy, you're so conservative, it hurts!"

"But that doesn't mean I'm not behind you, Arbie," I said. "Even if you are marching to defeat."

"Defeat is not in my vocabulary," Arbie said. "When am I going to see you, love?"

"Tonight, but I'll call you later," I said. "The man who tried to knife you is named 'Gabriel.'"

There was a pause. "Gabriel!" she laughed. "The avenging angel of the Lord!"

"Just be careful," I warned. "I don't think they'll use him again, but they'll try something else. They don't like the publicity you're getting."

"Who's they, pray tell?"

"When I find out, I'll let you know. See you, sweetheart."

I drove through heavy traffic to midtown and put my car in a garage in time to keep my appointment at the Algonquin on 44th Street. In the lounge, sitting in an upholstered Victorian chair and looking like a sexy character in a woman's pulp novel, sat Annie, the "librarian" of the massage parlor, puffing on a thin cigar. She gave me a bold, appraising look as I approached.

"What's happened?" I asked, sitting beside her. She looked over my shoulder at a waiter who had moved behind me. I ordered a daiquiri and a beer.

"Your name was mentioned," Annie said, lowering her voice. "I wanted to let you know you're in for trouble."

I looked round at the businessmen and ladies sitting on the sofas and chairs, and having a drink before lunch. There were a few artist types, Europeans on a visit to America, watching curiously.

"Who mentioned me?" I asked with a smile.

"Who else but that Poppin character," Annie said as if she wanted to spit. "He was talking to one of his union buddies while I was working with them. It takes him so damn long to get an orgasm, he could tell his life story, if anybody wanted to hear it."

I almost laughed out loud.

The waiter brought our drinks, and I paid him.

"So Harold Poppin was interested in me," I said. "I met him the other night."

"I know," Annie said. "He said you were spying on the Council, and he thinks you're working with Vine to embarrass the union."

"He's not all wrong," I said.

Annie sipped her drink. "He sounded really angry!" She continued fixing her eyes on me. "He wants to see you punched up. That's what he said. He's gonna have you worked over to find out what you know."

I swallowed hard. "How can he do that?"

"Easy," she said. "They'll pick you up when you're alone somewhere, walkin' down a side street. They think nothin' of killing you, Rudyard. They'd kill me if they knew I was squealin' on them."

"But did they say anything definite?" I asked, leaning forward anxiously.

"No, they don't usually," Annie said. "If I hear anything, I'll let you know. I just wanted to warn you." She swallowed the rest of her drink. "I've got to be at the parlor at half twelve." She stood up. "Take care."

I noticed that the men in the lounge watched her go. I wondered what I should do--wait for Poppin to make the first move or take the initiative and attack. All the great generals took the initiative and surprised their enemies, I thought, as I reviewed in my mind the military histories I was fond of reading. Napoleon defeated armies many times his force in size by surprise attacks. General Brock, with a handful of regulars and Indians, took Detroit in 1812 by surprise. But then, there was the Battle of Tiberias when Saladin enticed the Crusaders to attack him on the desert plains, then cut them off from water supplies, and watched them die of thirst. I had to know the resources of my enemy before attacking, and, at a guess, I put them at numerous and powerful. Better to adopt Saladin's strategy--entice them into the field where they'll be exposed to the elements.

When I got back to the Library, I found a message that Joshua Raikes wanted to see me in the President's office at one-thirty. I was going to meet my new boss. Somewhat alarmed by his reputation as an ex-CIA man, I was pleased that he would bring a professionalism to the problem of library security that Bugofsky lacked. I looked in at the guards' office. Ajax, his six foot five inches crowded into a chair, and his huge black hands brought delicately together finger tip against finger tip in front of him, stared at the monitors of the closed circuit television. He was one of the few guards entrusted with a gun, but his black eyes could look so murderous that he had never had to use it.

"Everything okay, Ajax?" I called.

"A-okay," Ajax smiled and waved. "All right, Rudyard, sir. It's been real peaceful this week."

"Must be the heat," I said.

Ajax nodded and looked back at the monitors. "Somethin' like that." He brought his hands together by the fingertips again. I was reminded that Ajax painted water-colors on the weekends. He was called "talented" by the *Staff News*.

I went to the cafeteria in the basement for a tuna fish sandwich and skim milk. When I took my food to the inside room overlooking the asphalt courtyard where the managerial staff and trustees parked their cars, I encountered Harold Poppin and Alf Landy, talking earnestly. I sat at their table.

Poppin grinned at me, but he was not friendly.

"Hey, you're the guy we just been talkin' about," Alf cried. "What the hell were you doin' at our union meetin' if you're the Library detective? First, are you the Library detective?" He looked at Poppin. "I work in a branch in the Bronx, so I don't know the Director from the floor washer in the Central Building."

I ate my sandwich.

"He's a detective," Poppin said with the hint of a sneer. "See that bulge under his left arm?"

"Christ!" Landy cried. "Did you wear that to our meeting?"

I took a drink of milk.

"You won't believe that your Local president is a fink," Poppin, still grinning, said to Landy. "Here's proof."

"Someone tried to kill her," I said. "I'm covering all possibilities."

"We're all under suspicion," Poppin said between his teeth. "Even Hector."

"It don't surprise me if Hector was behind that knifer," Landy said, frowning at Poppin. "He's a ruthless son of a bitch."

"Careful, careful," Poppin closed down his smile. "You think you're one tough radical, but Hector eats your kind for breakfast."

"Hector can't do nothin'," Alf said accusingly. "A guy who throws away all his union options to play management's game is worth fuck all. He's gonna weaken the membership so much it won't even have the strength to get rid of him."

"That suits me." Poppin returned to his hard smile.

"Whatever Arbie's reason for bringin' this guy to the union meetin', it must have been a good one," Alf said angrily.

"Why are you two here now?" I asked.

"I came down for book orderin'," Alfie said. "I come here to eat lunch."

"Had some business in the neighborhood," Poppin said as if he were giving an alibi. "I park my car here."

"Do you have a ticket?" I asked.

"Yeah." Poppin reached into his coat pocket, brought out his wallet, and fished out the ticket for permission to park at the Library.

I examined it. Bugofsky had signed it. I returned it without a word. Poppin looked as if he were swearing under his breath.

"I should've done the same with you at our meeting," Poppin said. "Then I could have had the pleasure of kicking you out the door."

"Dreams are always sweeter than reality," I said and stood up. "I'm surprised neither of you is happy that I'm trying to keep your Local president from being murdered."

"I'm satisfied that you're doing it," Alf said.

Poppin just stared in amusement at me.

"The killer went by the name of Gabriel," I said. "We're getting closer to him."

I saw a flicker of surprise pass over Poppin's face and his eyes looked intense.

"Good, Mack," Alf said. "I hope you catch the bastard."

"Ten to one he's from the Workers Party," Poppin smiled sarcastically.

"Fuck you," Alfie said.

Poppin laughed as I walked away. It was almost one-thirty. I took the elevator to the second floor and walked to the President's Office. Joshua T. Raikes was going to be a demanding fellow, I thought. The man had held several sensitive jobs in government and directed numerous companies, some of them transnational. I was nervous despite the careful preparation I had done for the interview.

The President's secretary smiled and asked me to go into the office. The fact that I appeared to be the main piece of business disconcerted me. I swallowed hard and walked over the thick red carpet to the President's desk to where a bald-headed man in his seventies was energetically writing on a paper pad. I cleared my throat, and Raikes looked up quickly.

"There you are, Rudyard!" Raikes' voice was mild but urgent as if he were impatient to get to the point at issue. "Sit down. I'll be getting an office down the hall-- just have this one for the day while our President is raising funds. Do you prefer Rudyard or Rudy?"

"Rudyard's fine, sir." I sat down, surprised by the energy coming from the man.

Raikes slipped off his spectacles and concentrated his sharp gray eyes on my face. "I'm determined we get along, Rudyard. I've looked into your background. You're a good man. I can trust you, can't I?"

"I hope so, sir."

"You've been going off on your own bat, though, haven't you? Looking into the sad affair at the Local Union Headquarters. Got anywhere?"

"Not yet, sir." I blushed.

"You're surprised I know," Raikes smiled quickly. His face was round and hard, as if the cheeks, the high forehead, and the jutting chin were packed solidly into place. The snub nose seemed to have been put on last. "Word gets back to us, here. At least to certain people. Since you are under my charge now, I have been asked to tell you to, shall we say, 'cool it.'"

"I had a hunch that would be the instruction," I smiled in turn, enjoying the humorous undertone that Raikes was setting.

"I hear you telling me," Raikes continued, "that you can't cool something you are hot on the track of. I agree. But we'll keep that as an understanding just between us. See here, Rudyard, I'm a new man on the Board. I have to find my way around, but it's going to be along paths I want to walk, not the way someone else wants to direct me. Understand?"

"Perfectly," I nodded.

"Now, I hold no truck with Unions, but there are other ways of dealing with them than killing their presidents if they don't conform. Thank God, most of them do know what side their bread is buttered on."

"You want me to continue my investigations then?" I asked.

"More than that. I'll help you," Raikes said, pursing his lips tightly. "I'll direct you if need be."

"Right," I said, controlling my amazement.

"If we want good security, Rudyard, we have to be on top of everything. That's why I admire the way you went after this case."

"Thank you, Mr. Raikes. Very kind of you."

"Now, this girl, Arbuthnott Vine, the Local President, she's been getting death threats, according to what the police tell me."

My surprise registered clearly across my face.

"It's true," Raikes said. "She's had them on her business phone and at home, trying to dissuade her from her protest march on City Hall. Find out who's making those calls."

"Aren't the police doing that?"

"Not the manpower," Raikes said quickly. "They think it's a prankster, but, then, they also don't think Vine was the intended victim of whoever stabbed the man who worked in the messenger service." Raikes grimaced. "I'll be working on the case when I find the time. We'll be in touch."

I rose on this note of dismissal.

"And," Raikes added, "forget about the general security operations. They'll run without you."

I went back to my office. I was charged with excitement but, at the same time, mystified by Arbie's hiding from me the threatening phone calls. I dialed her number and broached the subject immediately.

"How'd you find out?" she cried.

"The Library Administration."

"That's the cops for you," she said. "Anything they don't want to handle they pass on to the employer. I didn't want to worry you any more than necessary, Rudy. You've got enough crap as it is."

"But these calls could tie in with the knifer."

"Naw," Arbie said. "It's some dumbo out for kicks."

"I've been instructed to find out who's making them, so, what does he sound like? And is it the same guy every time?"

"The same guy--a phony, deep voice, sort of fruity. He calls me a Red Commie, screwball, and things like that. Look, I'm sorry, honey. I shouldn't have reported it."

"See you tonight?" I asked.

"It'll have to be my place. I got a meeting at an uptown branch tonight. I'll make us a dinner--about 8.30."

"Okay, sweetheart."

Who didn't want Arbie to lead a protest against the City layoffs? The bankers didn't. The Mayor didn't. Bratwurst and his union cronies didn't. Who else? Maybe some of the Library trustees didn't because of the bad publicity for the Library. The real estate business didn't. I wondered if Martin Slidsky was involved with the telephone calls. I had to find out who Slidsky was working for. But how?

As if in answer, my telephone rang. It was Tom Benbow.

"Sorry we had a misunderstanding," Benbow said gaily. "I want us to be friends, Rudy. If you knew me better, you'd see I run an honest business. I want us to be on good terms with the Library. We can contribute to scholarships for the Staff, and you can help us by understanding that massage parlors are just an insignificant part of all the real estate we handle. So, look, Rudy, come to our cocktail party beginning at six tonight, will you? It'll be at the Candy Hotel on West 54th. We're just opening it. See you there?"

"I'll be there," I said. "It's your profession of honesty that attracts me, Tom."

Benbow laughed, greatly amused, as if he were on a high.

SIX

I got to the cocktail party by six-thirty. It was in a corner of the hotel ballroom on the second floor. Benbow was jocular. He pumped my hand as if he were a long-lost friend.

"Rudyard, I want you to meet my partner Marty. He keeps the business going while I horse around."

Slidsky was a well-built man with a plain face scarred on the cheeks by acne. He looked on, quietly observant, and muttered a welcome to me with a quick, sharp handshake. A Puerto Rican waiter with a thick mustache, smiling and bowing, directed me to the

tables where waiters in short white coats served drinks. I took a scotch and soda and looked around, glad to have got rid of Slidsky.
  I recognized Alexander Mackart, the right-hand man to Bratwurst. Mackart was talking quietly with another black man. He held ostentatiously before him a cigarette holder, which he carried to his lips for a puff as if he were tasting wine.
  There were some local politicians--city counselors, state assemblymen and state senators--all celebrating the addition of a new hotel to the City's prosperity. There were plenty of women circulating amongst the guests. I recognized a couple from the Library massage parlor. I didn't see Annie.
  "Hello, Rudyard baby," said a deep female voice behind me. I turned to look into the amused face of Barb Janes. "Bet you didn't think you'd see me this soon. How you doin', baby?"
  "Just great, Barb," I looked at her full figure held high above her slim waist. "And you look great!"
  "That's what every girl likes to hear, baby." Barb took my hand. "Come on, I want to introduce you to Alex."
  Mackart rounded his eyes at Barb as she came to stand in front of him. They embraced, ostentatiously throwing their arms about each other.
  "Princess!" Mackart said. "Should have known a politician like you wouldn't miss this one!"
  "Alex." Barb reared back to seize me by the hand and bring me in front of Mackart. "This is Rudyard, my friend. He works for the Library."
  Mackart shook my hand. "Hope you're enjoying the party," he said politely. "Are you connected with the Democratic Club?"
  "No," I smiled. "I'm a friend of Tom's."
  Mackart said "Oh" and looked impressed. Mackart's companion stuck out his arm and introduced himself as a union man. I guessed he acted as bodyguard for Mackart.
  "I'm introducing you," Barb said to Mackart, "cause Rudyard's a good guy, and he might be needing your help."
  "My help!" Mackart raised his eyebrows. "Well, when the time comes, I'll do what I can. Is the Library in trouble?" he asked with feigned amusement.
  "No," I said, "but I may be."
  Barb Janes laughed shortly. "You can say that again. Oh, look Alex, there's Lanzetta. He never comes to these things."
  She directed our attention to a short, thin man in a dark suit who carried a cane to compensate for a limp. For such a powerful real estate figure, he looked disappointingly weak and insignificant.
  "I haven't seen him for two years," Mackart said. "I'm going over to say 'hello'. See you, princess."
  "See you, babe," Mackart's heavy-set friend said and followed Mackart.
  "Let's mix, Rudyard," Barb said. "I'll see you back at this spot in forty-five minutes, okay?"

"Okay," I said. I watched Barb go with misgiving. If I was to meet Arbie in the evening, I could not meet up with Barb again because she obviously had her own plans for me for the evening. I took another whisky and soda as I contemplated how I could slip out of the noose Barb was fashioning for me. I drifted over to the half dozen persons standing about Lanzetta. As Lanzetta gave his opinions on the fiscal crisis and the future prospects of the City, men and women would come to shake his hand and pass on. Lanzetta relished his power. Whenever someone suggested a solution to the City's problems, Lanzetta pooh-poohed it. Only he had the right answer, and he acted as if it were obvious to anyone who took the trouble to examine the situation the way he had. I watched the dark beady eyes, the tight prim lips and the long thin nose as I wondered if Lanzetta knew who had given the order to kill Arbie Vine. Suddenly, I found Lanzetta looking at me as if assessing me. I nodded at him and moved away. Lanzetta continued speaking in general, but I felt his eyes following me.

Feeling conspicuous, I walked in the direction of a sign reading "Gentlemen." The hall was shiny, new, spotless. I pushed the white steel door to the washroom and entered a large room arrayed with heads along two walls. The toilet booths were in another room at the back. I looked at myself in the wall mirror. Everything was so clean. I felt as if I was the first person to use the bathroom. I was about to address myself to one of the heads, and had just unzipped my fly, when three very tough-looking men in their thirties pushed through the door. Sensing a threat, I pretended I was finishing and zippered my fly. One man stood by the door while the other two, grinning, walked up and grabbed me by the arms. They pushed me back against one of the sinks. I felt the rim of the sink dig into my lower back. One of the men twisted my arm high behind my back so that I had to lean back and buckle my knees to reduce the pain. The other, with a thick broad face that seemed hacked from a block of wood, a furrowed forehead, and angry blue eyes, pushed his body against mine, pinning me motionless.

Recovering from my surprise, I realized that if I shouted I could not be heard by those in the party. I stayed quiet waiting for my captors to speak.

"You're making a nuisance of yourself," said the huge man pressing against me. "You're asking too many questions. You're getting into things that don't concern you." His voice was clear, well-modulated, unlike the gravelly tones usually associated with thugs. "We want to give you a message to mind your own business." He stood back and brought his right fist crashing into my stomach.

The pain was intense, as if a tight cord tying my throat to my bowels had been yanked, tearing all the muscles from one end of my body to the other. I blacked out.

When I regained consciousness, I was lying on the tile floor of the men's room. It took a good minute for my head to clear, but, while it was clearing, I sensed that I was alone and out of danger for the moment. I dragged myself to my feet by gripping onto a sink. Shoots of pain in my stomach and nausea weakened me. I pushed on a tap, cupped cold water in one hand, and spattered it over my face. As my strength returned, I paced the room, slowly at first. Then gradually I recovered my normal walking stride.

I had been warned good and proper, I thought, but by whom? Certainly by someone with a mundane imagination to have ordered this old style of thuggery. But then, maybe whoever ordered it didn't think me worthy of more sophisticated treatment. I had to remember, I told myself, it was not only how I regarded them that counted, but how they regarded me. If I ran away now, like a scared rabbit, they would think they were rid of me.

I walked out of the men's room, back down the shiny steel hallway, and passed by the fringes of the party, all of whom were talking animatedly, too occupied to notice my departure, except for Lanzetta, who was standing alone near the doorway, a drink in his hand, and a twisted smile on his little pointed face.

I was a bit early to meet Arbie, but I took the IRT Seventh Avenue uptown to her place and intended to wait in a coffee shop across from her apartment house. I noticed that people on the subway tended to look twice at me. I looked at my reflection in the windows and could see nothing wrong. My tie looked straight. Then I saw what it was. My face looked shocked. It was as if I'd just seen a ghost. I tried to relax my expression, but I couldn't rid myself of my alarmed look. It was absurd!

I met Arbie as I came out of the subway. She was hurrying by and carrying a large bag of groceries.

"Hey," I called. "I'll carry them."

"Rudy! Lucky my meeting ended early," Arbie said, giving me the bag with both arms. "How come you're so prompt?" She looked closely into my face. "Are you all right?"

"Fine," I said, trying to look nonchalant. "How are you?"

"Me? Oh, I'm sick of this whole stupid grievance business. The Library never fails to get the worst supervisors in the world, and then, when in their petty madness they put the screws on someone under them, management supports the supervisors without question. I'm really sick of it all. Let's just have a good dinner, play some music, and forget about everything."

"I'd like to forget about everything," I said.

When Arbie opened the door to her apartment, her telephone began to ring. She ran to answer it as I took the groceries into the kitchen. I put the milk, eggs and coke into the refrigerator. Since Arbie did not appear, I figured she was talking to a friend. I ambled out of the kitchen into her living room and saw her standing rigid, face white, and eyes staring as she listened to whomever was on the other end of the line. She beckoned to me. I took the receiver from her and listened. A male voice, sounding thick and fruity, was reciting a list of tortures in store for Arbie--barbarous suggestions, sadistic and frightening--in a slow deliberate manner. I thought the caller was reading them.

"What do you want, buster?" I cut in.

The voice paused, then the line clicked as the caller hung up.

I put down the receiver and took Arbie in my arms.

"It's so ugly, Rudy," she said as if in shock. "People are so ugly."

"What was it all about?" I asked. "Your rally?"

"Yes." Arbie pulled away. She looked determined. "No one's going to stop us from protesting. Not any sex-crazed nut, anyway!"

"That's the spirit!" I smiled. "Now, do you mind if I help you with the cooking. I'm hungry and it's almost 8:30."

Arbie laughed. "Okay, you make the salad. I'll do the cooking--fast."

As we prepared dinner together in the kitchen, I thought about Arbie, how much I loved her, treasured her companionship, admired her bravery and strength of character. Moreover, I really enjoyed making love to her. Now that her life was in danger, she became dearer than ever to me. I had to fight off the wish that she would give up the union rally, which, after all, was not going to effect changes in the City Government. But I knew I would be cramping her, denying her the right to be independent, and forcing my fears upon her, if I argued the issue with her. It was our respect for one another's independence which kept us together. I had to keep my faith in her ability to survive, as, doubtless, she kept her faith in me.

"That Lanzetta could be the key man," I said suddenly. "He could lead us to the character who's behind these threats."

"Sounds reasonable," Arbie said, as she put a chicken casserole into the oven. "The real estate interests don't want New York to default. Think of the billions they'd lose if the value of their properties were re-assessed, if they were forced to pay their back taxes, and if businesses moved away from the City. By making the workers take the burden of the loss, the real estate boys increase their control over City Government."

"How's that?" I asked.

"For one thing, the bankers who set up the economic council to govern the City are in cahoots with them. For another, when they created high inflation, the City could pay off its debts cheaper, real property became more valuable." Arbie put vegetables into boiling water. "Damn it, Rudy, when we finish paying for the mistakes of the moneyed classes, you'll see the real estate boys owning the biggest slice of the City. And then, try to pay the rent. Ha!"

"That's a gloomy picture, sweetheart."

"People don't see it though," Arbie cried. "If they'd only realize they've got to fight if they don't want to be pushed under. 'Stead they put all their hopes in a screwball like Bratwurst."

I laughed at her look of disgust. "You're really determined, aren't you?"

"You want to see the struggle at first-hand?" she asked with a half-smile. "Come to our rally in a union hall on West 43rd., tomorrow night. It's sort of preliminary to the march next week."
"The Left will be out in force," I smiled.
"Maybe Lanzetta will be, too," Arbie said. "On second thought, you'd better be there."

SEVEN

I entered the auditorium which the social workers and the librarians had rented from the hospital workers whose building it was. There was excitement in the air. Arbie had provided me with a union card to get me by the guards at the door. Everyone seemed to be talking. I saw Petula Simon Clarkson beckon to me. I came to her through the crowd. Taking my arm, she shouted over the voices: "Let's go down front."
I stayed slightly behind Petula as she bull-dozed her way down the aisle. I preferred to be near the stage where I could respond more easily should Arbie be in danger. An older genteel-looking black man moved his arm away from the backs of two seats he had been reserving. Petula sat beside him, and I took the other seat which was on the aisle. The older man was Petula's escort. He seemed to have been buffeted by the world and now clung in a weakened condition onto the rock-like Petula.
"There's all types here tonight, Mack," Petula shouted. "All the splinter groups on the left, Trotskyites, Spartacists, Stalinists."
Several people, Arbie among them, climbed onto the stage. The president of the social workers spoke into the microphone. A large bespectacled man, he subdued the gathering to relative quiet. He emphasized the importance of the march on City Hall to prevent lay-offs and called upon the social workers who were the greater part of the audience to turn up on Saturday morning.
A black man with a white beard in a toga and sandals came to the microphone to challenge the businessmen who had seized the City, administered its finances, and used the Mayor as their puppet. He represented a coalition of protest groups in the South Bronx where the citizens were victimized by arson instigated by landlords, roving criminal gangs and corrupt police. "The more we let them take from the City," the old man shouted hoarsely, "the less is going to be left for us. We've got to fight 'em." He received a smattering of applause which indicated sympathy, but the majority were impatient with these old-time representatives of the disadvantaged.
I watched speaker after speaker from blighted and beleaguered areas of the City speak of the absolute need to confront City Hall. But they had no constituency in the audience, which was disinclined to

sacrifice itself on their behalf. Just as the collective impatience seemed no longer containable, Arbie stepped to the microphone and caught the interest of the assembly with her fiery words and tough rhetoric against the capitalists, their political henchmen, their F.B.I. thugs, and their sweetheart union leaders. This was the speechifying they wanted to hear--words that grappled with the present and foretold of a future that they could bring about. As Arbie called on them to march the following Saturday, the meeting broke up. In one aisle a worker shouted, "It's a fraud, it's a setup! You're phonies!" Arbie looked astounded, and, before she could reply, the man, a mestizo, was lost in the crowd streaming out of the auditorium.

I called out to Arbie, who was gathering together papers from a chair, "Hey sweetheart, you're a fraud."

The others looked at me and laughed, but Arbie frowned, "You can bet that's what those Maoists are saying," she gestured at knots of people talking in the auditorium and in the hallways. "Trying to get socialists to trust one another is just impossible. We got a real problem on our hands," she shouted at the President of the Social Workers Local. "By letting the Trotskyites organize for us, we're alienating all the others."

The social workers President shrugged his beefy shoulders. "What can we do?"

"Don't worry, Arbie," someone said. "The meeting tonight was a pretty good protest on its own."

"Yeah, but who got the message," Arbie said. "Not the Mayor, not the bankers, not the public--only ourselves. And we already know it." She looked disgusted.

A young man, one of the Trotskyites that I had seen distributing leaflets, cried, "We need a general strike, but the unions won't do nothin'."

"Even the march," the President of the social workers said philosophically, as he started out the door near the stage, "is symbolic, at best."

Arbie, carrying her briefcase, came down off the stage and walked with me along the aisle to the exit at the front of the building. Cleaners were telling stragglers to leave and making unnecessary noise dragging waste bins behind them.

"I'm depressed," Arbie admitted.

"Be happy this evening was successful," I said.

"Maybe you're right, darling," Arbie sighed. "Everything counts regardless how small."

"Look at it this way," I reasoned. "Somebody wouldn't be trying to bump you off if he wasn't afraid of the protest march."

"How do you know it's the march?" Arbie asked. "Maybe it's somebody who just hates my guts."

"Not possible," I said and hugged her.

We made our way by a pile of black plastic garbage bags on the sidewalk looming in the light from the street lamp.

"At least no one took a shot at me tonight," Arbie said.

"Not yet," I said, "but there's a guy following us. As we turn the corner look to your right."

Arbie glanced back as we walked onto Eighth Avenue. There was a heavy-set man of medium height in a flowery sports shirt about twenty yards behind us in the dark.

"How do you know?" she asked, feeling uneasy and holding onto my arm more tightly.

"I saw him at the meeting," I said. "And he was waiting in the shadows when we left."

"God, I'm glad you're with me," she said.

"That's the problem," I said. "I'm going to pretend to leave you, then I'll circle back behind him."

"Rudy! Don't leave me alone with that man!"

"We've got to find out who's after you," I said. "This is our chance. Now keep walking south under the bridge."

I kissed her and whispered, "It'll be all right." I waved as I walked rapidly west on 42nd Street.

Arbie crossed the road and disappeared from view under the bridge.

When the man in the sport shirt crossed 42nd Street, I crossed in mid-block dodging a couple of passing cars and ran back to the Avenue. When I reached the corner, Arbie was nowhere in sight. The man running to a black car standing in the street. A car door opened to admit him, and I heard Arbie cry my name. The anguish in her voice froze me. The door slammed as the car started up, tires screeching. I caught two letters "I E" of the license plate as I ran up, and the car sped into the night. The enormity of my mistake struck me to the heart. That there would be more than one man never occurred to me. Fear struck me dumb. My mind went blank as I stared down the dark street flashing with the headlights of moving traffic. Then, shaking myself out of my paralysis, I ran to a sidewalk telephone and dialed the number for Detective Buckle.

EIGHT

I sat, feeling guilty and miserable on a bench against the wall in a narrow, neon-lit room in the Chelsea police precinct station. A wall clock pointed to ten o'clock. A police sergeant was showing me mug shots from a file of local criminals, but I did not find the thick features of the man in the flower-printed sports shirt among them. A thin, middle-aged gentleman with a kindly disposition and air of reticence came into the room. The sergeant greeted him warmly and introduced him to me as the resident head-shrink.

"Detective Buckle asked me to drop by before I went home tonight, Mr. Mack," the head-shrink explained apologetically. "He thinks I might help you to remember."

I swallowed hard. "Do you mean by hypnosis?"

"It'll last only for a moment or two," the psychiatrist smiled, and, unbuttoning his suit coat, he sat facing me on the chair that the sergeant had vacated. "Sergeant, would you please take a pad and pencil. We shall need a record of Mr. Mack's thoughts."

"I may not be any good at this," I said.

"We'll try, shall we," the psychiatrist smiled kindly at me. "Just relax. Lean back against the wall as comfortably as you can."

I settled my shoulder blades comfortably against the wall and began to worry what I might say under hypnosis. Arbie was in my thoughts as I focused on the watch swung before my eyes. I blinked and looked at the wall clock. It was 10:45. I thought of the passage of time as miraculous. Then I saw the reassuring face of the psychiatrist observing me.

"Did it work?" I asked.

"You did very well, Mr. Mack," he smiled.

"We got the full license number," the sergeant interjected.

I shook my head in wonder. "I thought I caught only two letters and that it was a New York plate."

"It was a New Jersey plate," the sergeant said.

The psychiatrist smiled and stood up to go when Detective Buckle entered the room, his short round body vibrant with energy and hustle.

"We've got the license number, Detective," the sergeant cried.

"Run it," Buckle said, and the sergeant hurried from the room.

Buckle shook hands with the psychiatrist. "Any thoughts?"

"I'll tell you tomorrow," the psychiatrist said as he nodded goodbye to me and stepped from the room.

"Who do you think did it?" Buckle asked with a half-smile.

"It could be Lanzetta," I said. "I think it was his boys who worked me over today."

"Oh yeah," Buckle said rounding his eyes. "You better be careful not to mention that name around here. He's got lots of friends." Buckle grinned. "What's his motive?"

"Stopping the march on City Hall, I guess," I said doubtfully. "But that's pretty weak."

"Yeah," Buckle agreed. "I dropped in on the meeting the planners of the march had with our guys to get the permit. Everyone with Vine was from the Socialist Party. She was the only *bona fide* union member. It looks like someone's setting her up."

"She's aware of that, but she wants that protest march to come off," I said. "The socialists have the capabilities and the will to organize it."

Buckle nodded. "Come on. Let's see what they've come up with."

He led the way down a corridor to a room at the end. The desks were angled about in several directions, and chairs were placed here and there giving the impression of the chaos that took place all day long when there were human beings to create it. The sergeant was staring at a monitor screen.

"It just came up," the sergeant said and pushed a button to print it.

"Don't recognize the name," Buckle said, staring at the screen. "Lawyer, nah, this is a bum steer. Better see if it's stolen."

The sergeant tore off the print-out and went with it to another room.

"What can we do?" I looked pleadingly at Buckle.

"We've got an alert out on the car," Buckle said in a matter-of-fact manner. "We just wait."

"I can't," I said. "I've got to get out and look for her."

"Where do you start?" Buckle looked amused. "Gonna pay Lanzetta a mid-night visit?"

I looked glumly at him.

The sergeant burst through a door into the large office and hurried toward us. "It's stolen all right," he said. "But they think it went through the toll onto the Queens Expressway about an hour ago."

"How would they know?" I asked skeptically.

"Our boys got an instinct," Buckle said. "Who do we know lives on Long Island?"

"Maybe Lanzetta," I suggested.

"Yeah, he does," Buckle nodded, his chubby face looking very serious. "Anyone else?"

"Hector Bratwurst?"

"Yeah," Buckle nodded. "We'll call Bratwurst and tell him one of his favorite union presidents has been kidnapped." He stepped to a monitor and typed rapidly.

"But won't you be alerting him that he's under suspicion?" I said in alarm.

"You want to move fast, don't you?" Buckle said. "We want him in the case--put pressure on him." He jotted the number on the screen into his notebook. "Sergeant, will you inform the newspapers that the President of the Library Workers Union has been kidnapped." Buckle dialed Bratwurst's number. "He ought to be in bed," he smiled. "His wife's probably giving him his hot toddy."

The sergeant began to call the night desks of the city newspapers.

Buckle told Bratwurst the " bad news." "Any idea who could have done it?" Buckle stared balefully at me as he listened to Bratwurst. "Just that we know you planned a protest march." I could hear Bratwurst's voice rise in denial. "We'll be in touch." He hung up. "Don't think he's in on it," Buckle said, "but he probably will be before long."

A telephone rang. I watched Buckle walk to a desk and speak into the receiver. I began to curse myself again for leaving Arbie alone for a moment. How could I have been so stupid? Buckle came up to me.

"The car's been found. In New Hyde Park. They must have had someone waiting for them." He sat on the edge of the desk. "I'll have a squad car drive you home, Rudyard. Get some sleep. I've got a few things to do before I pack it in."

I nodded. "I'll do whatever you want me to, but I want to be of use."

"We'll use you, don't worry." Buckle walked with me out the front door of the precinct to a squad car parked by the curve, and asked the driver to take me home. "She'll be all right," he said. "She's a spunky lady."

The cop who drove me across town brought up the subject of Arbie Vine. "We're behind her. We can't join the march but we're sending a big detail to walk alongside it." He pulled up to my apartment house. "We'll get her back." I found his assurance comforting.

The deserted street, the naked lights of the apartment entrance, the lonely atmosphere of the night made me sense how greatly I missed Arbie. I nodded to the doorman and trudged onto the elevator. There was a possibility I might not see her again, but I checked that thought the instant it came to me.

When I came into my living room, I poured myself a scotch and sat down beside the telephone. I decided not to go to bed. I could not afford to miss hearing the telephone ring, I thought. It was morning when I woke up. Pigeons were cooing outside my window. Daylight suffused the room in a low glow. A half glass of scotch remained. I was tempted to swallow it, but I carried it to the kitchen, put it on a shelf, and heated water for instant coffee. I went into my bedroom, took off my clothes, and stepped into the shower. It was when I was soaping myself that depression fell upon me. I stood staring at the enamel of the bathtub, the warm water splashing over me, the kettle whistling in the kitchen while I dreamed of Arbie being humiliated by thugs. When I could move again, I acted mechanically. The thought that the kidnappers might try to contact me at my office encouraged me to quicken my movements until I began to consider the foolishness of waiting for them to contact me. They would find me if they wanted me, I thought. Buckle had told me to stay put just to get me out of the way. If Arbie were in my shoes, she wouldn't stay put! As I ate breakfast, a determination to act welled within me. I began to lay a plan to invade the criminal world of Lanzetta.

NINE

There were two routes into the criminal world. One was through the bottom by way of police informants; the other was through the top by way of influential contacts, which was rarely used because it required ideological commitment on the part of the infiltrator. But this latter route was the logical one for me to follow. I telephoned Joshua T. Raikes at his home. I could tell from Raikes' slight pauses that I had caught him at the breakfast table.

"Kidnapped!" Raikes cried. "By whom?"

"That's what I hope you will help us to discover, sir," I said. "The order must have come from someone opposing the protest march."

"But surely kidnapping Vine is an absurd way to keep her from protesting," Raikes remarked in a tone that dismissed such an hypothesis. "There must be something larger at stake."

"These guys don't think on a very high level," I warned. "Can you use your contacts to find out who is behind it?"

There was a pause. "You sound quite emotional," Raikes said calmly. "You really are deeply involved in this case."

"I put one hundred percent into everything I do," I said.

"I'll do what I can," Raikes said dryly. "Where can I reach you?"

"I'll be on the road. I'll call you at the Library about noon."

I wondered if I could trust Raikes. Actually I wasn't trusting Raikes, I thought; I was trusting the liberal element that Raikes represented. While Raikes was looking for an answer in the respectable world, I decided to move among the less respectable. I called Harold Poppin's number at union headquarters. Poppin seemed genuinely surprised about the kidnapping. But I could not be sure; the man was a skillful dissembler. Arbie had told me that Poppin's method of selling a negotiated contract to the membership was to threaten the members with the need to strike if they did not accept the terms.

"Are you prepared to join in the search for her?" I asked Poppin.

"What can we do?" Poppin hedged. "Isn't that a matter for the police?"

"She needs your help," I said in a tone of impatience. "After all, she works in your department, and the union has resources. The least you can do is talk it over."

I could almost hear Poppin thinking as a craftiness crept into his voice. "Hector's in his office. Hold on while I call him."

Poppin seemed ready to show that he wanted to help Arbuthnott to disguise his true ill-feelings for her. Hector, too, would be put on the spot. Hector could not afford to appear to refuse help to one of his Local presidents when in need.

"You have it, Mr. Mack," Poppin's voice said. "Come to Hector's office down here on the sixth floor at nine-thirty."

I hung up with a certain satisfaction. By obliging the union leaders to help in the search for Arbie, I was narrowing the field of suspects; and if any of these leaders were involved in the kidnapping, I would be working close enough to them to flush them out.

At nine-thirty, I stepped off the elevator onto the sixth floor of the Council office building. I stepped along the neon-lit, carpeted hallway instinctively to Hector Bratwurst's office. Poppin's heavy-set form appeared beyond an office doorway at the end of the hall. I walked in and found Poppin with Alex Mackart and Ted McConnell, the happy-faced administrator, standing by the desk of Bratwurst's secretary.

"Our library detective, gentlemen," Poppin said with a twist of a smile. "Teddy, this is Mr. Mack."

I shook hands with McConnell, whose breezy manner seemed to conceal a wariness evident in the sharp look of his eyes and a tenseness in his face.

Mackart stepped forward casually. "We've met." He stretched out his arm and I grasped his long fingers manicured and ringed. "Our friend, Barbara, introduced us." He smiled as if there were a secret between us.

Bratwurst's secretary came from the inner office. She was short and dark-haired, and spoke brusquely. "Hector will see you now."

"Let's go then," McConnell said. "I'll lead the way into the lion's den."

I sensed the respect these union men had for Bratwurst's office, as if it were a sanctum. It was a respect founded on fear, I thought, because Bratwurst could dismiss them from their highly-paid employment with the snap of his fingers.

Hector was standing behind his desk. He smiled boyishly and asked me to sit. There were a number of wooden chairs with green seats facing the desk in a semi-circle. Poppin introduced me to Hector, but Hector made no gesture to shake hands, rather he stepped back, put his hands in his pockets and grinned at me.

"So you're the guy who's givin' me all this trouble," Hector said. "One of our trouble-makers disappears, we heave a sigh of relief, and you come along and prick our conscience." The company laughed with him, spurred by his emphasis on "prick."

"The membership of her Local will be pleased by your efforts to find her," I reminded them and watched as they looked suddenly serious.

"We could get a big spread in our newspaper," Poppin suggested. "You could write a piece expressing your concern, Hector."

Hector nodded. He liked the idea. "And what the hell we gonna do to find the girl. Sure, we got a reading membership of two hundred thou--at least we got a membership; whether they can all read is a fuckin' big question," he smiled. "But how the fuck do we find her?" He glared at Ted McConnell.

"First, we ask our sister unions to help," McConnell said, eyes twinkling with his bright idea. "We get sanitation, mail delivery, teamsters, the whole goddamn lot to keep their eyes peeled for this dame."

Hector nodded. He seized the back of his chair, bowed his head, and asked for more suggestions.

"Then we ask Louie where he's hidin' her," McConnell smiled, and the others laughed.

Hector explained the joke to me. "Louie's from the Italian-American League--comes round here for donations."

I noticed that Poppin was looking uncomfortable.

"Sounds like a good idea," I said.

"Aw, he's just a bum," Hector said.

"He's a soldier," McConnell explained, eyes still twinkling.

"Let's move this thing along," Hector said impatiently. "The Mayor's waiting for me. I got to see State senators at lunch and screw Mrs. Bancroft for tea."

The men laughed. She was a rich liberal philanthropist.

"You could go on television and plead for her life," McConnell suggested.

Poppin chuckled.

Hector frowned, his eyes looked murderous. "You tryin' to make me look stupid? Plead to whom? We don't know who has her? Sometimes, McConnell, you surprise me." His look warned McConnell, whose eyes lost their lustre.

"That trouble at her headquarters," Mackart said quietly. "Maybe her landlords know something. I could ask Lanzetta." Mackart widened his eyes with the significance of what he was saying.

Bratwurst looked uncertainly at him, paused as if caught off guard, and then growled. "You do it, Alex. I got no time for Lanzetta. You guys send me good suggestions. Clear out, you bums, I got work to do." Hector nodded good-bye to me sourly. I nodded in turn and walked in line out of his office.

"Okay, Alex," Poppin said, smiling derisively as they came into the hall, "the man's put you on to Lanzetta. Ted's going to contact the other unions, and I'll talk to the boys in the editor's office. That suit you, Rudyard?"

"It's movement," I said.

"Nothing sensational," McConnell said sarcastically as he moved away with Mackart, "but we'll get results."

"The Editor's office is on this floor," Poppin said breezily to me. "And here's your elevator."

The elevator light signaled red for down. I thanked Poppin and got on, but instead of pushing the lobby button, I pushed for the third level where I knew the Local presidents had their offices in this building. I wondered if Arbie's office would yield any clues. I doubted that the union officials would be of any help.

I walked from the elevator across the hall to a huge room which ran the length of the building. It was divided by seven-foot partitions forming a half-dozen office areas in which there were rows of desks running alongside the partition walls. These desks were for the presidents of the Locals. At the end of each row and in front of the windows which looked out on the Hudson River were the glass offices of the Division Chiefs. Since the desks faced the elevator, the backs of the Local presidents were turned to the office of the Division Chiefs, who could sit watching them through their glass walls.

"Librarians?" repeated a heavy-set, large-bellied man in a blue sweatshirt. "Two down." He pointed to a sign. "White-collar Division."

I guessed from the rugged looks of the men sitting at the desks that they were the presidents of laborers' Locals: sewer workers, tree pruners, parks maintenance, and so on. By comparison, the White-Collar Division looked as if a cyclone had hit it. The desks were strewn with papers. Files standing behind the desks were open and bulging with papers. No one was sitting at the desks. I approached the secretary at the back. She was a thin African girl from a race with rounded face and high, tight cheekbones, possibly from southern Nigeria.

"Where are all the Local presidents?" I asked throwing my arms out to the sides.

The secretary giggled, her eyes dancing with humor. "In the field." She looked at me waiting for my next question.

"Where does Miss Vine sit?"

"Third down on the right." The secretary pointed to the steel desk in question. "She didn't phone in yet."

I walked over to the desk and stared at the in and out trays filled with papers. There was a sheaf of papers in a red folder lying on the desktop.

"You can sit," the secretary said." If she calls in, I'll tell you."

I smiled my thanks and, sitting, looked casually through the red folder. Memoranda from the Library, instruction after instruction, met my eye. There were Library Administrative memos, Library Technical memos, Library Divisional memos, followed by a cache of memoranda from the Chiefs of Special Divisions who communicated with staff largely by memoranda on every conceivable subject. Arbie, I thought from the way she had arranged these memoranda, seemed to be emphasizing the plethora of contradictory instructions originating from the Personnel Division, the Business Manager, all the Library Division Chiefs, the Head Librarians in the Branches, and the Research Libraries. There was no coordination among them, yet it was difficult to prevent a Division Chief from issuing policy by memoranda because only through memoranda could he indulge his sense of power. But, at the same time, the Union had to have a clear idea of what was the true Library policy in order to conduct staff grievances.

I opened one of the file drawers and peeked at the folders crammed tightly into it; they comprised grievance hearings, step after step of the same complaint, the same defense, the same rejection by management, until the grievance reached an impartial arbitrator, when it took on a changed aspect and required a new file. I flipped the pages of Arbie's desk calendar and glanced at the jottings she had made: reminders for lunch, for meetings, telephone numbers. There seemed to be no clues. I sat back in the chair with a sense of hopelessness and frustration.

I heard a deep, heavy-accented voice talking to the secretary behind me and swiveled round to look. A thick-set man of medium height with a large throat, a broad nose, and dark hair slicked back to the nape of his neck was asking to see Harold Poppin. The man had come from another area along the corridor running alongside the Division Offices. I heard the secretary call him "Louie" and watched as Louie walked heavily, expressionlessly by me to the hallway and the elevators. So this was the representative from the Italian-American League making his rounds for collections, I thought. I waved good-bye to the secretary and reached the hallway as the down elevator arrived. Louie and I got on together. Louie wore a black raincoat. His face had no expression. He looked like a man who could kill on orders without questioning, without thinking, without even sensing what he was doing.

We were alone on the elevator. I caught Louie's eye and smiled. Louie stared through me.

"You're Louie, aren't you?" I said.

"What of it?" Louie said gruffly.

"I heard Hector talk about you."

Louie's face became alert. His eyes narrowed. "What'd he say?"

"He thinks a lot of you," I said.

Louie's thick lips turned down in a sneer. I followed him off the elevator, down the lobby corridor, and into the street. As I walked along with him, Louie suddenly stopped and looked threatening.

"Beat it!" he said.

"I've got a question for you, Louie," I grinned amiably. "Harold Poppin says you might know the answer."

Louie stared passively at me.

"Can you put me in touch with Gabriel?"

Louie looked suspicious. "A black guy?"

"Yeah, that's the man."

"Maybe. Why do you want him?"

"He can do a job for some friends of mine," I smiled. "Pay is good. He freelances, doesn't he?"

Louie nodded. "The family sees him from time to time. These friends, are they union people?"

"Oh no, no," I shook my head. "Business people. They got money."

"Cause if it's union, we look after all union business," Louie said in warning.

"No, these guys can't afford to risk using the family," I smiled. "Anyway, it's a job for only one man."

Louie nodded. "You know Dino's cafe on Hudson Street?"

I did not know it, but I said "Yes."

"Gabriel hangs out there most afternoons," Louie said. "What's your name?"

"Rudy," I said. "Tell me, Louie, why do you wear a raincoat in this hot weather?"

Louie looked surprised. He stared at me as if wondering if he should answer the question. "I got to carry things under it, if you know what I mean?" He looked darkly at me and turned abruptly to walk away.

I watched him move stockily down the street. I could not believe my luck at finding Gabriel. It was just mid-morning so that I had a few hours before going to Dino's. I went over to the west side subway and rode the train to Times Square. A cluster of boys tried to hassle me as I passed by. One boy nudged me sharply on my left shoulder while another reached into my inside coat pocket from my right. I felt my wallet being slipped out. I struck out with both arms, jabbed my assailants hard, and caught my wallet as it fell from the boy's grasp. The other boys jeered at the two who had failed in their maneuver and drifted away into the pedestrian traffic.

When I reached my office, my secretary looked relieved. "You've got messages galore," she said. "I put them all on your desk."

Many of them were from maintenance staff in the Central Building. I put them in an envelope, addressed it to the assistant business manager, who had returned from his vacation, and dropped it in the inter-library mail basket. One message I put in my pocket. It was from Annie asking me to meet her at noon for lunch at the Plaza Hotel. "Important" she had emphasized. I returned to Times Square, avoided the black kids clustered on 42nd Street, and took the BMT subway train to 59th Street. It was five past twelve when I walked into the Plaza Lounge and spotted Annie sipping a daiquiri at a corner table.

"How ya doin', Rudy?" she smiled happily, "Afraid you might not get my message. It was sort of last minute."

I ordered a beer from a passing waiter and sat down. "What have you heard?"

"Well," she paused, "last night when I was workin' on Poppin, I heard him tell one of his union buddies that Arbie Vine was goin' to disappear."

I felt my heart jump. "What time was that?"

"Round about seven, I think," Annie frowned trying to recollect. "Poppin usually pops in about that time," she laughed. "The girls have a joke. He pops in to pop off."

I smiled. "Did he say what he meant by disappear?"

Annie shook her head. "I was afraid they were gonna kill her, so I called you."

"Arbie's been kidnapped," I said and watched Annie's face register alarm. "It's interesting that Poppin knew about it before it happened. Did he say anything more?"

"Not really, except he made a comment about her not bein' able to lead a march of some kind."

I nodded. The waiter brought me a bottle of beer and a glass. The lounge was beginning to fill up with business people.

"Oh!" Annie said with delight. "There's one of my steady customers." She looked at a thin, elderly gentleman escorting a young woman to a table across the room. "He's a sweetie."

I took a long drink of beer. "You get some interesting customers, I bet," I said.

Annie giggled. "I don't pay much attention to where they're from. We're really too busy to talk much."

"Keep your ears open. I can't see Poppin acting on his own, and I don't think Hector Bratwurst is giving him the orders."

"Oh, Hector Bratwurst!" she exclaimed. "He comes in sometimes, but I've never had him."

I smiled. "Want another daiquiri?"

"No, Rudy, thanks a lot, but I've got to run. Besides, I already had two while I was waitin' for you. I hope you don't mind." Annie gave me a little wave with her fingers and hurried away.

I called for the check and, taking out my expense book, began to fill in the morning's expenses. That Poppin was involved in Arbie's kidnapping I half-suspected, but, nevertheless, I was shaken to have my suspicion confirmed. I suspected also that the players in this drama of Arbie's kidnapping were divided into factions; just how complicated were the connections among players and between factions I had no idea. I hoped that Gabriel would give me some insights. I left the Plaza and caught the subway train downtown to Dino's Cafe. I felt a spasm of cold fear with having to approach a violent killer. But I knew that killers could be engaging people and that a criminal like Gabriel who killed as a business might not be a psychopath.

TEN

Dino's was at the lower end of Hudson street, just below the cluster of homosexual bars. It had a narrow frontage but developed into a large room at the back where I sat at a small table among a crowd of patrons eating lunch. I ordered spaghetti and meatballs. By the time I was served, most of the working lunch crowd had left, and a more casual atmosphere was settling over the restaurant. I was eating my last meatball when a black man just under six feet, about 30 years old, walked into the room, looked sharply round at the tables, and threw himself onto a chair at a table by the wall. The waiter spoke familiarly with the newcomer and then came to my table to clear away the dishes.

"Is that man Gabriel?" I asked.

The waiter nodded. "You want him for somethin'?"

"Yeah, ask him if I can join him, will ya?"

I watched the waiter bend his tall body over Gabriel's table as he spoke confidentially to him. Gabriel gave a startled, sharp look at me, as if he were a wild animal wary of a trap, and then, nodding and beckoning to me with his arm, he sat up in his chair with a determined expression.

I realized that Gabriel expected he was being hired for a criminal undertaking. As I approached him, I wondered how I could keep that impression alive without actually mentioning a job or a price.

"Hello, Gabriel," I said. "The family told me I'd find you here." I sat at the table. "My name's Rudy."

"What do you want, Rudy?" Gabriel eyed me suspiciously.

I hesitated and looked around the room.

"Don't worry," Gabriel said. "This place is okay, and there's no bugs. The owner's a member of the family."

"They tell me you're pretty good with the knife," I said quietly.

"Yeah, I'm good," Gabriel frowned. "And I'm not bad with the gun," he warned. "So you better be on the level. Who sent you?"

"Louie," I said. I sensed just a shade of mental dullness in his personality, as if he lacked a level of perception that could detect deception. "It's your knife work that interests me. They tell me you were the guy who carved up the manager of a messenger service." I looked him squarely in the eye.

Gabriel looked stunned and then annoyed. "That was a mistake."

"I know," I said, "but to stab a guy almost a dozen times and not kill him, that takes talent--that's what we need for this job."

Gabriel looked at me in disbelief. "I was supposed to get rid of a dame. How could anyone think I did a good job?"

"I know all that," I said, looking annoyed in my turn. "The dame is a union leader who's been snatched by the mob."

"Yeah," Gabriel said, looking at me with curiosity, "they got her out on Long Island somewhere."

"We want to get hold of that dame," I said softly.

Gabriel grinned. "What for?"

I put my finger to my lips. "You'll have to move quietly to be effective," I said. "There'll be others with you."

Gabriel nodded, scratched his nose, and looked down at the calluses on his hands. "About a thousand would do me."

I raised my eyebrows. "I'll get back to you." I stood up.

Gabriel reached out his hand, and I shook it.

"It's a real pleasure," Gabriel grinned.

I left the cafe with relief. The sun was shining brightly in the street. The weather was drier, more comfortable. At last, I had made contact with someone who could lead me to Arbie, regardless how tentative the connection may be. But how could I follow through? I went back to my office in the Library and telephoned Joshua Raikes.

"Rudyard!" Raikes's voice cried. "I've been making enquiries about Arbuthnott Vine and think we've got an interesting lead."
"What's that?" I asked, surprised by the excitement in Raikes's voice.
"She's in Manhattan. A left wing group has hidden her away and won't release her until after the day of the protest march," Raikes said.
"But why would the Left do that when it's the Left that is organizing the march?"
"It's a far left group at odds with the socialists who are organizing the protest," Raikes chuckled.
"Don't believe it," I said. "I heard she's on Long Island in the care of the mafia."
There was a pause as Raikes considered this. "My sources are pretty knowledgeable, but they could be wrong."
"Can you tell me the main source?" I asked.
"Sorry, Rudyard, I must keep it confidential."
"Well, did they give you a clue as to how to find her?"
"No. They say she's all right, and they don't want to see her released until after the day of the march."
"I'll check it out and get back to you," I said.
"I'll look further too," Raikes said. "You're right, it does sound fishy."
As I settled down to think, my telephone rang. It was Buckle, sounding angry that he had difficulty locating me. "I thought you were gonna stay home," he complained. "Did you get a call from the kidnappers?"
No," I said. "But I got two leads. One, she's being held by Lanzetta's boys on Long Island somewhere. Two, she's in Manhattan held by left wingers."
Buckle gave a short laugh. "We heard she's in New Jersey."
I snorted. "I found Gabriel, the black guy who knifed the manager of the messenger service. He'll lead a raid on Lanzetta's place, but I need some guys to play his support group."
"You're crazy, Rudyard!" Buckle said sharply. "You been watchin' too much F.B.I. stuff on television."
"But it's one way of finding out where she is," I argued.
"You're emotionally involved in this case," Buckle said. "You're not thinking right. I'm not detailing men to help you make a raid on a house in Long Island."
"I just need one guy," I said. "We'll make a very quiet surveillance."
"Led by a killer!" Buckle cried.
"He knows the route," I argued. "I'll control him. Look, we can't afford to pass up an opportunity."
Buckle sighed. "All right, Rudyard. I'll play the other man-- undercover."
I explained that I would pick up Gabriel at Dino's Cafe and take him to Buckle's car in the next block.

"I'll wear a mustache," Buckle said. "Just in case Gabriel knows me."
"By the way, he wants a grand."
"Yeah?" Buckle said. "I'll get him a year."
I smiled as he hung up. At least, I had started the wheels of justice moving regardless whether they were moving in the right direction. It was better than waiting for a call from the kidnappers. As I left the Library, I saw young Bradley Tone handing out leaflets to the staff members as they left work. I picked up one that had blown to the sidewalk. "Elect Tone for Local President," it read, "and get the 30-hour work week." I dropped it into the waste basket on the corner. Arbie Vine, I thought sadly, was at a distinct disadvantage in the election campaign.

ELEVEN

While I was cooking dinner, the telephone rang. Alf Landy, Arbie's radical colleague, shouted excitedly into my ear. He had just heard about the kidnapping.

When I told him the left was suspected, Alf discussed left groups one after the other, discounting them in turn. The Progressive Laborites were disrupters; kidnapping was too positive an action for them. The Spartacists supported Arbie's efforts because mass protest was a first stage to revolt. The Union Leaguers were all hot air--too timid to do a kidnapping. Finally he settled upon the Maoists, who believed that all union leaders conspired with management against the workers. It was very possible, he concluded, that Maoists could be holding Arbie. I thought Maoists were terrorists like the Shining Path guerrillas terrifying Peru, but Alf said they had not reached that stage in New York. He and his fellow Trotskyites believed in Trotsky's idea of continuous revolution but opposed terrorist acts which Alfie attributed only to right-wing Catholics and Muslims and the far left like the Maoists who still read Chairman Mao's little red book.

"We gotta confront them!" Alfie exclaimed. "Go right down to their Headquarters and tell them we want to see her!"

"They might kidnap us," I suggested, amused at Alfie's impulsiveness.

"I'd like to see them fuckin' well try," Alfie said with a hard edge to his voice.

"We could be wrong."

"So what? At least we're tryin'. That's more than the fuckin' cops will do."

"Okay," I said. "We'll try it tomorrow morning."

"To hell with tomorrow," Alf cried. "We'll do it tonight. That's when they're all together, meetin' or somethin'."

"Okay," I said, encouraged by Alf's determination.

"I'll drive by your place and ring your bell in a half hour," Alf said. "It's near Gramercy, right?"

I went back to the kitchen just in time to prevent dinner from burning. I had just finished eating and was sliding my dishes into the sink when the buzzer sounded from the front hallway. Alfie's voice replied through the intercom. I made sure that I had my revolver. I found Alf sitting in his car with the motor running. The car door did not close properly. I had to slam it twice. The muffler needed repairing, I remarked, as we roared down the street.

Alf must have known what I was thinking because he said, "I drive an old heap because the car thieves leave it alone. I've had this for five years and the only thing I lost was a rabbit's foot from the dashboard."

Alfie drove down Broadway. "These guys hang out in the financial district. When their class enemies go home to Scarsdale at night, they come down near Wall Street to talk over how they're gonna close down the stock exchanges and the banks."

"How do you know where they meet?" I asked.

Alf smiled. "When you're on the left you gotta know your competition because after the revolution you're gonna have to deal with it forever."

"Funny you picked the Maoists," I remarked. "I thought it would be the Labor Party if any one."

"Naw!" Alf shook his head, his blond locks bobbing as he peered through the windshield for cross traffic. "The F.B.I. wouldn't let them do it. They gotta be careful or their source of federal funds will be cut off. They can't do nothing without wonderin' if they'll incriminate the government if they get caught."

I lapsed into silence as I considered the intricacy of left-wing politics. Alfie was right. A sincere left-winger had to know when he was dealing with those who were true to the political faith, and when he was being set up by a government agent or someone who unwittingly was acting for the government, or, at least, a particular faction of the government.

We came to the Old Trinity Church and Alf turned down a side street to find a parking place alongside the graveyard. The night air was hot and musty. A faint chemical smell wafted over the Hudson from the Jersey side. Alf led me across Broadway toward Wall Street and then down a side alley, the sign for which I could not read in the dark. We proceeded about twenty yards down the cobble-stoned alley when Alf stopped at a door faintly visible in the light from the lamp in the street they had left.

"You gotta take the ball from here," Alf said softly. "They know I'm a socialist worker, but you're an outsider, so they'll hear what you have to say."

The door opened in response to Alf's knock. A tall, thin man in a sweater and jeans looked at us. He knew Alf. "Who's the guy with you, Landy?"

"A library detective," Alf said. "He's okay."

"Wait." The thin fellow closed the door and left us to stand in the alley.

"I trust you," Alf said, "because Arbie told me you're okay. But I just threw these guys for a loop. If you were a real dick, there's no way we'd get in to talk to them! No way!"

"Do you mean we're going to address their membership and demand they release Arbie?" I asked in astonished amusement.

Alf looked at me askance. "What are you afraid of, man? They're not the Ku Klux Klan." He shook his head as if he doubted I had intelligence. "You conservatives. You always think leftists are the same as right-wingers except that you agree with right-wingers."

"All right," I said. "I'll take your word for it. We'll get to see them because you're a socialist and I'm a harmless library worker."

"Yeah, right," Alf said, looking around and up at the buildings in the alleyway.

The door opened. The tall lean fellow beckoned us in, led us down a hall, dimly lit by a naked light bulb in the ceiling, and into a meeting hall large enough to accommodate two hundred people. On a platform at the front of the room, and sitting at a table draped with a bright red cover, sat a half dozen men who looked to be in their seventies and eighties. They faced an audience of about fifty men and women. I noted the dark skin, long black hair, and stoic look of the Latin American predominant among them. The tall lean fellow asked us to sit on two chairs on the left of the platform so that we faced both the men at the long red table and the audience. There was an uncomfortable silence while the Maoists regarded us, and I studied the faces of the men at the long table.

"The guy in the center is Andres," Alf whispered. "He'll do all the talking."

As if taking a cue, the man sitting in the midst of the others at the long table cleared his throat. He was dark-skinned with flashing brown eyes. "Why are you here, Landy?" His voice was clear, modulated, pleasant, but with a hint of the forcefulness of his personality.

"My union president's been kidnapped," Alf said.

Andres nodded. "And you think we have her?"

"Yeah, I do," Alf said aggressively.

"What's your name, library detective?" Andres said looklng at me.

I said my name.

"You should know about Landy," Andres continued. "He's impulsive. It's a trait common to the members of his party."

Here and there in the audience men and women broke into laughter. A smile crossed the faces of some of the men at the long table. Alf blushed.

"But at least he puts all his cards on the table, and we can deal with him," Andres continued in the same level tone. "We heard the radio news today. We know Arbuthnott Vine was spirited away in a limousine. We don't support her rally next Saturday, but we're not going to try to stop it. As far as we're concerned, it's a waste of effort."

"I'm concerned," I spoke up, "about a woman whose life may be in danger."

"And you have come here to accuse us of taking her?"

"No," I said. "We heard she was taken by a left-wing group. Maybe you will help us find her."

Andres smiled, his white teeth glinting in the light. "I'm glad you don't agree with Landy."

"Rudyard's not had the experience of dealing with you like I have," Alf said sharply.

Andres face froze. There was silence. I thought swift retribution for the insult was to follow.

"Landy is outspoken," Andres said to me. "Let me be. We don't have Vine and we don't know who has her. We're not concerned about her. But we'll do you a favor. We'll look for her."

"Much obliged," I said.

"Don't cross us," Andres warned.

"No reason for me to do that," I said. "I don't work for the government."

The audience seemed amused by this remark. I smiled at the group.

"We don't work for the government either," Andres said.

The audience broke into laughter. All the men at the long table smiled. Alf Landy laughed.

"We'll be in touch with you," Andres said.

The tall lean fellow beckoned to us. We got up and followed him through the audience to the door at the back of the room.

"Next time, Landy," Andres called after us. "Wait till you're invited."

"I don't expect to have the pleasure," Alf shouted in a rare display of subtle sarcasm.

I sensed the good humor in the audience behind us. Back in the alley, I looked at Alf questioningly.

"We did the right thing," Alf said reassuringly. "Arbie's not bein' held by anyone on the left. Those guys would've known it."

"Do you believe them then?" I asked, surprised by Landy's change of tone.

"Of course," he snorted. "Andres isn't going to be caught lying to me. Those guys are too proud for that."

I considered the possibility that Andres had been telling the truth. "I wonder how my contact learned that Arbie was a victim of a left-wing group."

"Because he's a capitalist, that's why," Alfie said angrily, leading us back to his car. "They blame everything on the Left. Christ! We're happy when we find an activist who's progressive. It's fuckin' unexpected in a world of union sell-outs and big-mouthed yes-men."

We heard the low steady sound of a siren common to New York streets at night. A car thief had set off the alarm on a car parked in the direction we were headed.

"Jeez! I hope that's not mine!" Alf cried and broke into a loping run.

I loped behind him until we came to the Trinity Church graveyard and could see Alf's car sitting quietly at the curbside. The siren sound came from a new Chevrolet further down the street.

"D'ya see!" Alf said happily. "My old hag gets passed by when they got all these new beauties to pick on."

"Say, I've got a proposal," I said as we sat in Alf's car. "Tomorrow a small-time gangster is going to take me to a mafia hangout where Arbie might be held. Do you want to come?"

"Sure," Alf said gunning his motor and roaring down the street. "I'll take sick leave from work."

TWELVE

I met Alf Landy by prearrangement outside the Hudson Street subway at two in the afternoon. When we reached Dino's cafe, Alf waited in the street as I entered and looked for Gabriel, whom I found at his favorite wall side table. Gabriel was talking earnestly to a white girl who sat opposite him. He looked round with a nervous jerk of his body as I approached.

"Hey, Rudyard, man! What's up?" he cried with feigned nonchalance. "You got the job?"

"We're ready to leave now," I said with a thin smile at the girl. "Our boys are waiting."

"Now!" Gabriel rounded his eyes in astonishment and looked round at the girl. "We got action, baby, but it's all in the wrong direction. Maybe I'll meet you tomorrow." He reached over to pinch her cheek.

Gabriel looked askance at Alf Landy when I introduced them. "You ain't carryin' a gat. What you got? Special powers or somethin'?"

Alf laughed good-naturedly. I led them to a long black limousine parked in the next block. Detective Buckle, dressed in slacks and a pink sport shirt which hung loosely over his chubby frame, stepped out from the front seat. He was wearing a mustache and goatee, which appeared to be enough of a disguise to conceal his identity from Gabriel. At the moment of introduction, however, I sensed Gabriel stiffen in suspicion, as if an animal had caught a whiff of its predator in the wind. But Buckle shook his hand vigorously, and, patting him on the back, soon put him at ease.

Buckle drove us through the Queens' Midtown tunnel and along the Long Island Expressway as we discussed our plan of operation. Buckle knew where Lanzetta's estate was located, but neither he nor anyone he knew, police or criminal, had ever been in its grounds. Gabriel had been there a half dozen times with Martin Slidsky. He described the driveways and the landscape near the mansion, gesturing to make himself clear. He described the front part of the house and surmised the layout of the rest of it.

"They wouldn't put her in the cellar," Gabriel said. "They'd put her in the top floor at the back. Slidsky told me they got a detention center there. Any one of their guys gets out of hand, and they put him away for a while--till he comes to his senses."

"Did Slidsky want to do that with you?" I smiled.

Gabriel looked at me sharply. "Maybe he did." He laughed suddenly. "But man! I didn't wait around to find out."

We laughed with him. By the time we were driving over a country road running alongside the high stone wall of the Lanzetta estate, we had settled upon a plan of action.

"Let's hope we just have to deal with the custodial staff," Buckle said.

There was a note of caution in his voice as if the experience of a policeman was speaking out. Gabriel looked at him curiously.

As we neared the front gate of the estate, we saw a limousine approach from the opposite direction and stop by a black-uniformed guard. Buckle drove by as we all tried to see the faces of the men in the limousine.

"There *is* something going on in there," Buckle said. "Anyone notice who it was?"

"No," I said. "The windows had shaded glass."

"We've gotta get in there," Alf said. "We gotta see what's going on."

"Pull over here!" Gabriel cried, suddenly.

Buckle brought the car to a stop at the roadside and looked questioningly at Gabriel, who was peering through the window at the high stone wall.

"There's wire along the top which will probably electrocute you if you touch it," Gabriel said. "But right here there's a tree with a branch hanging over the wall. I'll climb it, drop over the wall, fix the guards, and open the gate."

"You can do that?" Buckle asked, alarmed.

"Many times I done that, my friend," Gabriel smiled. "They trained you to fight in 'Nam."

"Okay," Buckle said, "but take something for the guards with you." He opened a bag on the front seat and rummaged inside it. "Don't kill anyone!" He handed Gabriel a small bottle.

"Chloroform!" Gabriel read the label with a sarcastic smile. "You got a cloth or something I can put it on?"

Buckle gave him his handkerchief.

We watched as Gabriel shinnied up the tree, climbed carefully along the tree limb reaching over the wall, hung on as the limb dipped, and let go to disappear behind the wall.

"We'll give him three minutes," Buckle said, looking at his wrist watch.

We sat in silence. I looked at the thick foliage in the woods on the opposite side of the road. I thought of Arbie held in some bare room, taunted by thugs, intimidated by threats of death if she did not cooperate.

Buckle started the engine, turned the car, and drove back to the gate. The large iron gates were shut. There was no sign of life.

"Maybe we're too soon," he suggested.

We stopped before the gates and gazed through the iron grille at the guardhouse.

"Least, there's no guards," Alf said.

Then Gabriel appeared from the guardhouse, pushed a button on a post near the gate, and grinned at us as the gates moved apart to allow us to drive in.

"What'd ya do with the guards?" Buckle frowned as Gabriel came to the car.

"There's just two," Gabriel said. "They're sleepin' good. I tied them up."

"Okay, close the gate and get in," Buckle growled.

Gabriel went back to the post, pushed the button until the gates closed, and sat in the car which the impatient Buckle gunned swiftly along the driveway toward the mansion.

"Shouldn't we stop before we get there," I suggested. "And walk it to escape observation."

Buckle stopped. "Good idea. You and your friend, Alf, walk. Gabriel, you drive. I'll sit in the back seat."

I was amused at the arrangement which we effected quickly.

"Jeez!" Alf said as Gabriel drove away. "They're sittin' ducks."

"Buckle's gonna play a role," I said. "That may be the only way to get inside the house. We don't know what kind of electronic surveillance it has."

We ran into the woods beside the road and along a path we discovered which cut through the trees to bring us out on a great lawn, which fronted the mansion in the distance. We saw Buckle's car drive to a stop alongside half a dozen limousines. Gabriel got out to open the door for Buckle. Two guards approached them from the front door, spoke a few words, and escorted them into the mansion.

"I hope Buckle knows what he's doin'," Alf said in awe of the wealth of the place and its security.

"This is the time for us to make a run for it," I said, "while they're occupied by them. Let's run to that small cluster of trees over there."

"Okay," Alf said, dashing ahead.

I ran after him and reached the trees behind him. We caught our breath and peered out at the mansion again. With amazement we saw Gabriel standing at the front door and signaling us to come in with long sweeps of his arm.

"Let's go," I said.

We dashed across the grass. I felt exposed, like a sitting target, because it took a long moment for me to cross the lawn, the dirt driveway, and the threshold of the front door.

"What's goin' on?" Alf whispered as I gasped for breath.

Gabriel smiled, "We took care of the two guys at this door. Your friend is lookin' after a guy at the end of the corridor down there. I was lookin' out the window and saw you guys runnin' around."

"I hope no one else saw us," I said.

"They're meetin' at the back of the place, so one of those guys told us," Gabriel nodded at a room on the right of the hall. "There must be other security around here though." He began walking stealthily down the hall.

Buckle stepped out of a room. His corpulent body appeared strong and vibrant with energy. He beckoned us into the room with a twinkle in his eye. I saw a huge and powerful man lying face down on the floor, his arms taped at the wrists behind his back, and his ankles taped. He was unconscious. Along one wall there were fifteen closed-circuit monitors. I recognized the front lawn and the clump of trees on one screen.

"He was sleeping," Buckle chuckled quietly. "Lucky for us." He pointed to a monitor screen picturing the two guards tied to the furniture in the front room.

"Who's meeting here?" I asked.

"How should I know?" Buckle said. "We didn't have time to interview our reception committee."

Gabriel laughed loudly.

"Shut up!" Buckle barked. He looked at Alf. "You stay here and watch these monitors. We're going upstairs. Anything happens, you let us know. Understand? Don't try anything on your own."

"What if we get more fuckin' visitors?" Alf asked, frowning with alarm. "We can't lock 'em out."

"We can keep them waiting at the front door," Buckle said. "Rudyard, follow me. Gabriel, take the rear. You got a gun?"

"That's right, man," Gabriel said.

I noted the thick brown carpeting of the wide staircase and the brilliant colors of the Impressionist paintings along the wall as we ascended.

"The meeting room is down there," Gabriel whispered.

"You know the third floor?" Buckle asked.

"I never been there, but I got a good idea."

"See if she's up there while we take a look down here. Be careful."

"I want to go up," I said. "It's Arbie we're here to save, not to listen in on a meeting."

Buckle shook his head. "Gabriel goes alone. He won't get lost. Come on."

I reluctantly crept after him down the long hallway to the back of the mansion. I pictured Arbie locked in a small room somewhere upstairs. I was annoyed with Buckle for considering me not competent enough to search for her, and I began to question Buckle's authority. The detective assumed the leadership of this little enterprise without so much as a by-your-leave. I had to admit, however, the fellow had experience.

"Listen!" Buckle paused.

The muffled sound of voices came from a room on the right. Buckle crept to the door and peeked through the key hole. As I came up behind him, he moved aside and motioned for me to take a look. I could make out the faces of Lanzetta and Bratwurst. A man was talking in a nasal twang.

Buckle raised his eyebrows as I looked at him in wonder.

"I know that voice," Buckle said. "Kroneweiss, the banker."

I recognized it then. I had heard it dozens of times on television news broadcasts whenever the City's fiscal problems were being discussed. Kroneweiss was the chairman of the Economic Committee, comprised largely of bankers, which had been empowered by the State government to take control of the City.

Buckle moved to the end of the corridor and stood before the door which gave access to the room at that end. When I stood beside Buckle, the detective muttered that it was his duty as a police officer to hear what they were saying.

"Could be another Appalachia?" I smiled, referring to the notorious gangland meeting.

Buckle ignored the sarcasm. I saw that he was excited, and watched with amusement as Buckle carefully bent down the handle of the door and opened it a crack. Their conversation was now quite audible.

Kroneweiss was telling Lanzetta that the bankers could not get rid of rent control any faster without forcing half the population into the streets. Bratwurst argued that the wage freeze made it impossible for his members to pay higher rents.

"It's the market place," Lanzetta snapped. "You want rent control, you go to Russia."

"They're my people," Bratwurst reminded them. "You guys are decimating my union with these goddamn lay-offs. Why in Christ's name do you have to cut back so many in the hospitals?"

I had heard enough. I tapped Buckle on the shoulder, but he was too interested in the conversation to react. I climbed the stairs to the third floor and peered into the rooms leading off either side of the hallway as I went along. Then, smack in the center of the hallway were heavy mauve curtains and behind them a door sealing off further access. My heart leaped as I thought surely this was Arbie's place of imprisonment. I tried the door handle. It opened. I passed through, closed it behind me carefully, and stood in a narrow corridor at the end of which were two rooms. The daylight shone from them into the corridor through their open doors. I heard men's voices.

In the room on the left, Gabriel was talking to a burly young man. They were sitting at a plain wooden table near a window. Behind them was a cell, the iron bars of which ran from floor to ceiling, partitioning it from the front of the room. The cell door stood open. Gabriel looked round suddenly.

"Okay," he said to the young man who had started from his chair. "Come in, Rudyard. This guy is a friend of mine from one of the families. He was being cooled off in there." He nodded at the cell. "He done something bad."

"Yeah, like disobeying a command," the young man said with a twisted smile.

I sat in a chair by the door. "Where's Arbie?"

"They haven't got her here," Gabriel said.

"Lanzetta was in on the job," the young man said earnestly, "but he wasn't the brains behind it--least that's what I heard. It's somebody higher than Lanzetta."

"We'd better go," I said.

I led the way downstairs back to where Buckle was still standing and peering through the crack in the door at the conference. He closed the door quietly when we reached him. His eyes surveyed Gabriel's friend suspiciously.

"No Arbie," I said glumly. "We have to go."

We heard the front doorbell ring. As if at a signal we all moved swiftly down the hall. Buckle peered down from a front window and pulled back quickly.

"Two mafia bosses," he said quickly. "Waterfront and Teamsters."

Alf Landy appeared on the stairs. He looked worried yet relieved to see us descending.

"Open the door and send them to the back room on the second floor," Buckle said to Alf. "And for Lord's sake, check their identities as if you really were security."

Buckle signaled us to step into the front room where the two guards were lying bound to the furniture. The doorbell rang again with an insistence belying the impatience of the mafia chieftains. Buckle closed the door of the room as Alf opened the front door.

I heard Alf's voice ring out clearly, somewhat nervously, challenging the visitors, who responded in low tones.

"Okay," we heard Alf say. "Up to the second floor, back to the back room. They been waitin' for ya."

"Funny that!" said a deep voice with sarcasm.

"Here boy," another voice said, husky and demanding. "Take our coats and be careful with them."

I feared the delay. At any moment a servant could come from any part of the mansion and discover Alf. Every second seemed precious now that we were so close to getting away. We heard heavy footsteps climbing the stairs. Alf opened the door to the room, but Buckle signaled everyone to freeze. He listened until he heard the sound of men's voices in greeting suddenly cut into silence as the

upstairs door closed behind the visitors. Without a word, he led the way out of the mansion to our limousine, the keys in his hand as he reached the car. He started the motor as the rest of us jumped in and reversed as the last door shut.
"What you got there, Alf?" he asked, glancing at the back seat.
Alf sat smiling with two coats in his lap. "They said to take care of them, didn't they?"
We laughed. I took one of the coats. It was light for summer wear. I searched the pockets, and, finding nothing but a handkerchief, I took the other coat and searched its pockets.
"How the hell did those guys get in here?" Buckle said suddenly. "We got the guards at the gate all tied up."
A sudden fear passed through us as we wondered if the guards had broken free and were waiting for us to return.
"Wait a minute!" Gabriel said. "There's a way to open the gate with a card."
"That's right," his young friend agreed. "There's a few guys who got that privilege."
"Whew!" Buckle relaxed and brought the car to a stop as the young man leapt from the car and opened the gate by pushing a button on the post. Buckle drove through and waited for the young man to run up and jump in.
"I found a note in one of the pockets," I said. I held it to the light by the side window. "It's scribbled. 'Vine is at ....'" My voice cracked with excitement as I read the telephone number.

THIRTEEN

"At least we've got a lead to Arbie," I said. I sat elated watching the trees slide by as I wondered who were the men imprisoning Arbie and how we would deal with them.
"We'll find out about it right now," Buckle said and pulled over to a small eatery with a red roof and a large sign advertising hamburgers. I jumped out of the car and headed for the public telephone visible through the glass of the vestibule. I dialed the number nervously and listened to the ringing.
A deep male voice grunted on the other end of the line.
"Everything okay?" I asked. "Is that Vine dame okay?"
"Yeh, she's doin' fine. Beatin' the pants off me in pinochle," the man said with amusement. I pictured them at a bare table in a ramshackle room. "Who's this?" the man asked. "Martie?"
"Martie gave me your number and told me to get the address from you," I said. "Where the hell are you?"

The man gave his address without the slightest hint of suspicion. It was in Brooklyn, near the Verazzano Bridge. "You comin' to see us?"

"Later," I said. I could hardly believe my good luck. I had found Arbie! "We gotta get that dame off our hands."

"Yeh!" the man replied with a tone of disappointment. "Who'd you say you was?"

"Keep my name out of it," I said. "You never know who's listenin' in to us these days. We'll see ya."

I hung up sensing the puzzlement on the other end. I ran back to the car and told Buckle the address.

"It ought to take us about thirty minutes," Buckle said.

Buckle was full of what he had heard at Lanzetta's mansion. "Kroneweiss was telling them the Economic Council's plans for New York City--like Manhattan Island, a playground for the world's rich. It's gonna be a real estate bonanza. Lanzetta was so excited he could hardly ask a question without shouting."

Gabriel was giggling to himself. "Just think of the faces of those guys when they find their security all tied up."

"When they find me gone," said his young friend with a laugh.

"That's great!" Alf cried. "They're going to think whoever broke in was trying to rescue you."

"Right," said the young man, "and it's gonna be hard to figure out who'd bother to do that."

As we headed south into Brooklyn, we discussed the methods we could use to rescue Arbie.

"The less violence, the better," I said. "We ought to just walk in as if we were expected."

"And have our heads blown off?" Buckle asked scornfully.

"He must have been told you'd be calling," Gabriel suggested. "Least, he thought you was the guy who had the telephone number in his pocket."

"We could surround the house," Alf suggested. "And Gabriel could go in through a window."

"Yeh, I could do that," Gabriel smiled. "You're making me earn my grand."

"What grand?" Alfie cried. "You getting paid for this?"

"Aren't you guys?" Gabriel asked in amazement.

"We're all volunteers," I said. "You're the mercenary."

Gabriel looked uneasy. "I don't know about you guys. I smell cops, but I been too polite to say so, you know what I mean."

"Forget it," Buckle said. "You play square with us, we'll square with you."

Gabriel and his young friend pretended to look relieved by Buckle's words, but I could see that they were tense. Alf was mystified. He looked questioningly at me. I nodded to signify that he should remain quiet. We drove on in silence as the camaraderie induced by our success at Lanzetta's estate dissipated. Gabriel began to glance sharply about him as if he were preparing to strike out. The distrust emanating from him was palpable and threatened to disrupt our rescue operation. Buckle took a street map from the glove compartment and handed it back to me. I guided us to a tree-lined residential street. "It's going to be that big brown house on the next corner on our right."

"We'll drive by slowly," Buckle said. "Let me know what you see."

There was no sign of life in the house. Its tall windows were hung with white curtains. Buckle pulled over to the kerb.

"We'd better be sure that's the place," Alfie said. "There's a guy waterin' his lawn."

I watched Alf cross the street to speak to the old gentleman who seemed to respond in a friendly fashion. I remembered the brief exchange over the telephone with Arbie's captor. The man called me "Martie." Could he have thought I was Martin Slidsky?

Alf returned with an excited look on his face and sat in the car. "He says the house has been empty for six months or more, but he just saw some men leave it."

"How long ago?" Buckle snapped.

"About-ten minutes. There was a woman with them."

I felt a rush of disappointment.

"They must have got word to get the hell out," Gabriel spoke up. "After Rudyard called, they could have got a call from someone else who smelled a rat."

"It was Martie," I said angrily. "They were expecting him to call."

"We should take a look at the place anyway," suggested Gabriel's young friend. "If you circle the block and let me off on the other side street, I'll go in from the back."

Buckle nodded, started the car, circled the block, and stopped to let off the young man and Gabriel out of sight of the old gentleman tending his garden. I got out with them. I wanted to satisfy myself that Arbie was not there.

"We'll wait in the next street down," Buckle warned me. "There is a chance someone's still in there," he explained to me. "We don't want to be identified with any trouble."

I followed Gabriel through a wooden gate and up the steps of the back porch. Gabriel's young friend was working the door lock with a thin file. The door sprang open as I caught up to them. The young man stepped aside, and, with a flourish of his arm, indicated that I should go first.

When in the back hallway, I whispered that they should search the downstairs while I went to the upstairs. The house was deathly still. The stairway creaked as I climbed. I took out my gun as I entered the rooms, the doors of which were open. Sunlight streamed through the curtained windows and fell over furniture covered with sheets. I found a tube of lipstick on the floor touched it to my hand. The red color definitely belonged to Arbie. I pocketed it and searched for other clues. I was still searching when Gabriel, sweat standing on his black brow, joined me.

"Newspapers for the last three days are downstairs," Gabriel said. "Looks like they held her here. The bed is unmade."

I gave up the search. "Yeh, she was here all right. Where's your friend?"

"Skipped it," Gabriel smiled. "He's in a hurry to get back to his family and hide out. Do you blame him? I'd have skipped too, if you didn't owe me a grand." He looked darkly at me.

I nodded grimly. "You found nothing to give us a clue?"

Gabriel handed me a match folder. "This was near the front door."

I read the words " Macombo Restaurant and Bar" on the cover, pocketed it, and hurriedly led the way back to the street.

The late afternoon sun glinted in the trees and cast the shadows of their graceful limbs over the sidewalks. The atmosphere of residential respectability implied that crime had no place there.

Buckle started up as we got in. He was not surprised that the young mobster had fled .

"Probably thought I'd book him at the end of the ride," Buckle whispered to me. "I'm putting tails on those guys at Lanzetta's place. That Kroneweiss character interests me very much."

Alf broached the subject of the march on City Hall. "Arbie being kidnapped has definitely helped us. The Left is comin' out in full force."

"Trouble with that is," Buckle replied, "Miss Vine could be in a lot worse trouble, I mean, if she loses her value to her kidnappers."

I looked with alarm at Gabriel who nodded in confirmation. I thought of Martin Slidsky.

"Hey, let me off before you cross the Bridge, will ya?" Alf asked. "I got a meeting."

We dropped Alf, and, as we were crossing the East River, Gabriel asked for his money.

"You'll find it in your favorite bank account," Buckle said. "Just give me the number and the branch."

As Gabriel scribbled down the information for Buckle, I decided to go directly to Macombo's Bar. We came into Manhattan by the City Hall, sitting like a small white palace amid gray skyscrapers.

"Will you drop me here?" I asked.

"Oh sure," Buckle smiled.

Gabriel got out with me. As Buckle drove away, Gabriel snarled, "Was that guy a cop or wasn't he?"

"Did he arrest you?" I asked. "Use your head."

Gabriel still looked suspicious. "I'd better get that money, man. I'm disappearin' but I can come back to get you anytime."

I shook my head as if I were amused by his doubt and watched with relief as he moved away cat-like into the City Hall Park. I descended to the subway. The dirt and grime, the crowd and press of passengers on a hot day, the shrill cry of steel wheel grinding on steel track, all of it seemed to emphasize my disappointment that Arbie, despite our efforts, was still in the hands of her captors.

FOURTEEN

I found Macombo's Bar on 111th Street East near the north end of Central Park. The clientele was mostly black. There were some whites, some Hispanics. It looked new, not more than a year old. The furnishing was modern: a large sweep of bar, comfortable high stools with backs, low tables and low leather chairs, mauve in the subdued lighting.

I sat at the bar and drank Jack Daniels. From the bartender I learned that the place was run by a real estate company--Benbow and Slidsky.

"Never seen Benbow," the bartender said. "Slidsky comes round. 'Fact, he's sittin' at the back table."

I looked across the room to half a dozen men talking earnestly over a table. I recognized one of them as the dour-faced Slidsky.

I had an impulse to go over and shake the fellow by the shoulders until he confessed where he had hidden Arbie. But I turned back to the bar and took a long swallow of bourbon. I took my card from my wallet, scribbled "Can we talk?" on the back of it, and asked a waitress to give it to Slidsky. I watched Slidsky take the card, turn it over, and look at me. Slidsky said something to the other men at the table and approached me with a small smile. He held out his hand and gripped mine tightly.

"What's on your mind?" he asked tersely.

"Miss Arbuthnott Vine," I said, looking Slidsky in the eye.

Slidsky frowned. "Come to my office," he said.

I followed him up a stairway at the side of the bar to a door, which he opened with a key. The office was large with windows overlooking the street. Slidsky led me to leather-cushioned chairs by a glass-topped coffee table, and, reclining in one, signaled to me to sit in the other.

"Now, Mr. Mack, what are you accusing me of?" Slidsky asked, pleasantly.

"Kidnapping," I said. I took out my notebook and read the lines I had copied from Slidsky's diary: "Arranged for settlement with Local president."

Slidsky stared at the familiarity of the words. "You been snoopin' on me!" he cried in angry astonishment.

"I'm a detective," I said, as if in explanation. "You arranged today for her to be taken from Brooklyn to another location."

Slidsky remained silent. I saw that he was uncertain how to respond.

"Whatever the motive for kidnapping her, it was a foolish thing to do." My voice rose with emotion. I realized that my confronting Slidsky like this was an emotional response to my frustrations. "She hasn't harmed anyone. She doesn't deserve to be treated like this."

Slidsky looked at me with pity. "Take it easy. You're getting worked up to the point where you're making a lot of mistakes. First off, I don't know where the hell she is. Second, no one can come into my office and start accusing me of criminal activity. Third, you can't bully me into anything. But I'll tell you what I'll do. I'll let you walk out of here a man who can still enjoy life. Do you get my meaning?"

Slidsky stood up to indicate that our conversation was concluded. The door was being held open by a burly fellow with a sarcastic smile.

I went out without another word. I half-expected to be struck by my escort somewhere between the office door and the front door of the restaurant, but I survived the walk and stepped into the street. I looked back at the restaurant to see the burly fellow still smiling sarcastically as he watched me walk away. My foolhardiness may have served some purpose. If Arbie's captors knew that they were suspect, they would be less inclined to hurt her, I thought.

I stepped to a public telephone on the corner and called my office.

"Mr. Raikes has been trying to reach you," my secretary said excitedly. "Some trustees are meeting at seven tonight. He wants you to be there."

"Did he say what it was about?" I asked, fearing that they were dissatisfied with the security in the Central Building.

"He didn't," she said, "but I heard by the grapevine that they're very disturbed about Miss Vine's disappearance. It's been announced over the radio and in the newspapers."

"Okay," I said. "Aren't you working late tonight? It's almost six."

"Had to wait to give you the message," she said coyly.

"Much appreciated," I said. I thought of her wide hips with appreciation as I walked to the Lexington Avenue subway.

When I walked into the Trustees Room, Raikes turned me aside for a quick briefing.

"We think Miss Vine is a political hostage," he said sharply, his face tense and his eyes piercing. "The Board is split about doing anything. Some of the more liberal members agreed to discuss the matter tonight. Don't look surprised at what you hear. Feelings run pretty deep on the subject of City politics."

I nodded, eager to hear the opinions of those who had access to that intimate circle which ran the country, as it were.

Raikes turned abruptly to face the men chatting by a side table where they helped themselves to drinks. "Let's get our meeting underway, gentlemen." He went to the head of the table in the center of the room, and the others sat in the chairs at the table. Raikes directed me to sit beside him.

A guard closed the doors to the room. We were in momentary silence. I looked at the wall tapestries and hoped that I would not be called upon to speak.

Raikes adopted a formal manner as he opened the meeting. I sensed a reserve fall upon the room and reflected that these men, as executives, spent much of their lives in committee meetings.

"The Board of Trustees has asked me," Raikes said, glancing at notes on the table before him, "to chair this Ad Hoc Committee and has authorized us to meet as often as it is necessary for us to complete the business of the Committee." He paused to look at the members. "We shall not take minutes, unless, of course, you feel that portions of our deliberations should be recorded." When several members nodded in agreement with him, Raikes made a notation on a yellow pad. "I believe, with one exception, our Committee is complete. Our task is to find ways in which the Library can help the authorities to locate a staff member who is believed to have been kidnapped by persons unknown. She is Arbuthnott Vine, President of the Library Guild, whose salary is paid by the Library while she is on leave to conduct union business in accordance with the Mayor's Order on Labor Relations."

Raikes cleared his throat and took a sip of water from a glass beside him. I felt comforted by the mention of Arbie, as if these important men could help her somehow, but some trustees were making me uncomfortable by their looks of curiosity, even suspicion. Raikes, sensing this, added, "Mr. Mack has served the Library well for over twenty years; we shall be depending upon his expertise as an investigator in this matter of Miss Vine's disappearance."

Raikes's voice carried an authority that reassured me. The cleverness of the man, his decisiveness at Board meetings, and his nebulous past in the Central Intelligence Agency earned the respect of the other trustees, or so it was rumored throughout the Library. One of the members smiled kindly at me. I had spoken in passing to two or three of them on occasion. The trustees formed an austere group and had no dealings with staff lower than the chief librarian.

"Miss Vine," Raikes continued, "has been missing for three days. There has been no communication from her kidnappers, but she is believed to be in New York State somewhere. The police have assumed that her kidnapping is related to a rally she was to lead this Saturday. We have all read the news reports. Perhaps we should begin with your observations." He looked with a quizzical expression at the faces before him. "Mr. Edward Stinnes."

I recognized the name as President of the Rockefeller Foundation, and watched as a middle-aged man with sharp features and black hair slicked back over bald spots fixed his eyes intently on Raikes and spoke with slow deliberation. "We must do all we can to help the police find our missing staff member. I wonder, however, if it would not be wiser to try to understand the causes for her disappearance rather than to speculate on where she might be."

The others nodded deferentially. I recognized the wisdom of Raikes on calling upon the much-respected Stinnes to set the course of the discussion.

"I think we are in agreement," Raikes nodded. "Dickie Edwards." He looked at a thin, white-haired gentleman in his seventies, whom I recognized as a partner of a New York law firm and whose spryness in voice and gesture always caught my attention when he came to the Library. "What do you think?"

Edwards thought Miss Vine was a radical intent on making trouble at a time when City government was reeling from a fiscal crisis, but he was challenged by a bearded man who, raising his long bony arm, fluttered his fingers to get attention, and began to blame the City government for creating labor problems.

"Right on!" said a rather handsome, dark-haired man in his thirties.

"Tally Leyden," Raikes said, as if announcing him to the other committee members. "Mr. Leyden is President of Compumax. He joined the Board a month ago, I believe."

I knew Compumax as the name of a conglomerate which supplied computers to the Library. It was said to be in the forefront of the "information revolution." Leyden's jaunty attitude and breezy manner appeared abrasive to the other members. I thought that Leyden adopted his manner to conceal his nervousness.

"The City is run by an economic council which decides everything." He spoke rapidly. "I distrust some of the people who serve on it. The real estate interests in this City have altogether too much power. They will stop at nothing. And their job is made easier by our Mayor and Council who have capitulated to their wishes. No one, not even the police chief, dare stand between the economic council of bankers and their actions to shape the City in their image."

"You sound like a cynical, disillusioned young man," Dickie Edwards said with a smile.

"If you look at the history of government in this City, can you blame me?" Leyden cried. "The real powers in this City can get Vine released. But then I'm the new generation, gentlemen," he added with feigned apology. "I was in the S.D.S. not so long ago. I know how the left wing works. Miss Vine's disappearance is a practical solution to an irritation. She's in the hands of the powers-that-be, not political zealots."

"Do you mean," Raikes asked, "that if nothing is done to exacerbate the situation, she will be returned unharmed?"

"That's my reading of it," Leyden said cheerfully.

At that instant a young man in a black suit and clerical collar rushed quietly into the room and went to a vacant chair at the far end of the table. Raikes raised his eyebrows to intimate to the others that he did not know the visitor. I saw the gray eyes of the visitor glance shyly around the table as he respectfully waited for the chairman to address him. A secretary approached Raikes from the executive offices and handed him a letter, which, I could see, bore the insignia of the Roman Catholic Diocese of New York. "Gentlemen, the Cardinal sends us his regrets that he is unable to be with us today. He has sent us, however, Father Ian."

A brown forelock fell over the priest's forehead as he looked eagerly from one member to the other. "Forgive my lateness, please," he said as if trying to catch his breath. "The Cardinal is in Boston today."

Raikes glanced at the yellow pad in front of him, cleared his throat, and turned his sharp eyes on me. "At this point, perhaps Mr. Mack could tell us what he has found."

I sensed the coldness of the others as if they expected nothing intelligent from me. I had no thought of what to say and began with Leyden's suggestion that they do nothing.

"Miss Vine is in grave danger," I said more loudly than I intended. "I think criminal interests are involved."

"You do!" Stinnes said suddenly. "Can you enlighten us?"

"Not yet, sir," I admitted. "But we are pursuing certain leads."

Father Ian suddenly began expressing his fears that the political Right was involved.

"Are you suggesting that we are dealing with special police?" Tally Leyden asked sharply.

"Ten thousand disappeared in Argentina," Ian said simply. "In Peru, Colombia, Guatemala, El Salvador, they disappear in the tens of thousands. It is state terror on a grand scale." He looked apologetic as if aware of shocking his listeners. "Is it such an unlikely leap of the imagination to see our Government following the same policy with regard to our own people?"

"Come, come now, Father," Dickie Edwards chided him in a fatherly fashion. "We know that that can not happen here."

"It could, though," Leyden broke in. "He's right. This could be the beginning. How do we know what is really being done in Government? The Conservatives have the power. They talk patriotically about freedom, but they don't extend freedom of choice to our Central American neighbors, as the good Father points out."

"Kidnappings are quietly taking place in New York City all the time," Ian said persuasively. "I know it from my work as a priest. The newspapers report only the rare case."

"It's interesting," Raikes said, a glint of humor in his eye. "Mr. Mack is on the trail of organized crime, Mr. Leyden suspects the bankers, Father Ian points to the secret agencies of the Federal Government, and the rest of us blame the Socialists."

Amid the smiles of the members, Mr. Stinnes alone kept a serious face. He leveled a finger at Ian. "I find it hard to believe that the Cardinal sent you to this meeting."

"I am sorry," Ian said mildly. "Churchmen have more opportunity to become aware of changes because those who are in trouble come to us first."

"Are you one of those Marxist priests we hear about?" Dickie Edwards asked quickly. "A liberation theologist," he added contemptuously referring to priests in Latin America who supported the poor against the rich.

Father Ian turned to him. "One could argue that the bankers of this City would do anything to preserve the status quo because, if the City defaulted, a new class would come into power. Why should such arguments be labeled as subversive? Which is what you mean when you say 'Marxist', is it not?"

"We did not come here," Raikes interrupted, "for a philosophical discussion. May I bring you back to our subject, that is, the disappearance of Miss Vine. Let us make an effort in our spheres of influence," Raikes continued in his flat, methodical tone, "and give Mr. Mack our full support in his investigation. Meanwhile I shall draw up a statement of concern for Miss Vine's safety for the full Board to endorse at its meeting tomorrow afternoon."

As Raikes adjourned the meeting, the trustees broke into private conversations among themselves.

"I'll be seeing Bill Kroneweiss," Dickie Edwards said to Raikes. "I'll mention our concern, and we'll see if he can't do something."

Raikes turned to me. "Write me a memorandum on what you have discovered," and then stepped away to speak with Dickie Edwards.

I was walking from the room when Father Ian caught up to me.

"May I see you for a moment?" Ian asked pleasantly. "We can sit on this bench." He pointed to a marble slab bench in the hall under the portrait of a bearded trustee of long ago.

I did not know what to expect from this man. I found him disturbing.

"You know more about the disappearance of Miss Vine than you let on," Ian said. "Is she really a political hostage or what?"

I nodded. "It's political."

"But no one has demanded anything in exchange for her?" Ian queried.

"No," I said.

"What's to prevent her abductors from killing her or selling her into white slavery?" Ian asked, an intensity creeping into his voice. "We may never see her again. The only reason it hasn't happened yet is that someone on top hasn't given the order."

Tally Leyden walked by and gave us a look of suspicion.

"Those types," Father Ian said, looking after Leyden. "They know more than they'll admit. One of them in there, probably old man Edwards, knows the truth about her. In fact, I think the only reason she's still alive is because the march on City Hall is being organized without her."

"Do you fear for her life?" I gasped.

Ian smiled. "She would be released unharmed ordinarily. But she already knows too much, and there's such a high-level investigation underfoot that her captors may try to get rid of her just to cover their trail."

My heart sank. "What can we do?"

"Wait for a break, a significant clue," Ian said excitedly. "I'll notify you if I find one and vice versa. All right?"

I nodded and took the card Father Ian handed me.

"I see she means a lot to you," Ian said sympathetically. "I'm sure we'll find her."

I flinched in alarm that the priest had read my emotions, and Ian, seeing this, smiled reassuringly and walked away.

I headed for my office by the side staircase. I barely noticed the cataloguers diligently bent over their desks piled high with books as I passed by. On the mezzanine level, Bradley Tone detached himself from a group of serial procurement workers and cried out to me. "Mr. Mack! You got a moment?"

I stopped on the stairway as Tone approached. The young man appeared to be excited. His blue eyes were alight and his choir-boy face was alive with "Hallelujahs."

"Over three hundred turned up at my meeting last night. Isn't that good when people can't give up T V and are afraid of being mugged? That means our people do want the thirty-hour work week."

"Wait for the ballot return," I warned. "Appearances are deceiving."

"I thought you were goin' to help me," Tone complained. "You haven't done anything."

"I'm with you in spirit," I said, continuing to walk down.

Bradley Tone turned away in exasperation.

I went to my office and found my secretary sitting at her desk and holding out her arm for me to take a message.

"Detective Buckle wants you to call," she said archly. There was a sexy undertone to everything she did.

"Will you call him for me, please," I said apologetically, as if I felt that business should not be entering into our relationship.

I sat at my desk and picked up the telephone when it rang.

Buckle greeted me gruffly. "You know that young man we liberated from Lanzetta's mansion?"

"Yeah," I said, envisioning the fellow running away through the streets of Brooklyn back to his family.

"He was found in a parking lot. Bullet in the head."

I winced. "When did it happen?"

"Couple of hours ago," Buckle said with a sigh. "He wasn't tortured so I don't think he gave us away. Gabriel had better watch out."

"He's gone," I said. "Gabriel is changing his identity."

"Good luck to him," Buckle said, as if he felt Gabriel's luck had run out. "I called to see what you know about a guy named Harold Poppin."

I was surprised to hear the name from a detective. "He's a department head in Arbie's union."

"We're bugging Lanzetta. His name came up on the tape," Buckle said meaningfully. "Arbie Vine isn't his favorite woman."

"Does Poppin know where she is?"

"No, but we'll get Poppin to tell us what we want to know. Want to come down and watch? You'll find out what it's like to be a real detective."

"I can't refuse a free education," I said. "What are you picking Poppin up on?"

"Parking violation," Buckle said laconically and hung up.

FIFTEEN

I walked into the Chelsea precinct house to find Poppin talking animatedly to a policeman. Poppin's self-assurance had deserted him. His corpulent body no longer exuded complacency. Poppin gaped in shock at me, as if the connection between the police and the library detective had electrocuted him. I could almost see Poppin wishing that he had been nicer to me.

"In here," Buckle called from the door of a room.

Poppin spun round and walked to the beckoning Buckle. He smiled nervously and looked back at me following him. His eyes darted about as if he expected danger from anywhere.

Buckle acted with indifference. He pointed to a chair and Poppin sat down. I sat at the back of the room and wondered if Poppin was blaming me for his predicament. Poppin, although bewildered, would have gleaned that Arbie Vine was the point at issue.

"I'm not here because I parked my car in the wrong place," Poppin said, his voice sounding pleasant and willing to please. "You've got something more serious on your mind."

Buckle continued to look at him mistrustfully.

"Look," Poppin said, "if I've done wrong, I'm ready to atone for it. You guys won't find anyone more willing to cooperate."

Buckle cleared his throat. "Lanzetta," he said.

Poppin reddened. "Yeah, I know him," he admitted.

"We know you know him," Buckle sneered. "Tell us about him and Bratwurst."

Poppin squirmed. "They're in contact because of the maintenance men in Lanzetta's buildings. We negotiate their wages. Hector meets with him sometimes."

"You're the go-between," Buckle said.

"I'm a liaison man," Poppin nodded, "but I'm not the only one."

"It's not all union business, is it?" Buckle said.

Poppin shrugged. "Hector has a lot of interests."

"One of them is keeping labor peace in the City," Buckle suggested. "And Lanzetta also has that interest."

"Lanzetta is a spokesman for a lot of City business," Poppin nodded. "He's big with the boys in mid-town."

"And with the mob," Buckle added.

"Yeah," Poppin smiled, darting a look back at me. "You don't fool around with Lanzetta."

"Did Lanzetta tell Bratwurst that he didn't want to see unions marching on City Hall?" Buckle asked.

Poppin nodded. "No one wants that."

"Arbie Vine wanted it."

"Hey, wait a minute, detective, are you suggesting Lanzetta is involved with Vine's disappearance?" Poppin looked shocked.

"More than that," Buckle smiled coldly, "I'm suggesting you're involved."

Poppin held up his hands placatingly. "I don't like Vine but I wouldn't go that far."

"You talked to Lanzetta about her though," Buckle said.

"He asked me what she was like, that's all."

"How does Bratwurst feel about her?"

"Hector's not happy with her. She's too radical."

"She doesn't kiss his ass," Buckle suggested.

Poppin shrugged.

"We can hit you with a two hundred dollar fine," Buckle told him.

Poppin sighed. "I don't know if Hector is involved in the kidnapping, but it's not likely."

"It is likely he'll know where Vine is," Buckle said. "I'd like you to find out and let us know."

"Sure, if I get a chance," Poppin smiled genially.

"Chance doesn't come into it," Buckle said coldly. "You find out, that is, if you want to drive in this city."

Poppin shifted on his chair and darted a look back at me. "If I knew where she was, I would have sprung her long ago. Her disappearance has nothing to do with union politics. Lanzetta's a big man in the Democratic Party. He wouldn't be kidnapping anybody, especially a broad like Vine."

"Lanzetta has ties to the mob and the mob kidnap people," Buckle said. "We'll give you 48 hours to find her." He pointed to the door.

Poppin reddened sheepishly and stood up. He turned to give me a broad smile, which I saw as a thin veil concealing his anger. He seemed to be blaming me for his predicament, but he nodded genially and left the room.

"I thought you were going to break him down and make him confess like they do in the movies," I said, approaching Buckle.

"First lesson," Buckle said. "If you have horses, make them work for you. Harold Poppin hates Bratwurst's guts because Bratwurst humiliates him in front of others--that's how Bratwurst controls his staff. If he could implicate Bratwurst safely, he would."

"Meanwhile," I said, as if speaking to myself, "Arbie is at the mercy of those criminals."

Buckle looked at his watch. "The whole city is at their mercy. See you, Rudy. I've got half a dozen other cases to settle."

I left the station house with a nagging disillusionment in the police. If Arbie were to be found alive, I alone would have to do it and quickly. Poppin's reference to Lanzetta and the Democratic Party had given me an idea. I stepped into a telephone booth and called Petula Simon Clarkson.

She was cooking supper after which she was going to the Bronx Democratic Club for an important meeting. Sure, I could come with her. If I hurried up to her place in the Bronx, I might get some supper too.

I realized that my conservative bias was hindering my search. I had to tear away all those assumptions instilled in me from childhood, that, first of all, there were only a few rotten apples in a barrel and, second, that the upper classes were as concerned about the welfare of all the people as their own. Arbie had tried to make me see how "Society" worked, and, despite my rejection of her argument, I retained some of it. A strong showing at a protest march could very well have changed the public mind from accepting the gradual squeezing of the middle and lower classes to demanding the disinvestment of the ruling class. The people's protest against the Vietnam War was the prime example of people power. But, as Arbie complained to me, the people had not followed through on the home front, and, consequently, they were going to suffer more Vietnams.

I found Petula Clarkson's apartment house off the Grand Parkway. The hallways were long, dark, and dingy, but when she opened her door, her apartment looked bright and clean.

"We just finished eatin'," she said breezily and moved her large body to the side. "Mr. Mopes couldn't wait no longer." She nodded to a mild-looking black man in his sixties who was sitting in an easy chair. "But I saved yer a plate."

"No, thank you, Petula," I said. "I feel too much on the move to take time out for a meal." I nodded at Mr. Mopes who nodded back with a courteous smile.

Petula took an apple from a plate of fruit on a sideboard. "Put this in your pocket, Mack. We're going to have a long session and you're going to need it." She gave it to me with authority. "Any cooler out there?"

"Still hot but not so humid," I said, pocketing the apple and catching a glint of humor in Mr. Mopes's eye.

" I don't need yer tonight as a escort, Mr. Mopes," Petula announced. "You stay here and rest your bones. Mack's gonna be my escort."

"All right, honey," Mr. Mopes sang. "You take care now."

We walked the several blocks to the Democratic Party Clubhouse. Petula, although well-known in the district, watched the street. She was always on the alert for a sign of trouble. When we approached a group of boys loitering on the sidewalk, she hesitated, recognized one of them, and cried a greeting like a password which opened a passageway for us.

I was touched by her concern for my welfare. She may have been a party hack, as Arbie said, a loyal Democrat in return for the favors the Party could bestow on her, but she was a good sort.

"You just keep your ears open," she said as we climbed to the party headquarters on the second floor. "You just might get a clue to where Vine's at." She stopped on the landing to catch her breath.

"They gonna have to move to the first floor if they want me to continue my patronage."

I smiled in agreement and opened the headquarters' door which led into a hallway whose walls were covered with promotional material of past campaigns. The cool air hit us.

"Just follow me now," Petula said moving her large girth down the hallway like an advancing tank.

We proceeded into a very large room, windowed on one side and clustered with wooden folding chairs. I estimated there were forty people assembled, mostly white and talkative. I saw the short thin figure and beady-eyed look of the man who controlled this Democratic Club, the man I had come to hear, the man whom I was convinced held the key to Arbie's release. Lanzetta rested his rump on the back of a chair and talked lazily to a dozen club members gathered around him. Afraid of attracting Lanzetta's attention, I stayed back and listened. Petula whispered that she would meet me at the end of the evening. Feeling as if cut adrift, but, at the same time, less conspicuous away from Petula's company, I mixed with the men sipping coffee and nibbling cookies. People were arriving constantly. I helped myself to coffee and looked at photographs on the wall, which took me back through the Al Smith and Roosevelt days until I heard a familiar voice at my shoulder.

"You enjoying yourself, detective?"

I turned to see the long bony face of Alex Mackart, an amused look in his black eyes, and the slight twist of a smile.

"You remember meeting me with Barb Janes?" Alex said.

"Of course," I reached out and shook Mackart's slimly tapered fingers.

"The occasion was grander, but the principal was the same, meaning our real estate friend," Alex said, his eyes still looking amused. "He's why you're here, isn't it?"

I shrugged. "I'm interested in working for the next election."

"Balls!" Alex said softly. "You're interested in finding Arbie Vine and so am I."

I looked cautiously around, and, finding that our neighbors were too involved in conversing to overhear us, I asked: "Why are you interested?"

"It's a long story, goes back to slave days," Mackart said, "but I'll make it short and sweet. She's the only Local president who can stand up to Bratwurst and the only hope we blacks have of throwing off the Bratwurst yoke. We can't do it ourselves, at least just yet. Necessity requires we play Uncle Tom until we're ready."

"But there are a lot of black Local Presidents," I said in disbelief. "Why don't you get together?"

"We're not promoting a revolution," Mackart smiled, "We still need a whitey to do business with the City."

I nodded. "Not all of you are *playing* Uncle Tom, though."

"True," Mackart sighed. "Some of us *are* Uncle Toms"

I smiled and snorted a short laugh at Mackart's disgusted expression. Some club members were looking over at us. Alex suggested we move to some chairs by the window and out of earshot.

"Is Lanzetta behind the kidnapping?" I asked as we sat down.

"It's complicated," Mackart said, pausing to fit a cigarette into his cigarette holder. "These types function by suggestion, innuendo, second-hand reports; they have to, because, like in all leaderships, the different factions have to be made to move in concert." He lit his cigarette. "Lanzetta doesn't act on his own. Even if he did give the order, he got the initiative to go ahead from a half dozen sources. But you don't care about that crap. You want to know who's holding Arbie?"

I nodded expectantly. I was surprised by Mackart's forthrightness as I had thought of him as a flunky to Hector Bratwurst.

A tall, heavy-set, black man moved up behind Mackart's chair. I recognized him as Mackart's bodyguard.

"Slidsky just came in," said the bodyguard in a deep, muffled voice. "He's deliverin' a message to Lanzetta."

I caught sight of a slight, smiling Lanzetta following the menacing-looking Slidsky to a back room.

"Tell me when either of them leaves," Alex said and turned back to me as his bodyguard glided after Lanzetta. "I have a hunch this is important. Slidsky would never interrupt Lanzetta's political business otherwise."

I saw Petula Clarkson wave her fingers at me from a distance. I signaled to Alex to wait a moment and went over to explain to Petula that I could not escort her home.

"That's okay," Petula said reassuringly. "I'll call Mr. Mopes."

"She friendly with you?" Mackart asked when I returned. "You be careful. She works all the angles."

The bodyguard loomed before us. "They leavin' now," he said urgently.

"Both?" Alex said standing up. "Come on."

I could see Lanzetta speaking hurriedly to a florid-faced man as if he were instructing him to run the meeting. Slidsky was waiting impatiently by the door.

"Get the motor running, Joseph," Alex ordered his bodyguard. "We'll come out after them."

The bodyguard stepped through the knots of people and pushed by Slidsky who stared after him. Lanzetta moved deftly past well-wishing club members and, reaching Slidsky's side, replaced his grin with a glower. Mackart and I walked toward the door as the sound of a gavel and a hoarse cry of "to order" caused the members to look for seats and compose themselves for the meeting. When we reached the stairs, we heard Lanzetta's angry voice on the street level.

"Somebody's messed up," Alex said, flipping his cigarette onto the floor and mashing it with his heel.

I had a fleeting doubt whether I should be following two dangerous criminals into the unknown in the company of a dubious union leader, whom I hardly knew, and his bodyguard, who looked as if he could kill without blinking an eye.

As we reached the street, we glimpsed Slidsky pulling shut the door of a long black limousine, which immediately glided away. Mackart pointed to a light brown Pontiac turning the corner, ran across the sidewalk, and snapped his fingers impatiently waiting for it to pull up.

"Get in," he said and held open the back door. He scrambled in behind me. "You got' em?" he shouted at his bodyguard.

"Yeah, I seen where they went."

I admired the way Mackart's bodyguard followed Lanzetta's limousine, although its extravagant length made it conspicuous in traffic. Lanzetta could not have known that he was being followed, at least, not while we passed through the Bronx, not while we drove on the highway for two hours, and probably not as we ducked along a minor road into Connecticut in the darkness.

Mackart discouraged conversation until we found ourselves careening on a winding road past lighted villages and solitary farm houses. "Obviously they are going to a very private place where they could be harboring Arbie Vine. But I don't intend to walk into a trap, Mr. Mack. We've got to lay a plan."

Keeping my eyes on the tail light of the limousine ahead, I sensed the strain we had been under as Mackart's words weakened my concentration. "First, we've got to make sure Lanzetta has her," I murmured.

"However," Alex warned, "if we go blundering in after them, she could be killed and so could we."

"Blundering is not in my nature," I said tersely.

Mackart stared at me in the dark of the back seat and said in a patient tone, "Vine's safety is not the only issue at stake. We've got to find out who's behind her kidnapping and how far into City and State Government Lanzetta and his boys have penetrated."

"We can worry about that later," I said sharply.

"No, we cannot," Alex responded with a hint of anger in his voice. "If we don't locate the composition of this faction and all its tentacles, it'll kill us in the end."

"All right," I said. "I'm willing to believe the borough presidents, the Mayor, some of the police, the Governor and his aides, and maybe even the White House are behind Lanzetta, but I'm not going to let Arbie stay in their hands a moment longer than necessary."

"It's not the politicians that worry me," Alex said tersely. "They're so corrupt they can be turned like a weathercock, as the bard has it. But it's the banking people, the ones with the real power who are only too glad to get those crooked politicians in office who'll do their bidding on the real issues."

"Such as?" I asked.

"Such as who's really gonna pay for the breaking up of the welfare state," Mackart said with vehemence. "And how many of them specially-constructed limousines are gonna cruise the New York streets while the rest pick through garbage cans, sleep in shelters, and fight to work for less than subsistence wages."

"Do you think this is what Lanzetta's all about?" I asked, amused that Mackart could identify with the dispossessed while owning a limousine not much shorter than those he was criticizing.

"I know it," Mackart snapped . "Look, husband and wife working in City jobs can't afford a City apartment, have to live in a City shelter with their children. The Mayor acts like a ring master at a circus, while real estate gangsters like Lanzetta are getting disgustingly rich."

I sensed his deep, brooding anger. "How does Arbie fit into it?" I asked quietly.

"She was ready to fight back when Bratwurst and his ..." Mackart paused for the right word and, in exasperation, cried, "sellouts are working with the bankers to crush us." He pressed his hand to his forehead, his long thin fingers catching the light flickering through the window. "They made a mistake in kidnapping her. If we're smart, we'll use it to catch them."

I questioned how it was to be done, but he said nothing. Mackart was not very realistic, I thought. "Why weren't you black leaders behind her when she organized the march? I didn't see any of you at the big meeting where they planned it. And you've got thousands of members behind you."

"That would've been suicide," Mackart said. "Only the socialists were ready to fight; the rest of us didn't know what was going on. Anyway, Bratwurst has got us under his thumb. Don't ask me any more; it's depressing."

"Hey, they're turning," the bodyguard announced.

"Slow down, Joseph," Alex said and peered ahead at the limousine's red tail-lights disappearing up a lane into the blackness of the trees. "Drive by and stop up the road."

I thought I saw a house in the distance.

"Stop here," Mackart said.

We pulled onto the shoulder of the road.

"I'm cutting across the field," I said. "I think I know where the house is."

"Wait," Alex held up his hand. "We should get the police."

"It'll be too late," I said, opening the door. "They'll be long gone before we can find any policemen."

"Joseph, go with him," Mackart said. "I'll wait in the driver's seat."

Joseph got out, leaving the door open for Mackart to get behind the wheel. He jumped the roadside ditch, climbed over the fence, and ran to catch up to me in the field.

"We'll play it by ear," I said. "Stay together till we know what's going on."

Crickets were orchestrating the countryside. As I moved into the trees, the cacophony of sawing beetle wings died away. We came onto a driveway and ran along it to where it turned sharply. I put my hand on Joseph's arm to stop him.

"They'll have a look-out. Go that way." I pointed into the trees on the left side of the lane. I went stealthily into the right side, avoiding the low branches and stepping around the bushes which were barely discernible in the night light.

I had not gone far when I heard a sharp low cry as if a small animal had been trapped by a predator.

"Okay," I heard Joseph's deep voice call to me.

I stepped back to the lane and saw the great frame of Joseph loom in the darkness. A man lay at his feet. I kneeled to look closely at him and noticed that Joseph was gripping the barrel of his pistol by his side.

"You hit him too hard," I said. "You could have split his skull."

"I had to," Joseph said. "He saw me comin'."

I took the man's rifle which had fallen a few feet away and turned round at the sound of an angry shout. It was Lanzetta. His voice was coming from inside the house about thirty yards ahead of us.

"Let's hurry," I said.

We ran lightly up to the back part of the house where we could hear Lanzetta shouting furiously at someone. There were two floors. Lights shone from the second story windows.

I crept up the steps of the back porch and tried the door. It was locked. Joseph cleared his throat to get my attention. He pointed to a darkened window on the second floor over the porch and gestured to suggest he climb a drainpipe running down by it, go through the window, and come down to open the door from the inside. Coming to stand beside him, I could see that the window was open a crack. I nodded, and Joseph, getting onto the porch, seized the drainpipe to draw himself up. But he hesitated and let himself down.

"What's wrong?" I whispered.

"It's not strong enough."

"Wait," I said, setting the rifle on the porch floor. "Let me get on your shoulders."

Joseph cupped his hands for me to step on. Taking off my shoes, and using the wall and the drainpipe to support myself, I gingerly climbed onto Joseph's shoulders. By standing on my toes, I reached the window shelf with one hand and the drainpipe with the other. There was a fixture holding the drainpipe to the wall up to which I could climb. The thought crossed my mind that a middle-aged man should not be attempting this, but I stepped on the fixture with my toes and shakily pulled myself up level with the window. Slamming my elbow on the sill, I carefully slipped my hand under the open window and raised it quietly up as far as I could. Then, grabbing the sill with both hands, I pulled myself into the open window space and crawled onto the floor of the room. I heard men's voices arguing in the next room.

There was a stirring as if someone were moving on a mattress, and a woman's voice said in half-whisper, "Who's that?"

I paused, not daring to hope, and whispered, "Arbie?"

"Rudy! Oh God, Rudy! "

Shaking with joy, I rushed to where she lay on a bed in the shadows in a corner of the room.

"Ssh!" she hissed, "they'll hear us. Oh, Rudy, thank God, you've come."

I put my hands on her, scarcely believing it was her.

"My hands are tied to the bed," she said.

I fumbled with the knots at her wrists.

"It's a slipknot," she said, "just push the end back through the knot."

Unable to see what I was doing, and terrified that someone would come into the room, I cursed under my breath until I slipped the knot, and she was free.

Arbie threw her arms around me. "Oh, Rudy, Rudy, let's get the hell out of here."

Tense with excitement, I took her to the window, opened it wide, and hissed for Joseph's attention. I helped Arbie climb out the window and held her by the arms as I lowered her down to Joseph, who grabbed her by the legs and brought her safely down to the floor of the porch. I dangled from the window an instant later, and Joseph reached up just in time to help me to clamber down the wall to the safety of the porch.

I saw that Arbie was wearing just a thin dress and no shoes. Her hair was awry.

"Can you walk?" I asked.

"I think I can," she said faintly.

Slipping my arm behind her back, I led her quickly down the porch steps and round the side of the house to the driveway. Joseph picked up the rifle and my shoes and followed us. I looked back at the house to see if we had been observed, but there was only the sound of Lanzetta's voice, not as loud but angry.

"Damn it!" I cursed as I stepped on the sharp gravel.

Joseph handed me my shoes with a grin. I took them and put them on hurriedly as if the delay could cost us our lives. I picked Arbie up in my arms and ran with her down the driveway, past the crumpled figure of the look-out, and under the trees. Joseph jogged alongside us.

"Get the car and meet us at the foot of the lane," I cried. "We'll be all right."

Joseph dashed ahead and disappeared into the darkness.

"Let me down, Rudy," Arbie said. "You're too little to carry me. I can manage."

"No, you're too weak," I gasped. I clenched my teeth and kept running.

Arbie planted a big kiss on my forehead. I burst into laughter and almost dropped her, but kept running. God! I thought, it's good to have her back again. I heard an engine start up, and, catching my second wind, increased my speed, and ran suddenly onto the road. Mackart's car approached us, its headlights pin-sharp in the darkness. I let Arbie stand and turned to catch the name on the mailbox in the car light: "Haliburton."

"Jump in," Joseph called through the driver's window.

Alex Mackart was looking round-eyed over his shoulder.

I opened the back door and helped Arbie into the back seat. I got in beside her and held her in my arms.

"Arbie, baby," Mackart laughed gleefully and reached behind to shake her arm. "How you doin'?"

"Let's get the hell back to New York," she said, "then I'll tell you all about it. There's lot worse in this world than listening to Bratwurst's speeches, Alex."

Mackart laughed and clapped his hands. "Put your foot on the floor," he told Joseph. "This lady's had her fill of this joint."

They sped through the night. I kissed Arbie full and long. She pulled back and looked me in the face. "What brought you here tonight?"

"That guy who was shouting, that was Lanzetta, the real estate mogul," I said. "We followed him on a hunch."

"Is that who it was!" Arbie said. "He was giving them shit for trying to rape me!"

"What?" I grabbed her tighter.

"Don't worry, sweetheart, I screamed and kicked until the guy who'd gone out for a walk heard me and pulled this big brute off me. It was the second time he tried it. I guess his fellow warden had enough and told on him."

"Who were they?" Mackart asked.

"The mugs? Who cares? Whenever anyone important came, they blindfolded me."

"We're going to get them," I said angrily. "I'll call Buckle and tell him where they held you."

"Oh, I've got some good clues," Arbie said, snuggling her face into my neck, "but I want to go straight to your place before I say another word."

My arm tight about her, I swore to myself that I would not rest until Lanzetta and his friends were behind bars. Alex and Joseph sensed my determined anger, and they, too, stared ahead into the night as we sped back to the City.

SIXTEEN

After putting Arbie to bed, I called Buckle at his residence. The city detective, emotionless, said I did the right thing, and that he would notify the Connecticut police about the farm house, and the possibility of their finding no one there. I also called Joshua Raikes. Sounding exuberant, he volunteered to inform all concerned--the trustees, the Library staff, the press--in the morning. I fell into bed and slept deeply for the first time since Arbie's disappearance. As I shaved the next morning, I noticed that I felt marvelously relaxed, as if I had just thrown off a heavy burden. Much of that burden, I thought, was guilt. The night of Arbie's kidnapping flashed through my mind like a pain--the car speeding away, my helplessness in watching it go. I looked into the bedroom to assure myself that she was really there.

I let Arbie sleep late. She was bruised and cut from defending herself from her guards. She was thin, and, despite her calm behavior, she was nervous and frightened to the core. It would take her some time to recover emotionally, I thought.

I was reading Thiers' *The French Revolution* and was immersed in the masterful portrayal of events when two arms gently encircled my neck, and Arbie put her cheek next to my ear.

"I have to treat you like my hero from now on," Arbie said.

I pulled her round to sit on my lap. "You're the hero. Do you realize how many people will be glad to see you back?"

"I don't care about that now," she said. "Just hold me, Rudy. I've got to persuade myself that I'm not tied to a bed waiting for an ugly thug to bring me something to eat."

I rocked her gently in my arms. "This ugly thug has breakfast waiting for you. The coffee's hot."

She kissed me and stood up, stretching and yawning. "Good Lord! I feel almost normal!"

We sat at the kitchen table, and I gave her grapefruit and the eggs and bacon I had prepared. She ate as if famished.

"You're a hell of a better cook than they were, Rudy. Another week with them and I would have given up on food."

"Did they move you around from one house to another?"

"A couple of times," Arbie nodded. "I'm going to write out every detail I can remember so you and the police can read it before you question me. All I want to do is find out who gave the orders and why. By the way, what's happening to the march on City Hall?"

"It's still on. I think it starts at noon."

"An hour from now," Arbie cried, swallowing her coffee. "I've got to get down to Union Square. Hurry Rudy, help me get dressed."

"Are you sure you're strong enough to march?" I frowned.

"After all that time lying around doing nothing?"

While Arbie took a shower, I took some clothes out of the cupboard for her. She had only jeans, several blouses, and a pair of flat shoes which she kept at my apartment for emergencies.

The telephone rang. It was Buckle wanting to debrief Arbie. When I explained that she was marching on City Hall, Buckle did not sound pleased because that meant he had to provide more protection. "The City spent a lot of money looking for her," he complained. "Now she makes us pay for protecting her so she can bad-mouth the Mayor."

"There's no way anyone could talk her out of marching," I said. "I'll walk beside her all the way."

"If she gets shot, it's not our fault," Buckle warned. "We're not miracle men."

I cleaned my gun as I waited for Arbie to dress. It was possible that Lanzetta would try to kill Arbie during the march.

"Okay, Rudy, I'm ready," Arbie sang out from the hallway.

I grabbed a light summer coat to cover my shoulder holster as I hurried to the door which Arbie was holding open.

"Just in case you don't get a chance to tell me," I said as we waited for the elevator, "what did you find out about your captors?"

"They're working for someone bigger than Lanzetta," Arbie said, "someone who has a dozen Lanzettas working for him. They asked me a lot of questions about my union membership and what we expected to achieve by marching."

"Who's they?"

"A couple of young guys, in their thirties, lawyer types. They used to sit me at a table and take turns quizzing me. They seemed really concerned about how the workers were going to respond to the cutbacks, the inflation which the government is engineering, and the fall in real wages. I don't know why they thought I was so important, but one of them suggested I might like to change sides and work for them. Good money, they said. 'Course I played along because I thought they were going to kill me if they couldn't control me."

We reached the street. The heat of the day made me think of the effort of marching. Union Square was only a ten minute walk via Gramercy Park.

"If you hadn't rescued me," Arbie said, "I wouldn't be alive. They seemed to be waiting for orders."

We walked by the iron grille fence encircling the park and side-stepped the dog droppings.

"Who do you think was behind it" I asked.

"Some screwball, like an international banker," Arbie said. "When my wardens spoke over the phone to whoever was directing the operation, they mentioned New York City bonds and the City's possible default. I thought that was unusual for your average thug."

I laughed. "You don't think they were talking directly to their banker, do you?"

"No, they were talking to Slidsky or somebody, but they definitely connected labor unrest to bankers' profits--which is where I came in."

"We'll have to get at the truth through Lanzetta," I said.

"He could be a blind alley, Rudy. The real power is wrapped in clouds well over Lanzetta's head."

We came onto Union Square by Park Avenue South. The farmers' market on the north of the Square was doing a good business, but there seemed just as many people gathered at the south side where unionists had agreed to assemble for the march on City Hall. Arbie and I walked unnoticed to where the Library Guild's banner lay propped against a railing. Alf Landy let out a shout of disbelief when he saw Arbie, and, suddenly, there were cries of surprise and jubilation around her as people ran to greet her, kiss her, shake her hands, embrace her.

"It's a miracle!" Petula Clarkson announced.

The presidents of other union Locals came to her and learned of her hair-raising escape. It was marvellous to see the happiness in their faces. It brought tears to my eyes, and I had to turn away so that no one could see them. A reporter for the *Times*, a distinguished gray-haired gentleman who could have been the chairman of the board, took notes on whatever he overheard, and then asked Arbie if she thought that less than three thousand protesters was enough to make City Hall listen.

"Considering the opposition we faced," she said, "the fact that three thousand turned out is fantastic!"

"What do you feel about allying your union with Socialists," the reporter asked, and nodded at flags and banners advertising the Socialist Party.

I could see that he was baiting her to say something that could be used to discredit her.

"They've got guts," I intervened. "Which is more than you can say for a lot of people."

The reporter took a step back and looked at me in mild amusement. He mistook me for an ardent unionist, and, ignoring me, looked back at Arbie for a reply.

Arbie shouted over the cries of the marchers who had become vocally alive with a new-found excitement now that she was back among them. "They see the co-opting of the unions by the bankers and politicians as the first step in getting an iron-hand control over the worker in order to lower his standard of living back to where he was in the mid-nineteenth century." Arbie stared angrily at the elderly reporter. "Will your *New York Times* print that?"

The reporter, jotting everything down, smiled noncommittally.

"Yeh, let me tell ya," Alf Landy, who had overheard Arbie, broke in. "We got over three hundred in our Local alone who got pink slips to be laid off at the end of the month. Not one of them is here! They're scared shitless to show themselves 'cause they hope for a reprieve like happened last time."

"There'll be a reprieve," Arbie said. "The Library would have to shut half its branches if there weren't."

A drum sounded the beat for the march. The Socialist Workers Party took the lead and formed the column eight abreast. Police fanned out over both sides of 14th Street. The unionists fell in line and held up their banners. The *Times* reporter disappeared, and I steered Arbie into the third row.

Passers-by stopped to watch. Storekeepers looked out of their windows, and, sometimes, as the march passed through the narrower streets of the East Village, people perched at their apartment windows. Many of those marching had been in the protests against the Vietnam War, and they raised the chants, common to that era, but with different wordings, such as "One, two, three, four, stop the war on the poor."

I watched the sides of the streets, the windows of the houses, and the marchers near me. At any time someone might try to hit Arbie, though he would have to be an excellent shot, I thought, to make contact in this crowd. There was always the "Sirhan possibility," that someone could step up from behind us. The police seemed to be aware of the danger because several officers were concentrated about the first few rows of the column.

"We were supposed to get ten thousand," Arbie said to Alf Landy. "Who messed up?"

"No one messed up," Alf remonstrated. "Jesus, we just couldn't persuade people of the importance of this. Bratwurst threatened to cut funds to a lot of organizations who were ready to join us. When that happened, all we had was the Party. If it weren't for it, nobody would have showed."

I looked for the community leaders who spoke at the rally in the union meeting hall the night that Arbie was kidnapped, but they had not come.

We attracted some attention on the way to the City Hall. The police had an area at the tip of the City Hall Park ready for us. A truck with loudspeakers was hooked up and waiting. Television cameras and radio reporters hovered about. I listened to the speakers trying to be heard over the foggy loudspeaker system. No one seemed to care what they were saying as long as something critical was being said. When Arbie stood on the roof of the truck, however, she spoke with such passion that the protesters stopped talking and listened. Arbie attacked the Mayor and his connection with the bankers and real estate moguls, who were taking over the City government with dictatorial committees, and sacrificing the citizens in their plans for maintaining profits .

"All done in the name of saving our City!" she cried. "Hypocrites! They're doing it to save themselves, and only themselves! We pay for their mistakes, and for their greed. We'll pay and pay and pay ad infinitum until enough of us stand up and cry, 'Enough!' We need a general strike! But what we see are union leaders carping at one another and intentionally dividing their members. You're being sold down the river, brothers and sisters, and Big Brother is doing the selling!"

I admired her courage, her clear speaking voice, and her great energy which kept the protesters enrapt. Petula was right. Arbie's appearance at the rally, which she had done so much to promote, was a miracle! I scanned the buildings in the distance to see if there was a rifle at one of the windows. I pictured Lanzetta, short and skinny, fuming with anger at his subordinates. "The bastards behind the kidnapping must be cursing themselves for not putting her away for good," I shouted in Alfie's ear. I stood beside her as she climbed down from the truck and spoke into the microphone of a radio reporter.

"We went to Bratwurst and begged him to come," she spoke into the microphone excitedly, accusingly. "But he wouldn't budge. He wouldn't support us."

"Is your union split?" asked the reporter, a girl in her twenties, fishing for a good piece of news.

"No!" Arbie cried. "We're sticking together. We've got a common enemy, and he's become very visible."

"Who kidnapped you?" asked the reporter.

"We'll find out," Arbie said. "Rudyard Mack rescued me. Ask him?" She stepped aside and left me exposed to reporters who were satisfying the public's right to know, up to a point.

"How'd you rescue her, Mr. Mack?"

"The police don't want us to say just yet," I said as nicely as I could. "They'll make an announcement."

"But you tell us how you did it? I mean by car or plane?"

"By car," I said stepping away. "I'm sorry."

Alf Landy confronted the reporters and began shouting into their microphones.

I caught up with Arbie talking to unionists from other Locals, assessing the impact of the march, telling about actions to be taken in the weeks to come.

"I'm very afraid," cautioned a bespectacled civil servant, "the public will see us as socialist revolutionaries. Watch the TV news tonight. They'll only show the socialist banners and they'll report nothing of what we said or what we stand for. But, glad to see you back, Arbie. It was a good rally."

Others agreed and the meeting disbanded. The unionists rolled up their banners and headed for subways and buses. Arbie and I walked through Foley Square, by the courts and into Chinatown.

"Well Rudy? Was it worth it?" Arbie looked disappointed.

"You made a stand, sweetheart." I put an arm about her shoulders. "Without people like you, the rest of us would be trampled on."

Arbie smiled at me. "I love you, Rudy. You're always ready with a kind word when a girl needs one."

"It's not kindness," I said, drawing her to me and kissing her.

We continued walking through the crowds of Canal Street, along the side streets towards home. We needed the walk to dissipate our excitement.

"First thing," Arbie said, "we've got to find out who's been trying to kill me."

"First thing," I said, "we pick up clothes from your place, and you move in with me. That is, if the cops don't insist on hiding you."

"Oh, bugger hiding!" Arbie cried. "I'm staying with you."

"Be prepared to argue with Buckle," I said, and turned to watch an automobile pull up alongside us. With my heart in my mouth, I reached for my gun.

"Hold it!" Buckle poked his head out the window. "Get in the back. We've got a lot of questions to ask you two."

SEVENTEEN

I sat at the back of a room in the Chelsea police station as Buckle and another detective questioned Arbie up front. I admired their precision. They ferreted out details, pin-pointed scenes and actions, and brought Arbie to remember words and phrases in conversations she had heard, which meaning nothing to her, could be helpful in piecing together a larger picture. She had been blindfolded when moved, and, aside from two young lawyers, she had seen only the three men who guarded her.

Buckle beckoned to me to come forward to sit beside Arbie.

"The Connecticut cops went to the Haliburton farm house and found it to have been abandoned in a hurry," Buckle smiled. "The owner lives in the south of France. We're trying to contact him. We have one of the men. We found him lying unconscious off the side of the driveway, and took him to a hospital where he was brought round." He took a photo snapshot from his wallet. "But he's lost his memory." He gave the snapshot to Arbie. "Recognize him?"

Arbie looked at the thick features and heavy-lidded eyes of one of her guards. "That's Salvatore," she said with a shudder.

"He's a member of one of the Costra Nostra families," said the other detective, lean and taciturn. "He'll begin to remember." He picked up his hat, put his hand on Buckle's shoulder, and left the room.

"You don't know how Salvatore got hurt, do you, Rudy?" Buckle asked, arching an eyebrow.

"I found him unconscious," I said truthfully.

"Convenient," Buckle said. "Are we to infer that you rescued Miss Vine all by yourself?"

"You are to infer that," I said.

"The newspapermen have been asking for you," Buckle smiled. "They are more persistent than me on such matters."

"Arbie and I are taking a short vacation," I said.

Arbie stared at me.

"She needs it and I deserve it," I said. "We're leaving as soon as you drive us to a Rent-a-Car and we pick up some clothes."

"Keep your destination a secret," Buckle said, "but tell me."

"Monhegan Island off the Maine coast," I said cheerfully, feeling suddenly relaxed as I thought of the rocks, trees and the ocean, a refuge from this Manhattan steam bath with its drugged and dirty denizens of the streets.

The lean detective re-entered the room. He carried a square box under his arm. "Our friends from Hartford sent us a picture and prints of your friend, Salvatore," he said, and putting the box on a table, took out some photographs. "These are believed to be his friends." He passed them to Arbie.

She looked at several of the photos, some full face, others of groups, and passed them back to the detective. "Those were the two other guards. The ugly one with the cut above his cheek tried to rape me." She continued to study the other photographs.

"The rest of them are soldiers in the Cantata family," Buckle informed her. "You won't see any of them again. They're in disgrace."

I smiled. "And Lanzetta?"

"That depends on you." Buckle looked steadily at Arbie. "If you give up your union protest, you won't hear from him."

"I'll be hearing from him then," Arbie said. "Or let's say he'll be hearing from me."

I grimaced. "I'll phone you, Buckle, just to get the latest."

Buckle took us to the door of the precinct house, pointed at a Rent-a-Car sign down the street, shook hands and wished us luck.

"Who's paying for this vacation?" Arbie asked as we walked. "And why Maine?"

"We've got to give it time to die down," I said. "I have a standing invitation to stay with an artist friend. So I'll pay."

We rented a Honda, a two-seater, shiny red. I liked the way the car handled. We stopped at my apartment while I packed a bag for a week's vacation. When we stopped at Arbie's apartment, I had a feeling that we were being watched. I was impatient for Arbie to pack her things, answer her mail, pay her bills, and water her plants. But I said nothing. I just looked worried.

We drove to the FDR Drive. There was a long route ahead and plenty of time to shake a tail, I thought. On the freeway near to New Haven, I turned off at a rest stop.

"Hungry?"

"That's an understatement," Arbie said. "It's seven already."

I drove to the self-service gas station and filled the tank while I cautiously glanced around for any tell-tale signs of pursuers. Cars glided by, all very much the same. When I drove to the restaurant, I found a parking space close under the restaurant windows. I noticed that Arbie was watching me.

"If you think we're being followed," she said, "you're right!"

I looked quizzically at her.

"Two rows back to your left," she said. "Look through the rear view mirror."

I could see three men in a brown Lincoln. "When did you notice them, Arbie?"

"When they pulled up alongside us at a stop light about an hour ago," she said. "I thought they looked like the Cantata family." She got out and waited while I locked the car. "How can we lose them?"

"Let's think while we eat," I said, gazing dreamily over the parked cars and trying to distinguish the features of the men through the car window in the distance.

I suspected they would make their move when it got dark, which would be about 8:30. But what was their object? to kidnap? or to kill? And why? We chose a table by the window from where we could see their car and observe the men in the Lincoln who appeared to be talking and smoking. I ordered full course dinners.

"We can't drive away from them, can we, Rudy?"

"We can try. We can also tell the highway patrol, but we have no proof."

We ate in silence, each trying to come up with a plan for escape.

"I feel so helpless!" Arbie said. "It's like being a prisoner again. I hate those brutes."

"Maybe we're wrong," I said. "Maybe they're just travelers relaxing after a long drive."

Arbie gave me a careful look. "They look like the men in Buckle's photographs!"

"Ah!" I raised my finger and stood up. "I'll call Buckle."

I was lucky Buckle happened to be at the station house.

"In trouble so soon!" Buckle cried. "Look, drive down the main street of New Haven right by Yale University. Give me your license number." I read him the number from a tab on the car keys. "Now, describe their car in detail."

I looked relieved when I returned to Arbie. "We'll leave in a half-hour, after dessert and coffee. The Cantatas will be intercepted by the New Haven police."

"On what charge?" Arbie asked surprised.

I shrugged. "Drunken driving or something like that which will take them a couple of hours to clear up."

"I hope those bozos get the right car," Arbie said. "I don't want to spend the night in the New Haven jail."

Arbie skipped dessert. She was nervous. I looked at my watch and glanced out the window. One of the men from the car was approaching the restaurant.

"He's probably going to the rest room."

"Shall we be cruel and leave now?" Arbie suggested.

I nodded. "After he goes to the restroom. We can cut our pursuers down to two."

The Cantata brother, or so we identified him, had a large florid face, protruding stomach, and heavy build typical of the thugs who had guarded Arbie. I watched him pick up a chocolate bar near the cashier, throw down some change, and lumber into the men's room.

"I'd like to go in after him and make him tell us what their game is!" I said angrily.

"Don't Rudy! You won't come back alive," Arbie stood up. "Let's go."

I dropped our check with the exact change at the cashier's counter and followed her in a half-run to our car. As I unlocked the car door, I sensed consternation in the Cantata's car. I opened the other door from inside and Arbie slid in with a look of fright.

"They look furious!" she cried.

I spun our Honda away with the sound of the Lincoln starting up in our ears. New Haven was fifteen miles away. It was darkening. Some drivers had their headlights on. I kept our lights off in the hope that we would be harder to follow. I weaved between the slow and fast lanes.

"Can you see them back there?" I asked Arbie.

"They got us in sight," she said, gazing through the back window. "They've got to be figuring out what to do next. There's too much traffic to run us off the road at this point."

"If you see them coming up fast, shout," I said.

"I'll scream!"

I decided to stay in the outside lane and speed.

"They're staying up with us," Arbie said. "One of them is using their car telephone."

"Damn it!" I swore. "They're probably laying a trap for us. I hope Buckle got in touch with the New Haven cops."

I glimpsed a highway marker: exit in 2 miles for the City Center. I cut over to the right lane to be ready for the turnoff. The Lincoln was right behind us now, all pretense having been dropped. I saw the intense stare of the driver of the Lincoln in the rear-view mirror. I figured that whatever they were planning was due to take place any moment. The "main street," Buckle had told me. But just as I slowed to take the turn at the sign into New Haven, a black-shirted motorcycle cop left his motorcycle at the roadside, hailed out to us, and ran towards our car.

"Jesus! They have made a mistake!" Arbie cried. "They're going to arrest us!"

I slowed the car to a crawl, glimpsed a malicious smile on the face of the driver of the Lincoln in the rear-view mirror, and squinted at the policeman hurrying forward in the dusk. Something about the cop's dress or the way he was running looked strange. I instinctively stepped on the accelerator as the cop reached the side of the car.

"He didn't even try to stop them!" Arbie shouted.

"That was the trap," I said between my teeth as we reached the toll booth. I paid the toll, flipped on our headlights, and sped through the slower moving traffic. "If there are any real cops, they'll stop us for speeding."

"They're still behind us," Arbie announced, "but it's getting too dark to see clearly."

A tower of Yale University rose ahead. I heard the siren of a police car and pictured the cops arresting us, the ensuing argument, the confusion.

"At least we'll be out of the clutches of the Cantata family," Arbie said ruefully. "You better slow down and pull over."

In the rear-view mirror, I saw a police car pull alongside the Lincoln, and signal it to go over to the kerb. I dodged behind a slower moving car, the siren stopped, and we moved inconspicuously with the traffic.

"They'll arrest them for speeding," I said with a sigh. "We'll drive till about ten o'clock and look for a place to spend the night."

"Nothing doing," Arbie said. "I can't sleep. I'm too nervous. You sleep in the back seat, I'll drive."

"Are you sure that's wise, honey?" I asked.

"Wiser than risking another meeting with those guys. I want to put a lot of road between them and us."

I nervously gunned the car into the turnoff leading back onto the highway, and wondered who was behind this latest attempt to disrupt our lives.

EIGHTEEN

As we drove through the night, I thought of the larger issues facing us. Three-quarters of the American people were affected by the downturn in the economy of the country. Cities with financial structures smaller than New York's went bankrupt. Municipal bondholders lost their money across the nation. But in New York, the large banking institutions held most of the City's debt certificates. Their control of the economy reached beyond the U.S.A. into Europe and many third world nations. They argued in the economic committees hastily set up to contain the crisis that if they lost money on their investments they would be bankrupt and cease to keep the third world afloat with further loans. Then would Spengler's prophecy of the decline of the West become a reality. Civilization nurtured by thoughts from Aristotle and the Judaeo-Christian ethic down to the present day would be displaced by the anarchy of the modern barbarian hordes. Only by reducing the workers' share of the economic pie would entrepreneurs be able to garner the profits required to fuel the great engine of capitalism, and, by extension, "Freedom."

As we drove into Maine early in the morning, Arbie explained that the neo-colonial American empire had received a severe blow by the loss of Vietnam and by the nationalist movements in Latin America, which had gradually undermined the power of American capital and its alliance with the comprador bourgeoisie of those countries. "When you begin losing your power to exploit other peoples, you have to exploit your own," she said.

I yawned. "There is always a ruling class that exploits the others whether it's American capitalists or Latin American nationalist heroes. I prefer American capitalists."

"You can prefer whomever you want, Rudy. But the facts are that American capital has to consolidate to survive. That's why we've had thousands of bankruptcies, amalgamations, and take-overs every year. There's a diner! Let's get breakfast." She pulled over to a roadside restaurant.

After we ordered breakfast, I suggested that she was tired from a night of driving.

"No," she shook her head with determination, provoking me into remembering how much I loved her. "I needed the solitude and the concentration. It gave me more rest than a deep sleep. Rudy, I think we're getting death squads from the political right in the States just as they've got them in Latin America."

I put my coffee cup down and stared at her. "Do you call that thinking or dreaming?"

"Why did the ruling class torture and murder thousands and thousands in Argentina? Because the fascist rulers fear the people. Besides, right wing death squads are not new to us. The Ku Klux Klan is just one of the many."

I had to concede that it was possible. "But you can't tell me that New York cops are kidnapping and torturing our citizens."

"You don't need cops! Here we've had networks of organized criminals who are connected with every level of government including the White House. Nixon's Watergate, Reagan's Contra Progam, they both had plans for military control of the United States. Hell, Rudy! if the CIA can work with the mob to assassinate leaders of other countries, why do you think it won't work with the mob to silence the Left?"

I shook my head slowly in bafflement as the waitress set our breakfast before us. "So guys like you and Alf Landy are targets."

"Remember what a State governor said in Argentina: 'First we get the activists, then their collaborators, then their sympathizers, then the timid'...."

"Stop it!" I said. "You're up to me already."

"I think they are just starting with the activists, so they're a long way from you," she smiled.

"We're too big a country for that sort of thing to be controlled by the government."

"With electronics and computers we're just as small as Argentina," Arbie said. "I, for one, am not going to let it happen. Look at the misery McCarthy caused because the people were afraid to challenge him. The hundreds who went to jail, the many who lost their livelihood, fled into exile, committed suicide. Why? Because a bloody pervert was allowed to take over the country! through fear! We've got to stop what's going on, now!"

"You can't be sure you're right," I said calmly. "Let's enjoy a few days in the sun and then take another look at it."

Arbie paused, feeling the calming effect of my voice, and reaching to take my hand, she agreed. I turned the subject to baseball, to which Arbie responded with growing enthusiasm.

Her enthusiasm for nature and walks in the woods, for the sea and swimming, for the solitude in an old house whose owner was in Europe, and for the contacts with artists on the Island transformed her from the pale and worried young kidnapped victim to her usual robust and satirical self. I enjoyed the four days of her company, our love-making, our common interests, more than at any time I could remember. Our only contact with the mainland was a ferry which ran once a day. All of our worries about right-wing politicians and murder plots vanished as if they were a part only of the mainland.

It was on the fifth day that we received a visitor who arrived unannounced. I could not believe my eyes. Father Ian was standing on our porch at ten in the morning. We were just finishing a late breakfast.

"Hello, Rudyard," Father Ian cried through the screen door. His eager young face beamed in good will.

I jumped to my feet in surprise. "Father!" A flood of trustees' faces engulfed me. I felt the frustration and worry of searching for Arbie once again.

Arbie looked at him in surprise and puzzlement.

"Come in," I cried and opened the screen door for Ian who entered wearing slacks and a blue sport shirt. "Where did you come from?"

"The ferry boat," Ian smiled. "I'm here just for an hour, just to see you, actually." He stepped up to Arbie who was looking at him curiously from where she sat at the table. "I'm the Cardinal's representative. Congratulations on your escape from the gangsters."

Arbie took his proffered hand and squeezed it. "Thank Rudy," she smiled brightly. "Coffee?"

"Please," said Father Ian sitting down as I fetched him a cup of coffee from the kitchen. "Detective Buckle gave me the details."

"Did he tell you that we were here?" she frowned.

"Yes." Ian lowered his eyes guiltily. "He's been keeping tabs on you. I am sorry to disturb your bliss." He took a cup of coffee from me with a word of thanks.

"What now?" I sighed.

Ian took a drink of coffee.

"It must be urgent for you to come all the way from New York," Arbie said.

Ian laughed. "I have church business in New Brunswick. This is a side issue, though an important one, nevertheless."

"More trouble?"

"Well," Ian frowned. "The police have the men who kidnapped Arbie in custody, and they've been questioning Slidsky about what he knows. Apparently he's far down the ladder."

"He knows about massage parlors and mysterious knifings," Arbie said sarcastically.

"Lanzetta has disappeared. His office says he went on vacation. Nobody knows where."

"I hope it's not here," Arbie said.

"None of that news seems urgent to me," I said sourly. "Did you have to break our peace of mind for that?"

Father Ian blushed. "The urgent thing is that the men who were pursuing you in New Haven were found to be connected with a clandestine paramilitary force based in Arkansas. They are suspects in a number of disappearances."

"Do you mean this has been going on here and the press hasn't said a word about it?" I cried in alarm.

"No one is certain," Ian warned, "but the Cardinal wanted me to inform you, for your own safety."

"I have my bodyguard right here with me," Arbie said, reaching over to pat me on the knee. "And since these guys are operating interstate, I guess the F.B.I. is watching over us."

"That's the trouble, I'm afraid." Father Ian looked at the floor. "We think that someone in the Bureau is giving the orders to help them do the kidnapping. You see, it's hard to tell. There are hundreds of disappearances in our country every month, and no publicity. Many are absconded by the white slave traders whose trade has increased enormously with the rise in Near Eastern oil money and demand for pleasure. We have evidence that certain persons in government are involved." He smiled reassuringly at Arbie. "In your case, people want to stop your re-election as Local President and silence you that way."

"When you say 'people,' you mean the ruling class, don't you, Father?" Arbie said expressionlessly.

"Well," Ian hesitated, "their surrogates."

"Oh, there are plenty of them," Arbie said. "Rudy would be one, if I let him."

I pretended to laugh but I felt uncomfortable.

"That's all right, Rudyard," Father Ian said. "We priests are accused of the same thing. The fact is, some of us are diametrically opposed to our ruler." He stood up. "Thanks for the coffee; I've got to be sure I don't miss the return boat."

"No instructions?" I asked in surprise. "Just a warning?"

"Will you walk with me to the wharf?" Ian asked me. He waved his hand slightly at Arbie and preceded me through the door. "I didn't want to alarm Arbie," he said as we walked along the narrow path snaking among fishermen's cottages with their blue and yellow shutters, "but her speech at the rally has infuriated certain people so much that she may be a target for assassination. One of the socialist papers printed it in full. She's becoming a sort of folk hero on the left."

"Oh no!" I groaned.

"My church is active on the political right these days. I get the news." Father Ian smiled. "Actually, my instruction is for you to return to the Library right away, on Mr. Raikes's orders. Bugofsky, the business manager, is in the hospital with a liver complaint. Mr. Raikes is worried about library security. Sorry." Ian held out his hand as we reached the wharf. The only sound was the ferry boat's motor in the silent scene. "Looks like they're waiting for me."

I shook his hand, watched him board, and waved as the ferry steamed into the ocean. I made up my mind that the Library was secure enough for us to spend one more night on the island. I looked up at the cottages on the hillside and caught sight of Arbie watching from the window of our house at the top of the hill. She looked lovely, I thought, like a beacon of beauty in a sea of treachery. I wondered when I should break the bad news that we had to return. Not till tomorrow morning, I decided, that is, if we were not assassinated in the meantime. I grimaced, and a fisherman passing by, mistook it for a greeting, and nodded politely.

NINETEEN

Two days later, when I walked into my office, my secretary greeted me warmly, and, arching her eyebrows, she pointed out the pile of letters and telephone messages I had received while away.

"But before you do anything," she said with a flirtatious smile, "Mr. Raikes wants to see you. He's waiting in his office."

"But it's just nine o'clock," I gasped.

"He's been here since seven, so his secretary tells me."

I glanced through my mail for the important pieces, which were few, put them aside, and proceeded to Raikes's office on the second floor. The long marble hallways and the great staircases glistened in the morning light falling through the tall Fifth Avenue windows. In the morning, before the doors opened to the public, I enjoyed walking these halls, deserted, except for the occasional guard or maintenance man passing through to some obscure duty. I felt as if the building belonged to me, as if a patrician character reasserted itself after generations of plebeian living and possessed me.

Mr. Raikes's secretary motioned for me to proceed into Raikes's office. The short, balding, intelligent-looking Raikes bounced from behind his desk and seized my hand. "Welcome back, Rudyard. You had us worried, but you worked a miracle. Where's Miss Vine?"

"She's living at my apartment for the time being," I said looking around for a chair. Raikes stuck his arm out at the chairs at his conference table and we sat. "She insists on acting as if there were no danger," I continued. "I wish we could find out who's behind these disappearances."

"We'll find out," Raikes assured me. "Miss Vine's case woke up the whole police establishment to this mysterious alliance between criminal and government agents. I'm alarmed by the political implications. We have to be on guard always against the radical right in this country. We're forming a Task Force to deal with it."

"Looking for volunteers?" I asked.

Raikes laughed. "You're needed at the Library, Rudyard. Bugofsky hit the bottle too hard. I hope some day we can persuade him to retire."

I looked glum. "So I'm just to patrol the halls and keep the guards looking sharp."

"The Trustees think you do a good job. Without you, there was more purse snatching, book thievery, and all-round mischief-making. You're doing an important job, and, incidentally, that's what we're paying you for."

I nodded gratefully. "If I get certain leads as I did with Lanzetta," I ventured, "do I have your permission to take the time to follow them up?"

Raikes made a moue. "Well, if they really look important," he said reluctantly, and, standing up, held out his hand.

I left feeling that I had been dismissed from the case. I was considered just a library detective unworthy of higher assignment. The thought made me angry. But I had no recourse. I walked into the stacks and paced the long walkways between the rows of books as I pondered my disappointment. By the time I climbed from the seventh floor stack to the main reading room, the general public had been let into the building and was scurrying to find books and sit at the long, lamp-lit tables. I stood watching them as the staff took their places behind the light indicators and the book delivery lift. There seemed to be no sign of danger, no pickpockets or shady-looking readers, no revolutionaries planting bombs beside the reading desk. It was, I remarked, like a Joseph Conrad story, when the sea was calm, and peacefulness lay claim to the atmosphere, yet there was a ship sinking and desperate survivors were about to go under. I had no sooner thought of desperate survivors when I realized with a start that I was staring at one. Gabriel, seated at a reading room table, had riveted his eyes on my face, and, now, having caught my attention, he beckoned to me.

I drew up a chair and sat beside him.

"We can talk 'cause there ain't 'nuff people yet," Gabriel said. "Lucky you were here. I was thinkin' I'd have to wait all day, or send a message to your office."

"You could telephone," I said.

"I bin phonin'," Gabriel complained, "but I couldn't leave no message."

"Lanzetta's on the run," I informed him. "You don't need to fear him any longer."

"Yeah, I do," Gabriel smiled, his black face lighting up with humor. "I've got on to something special. That's why I had to see you. Listen." Gabriel looked around and lowered his voice so that I had to strain to hear him. "You know Kroneweiss? He's not just acting for the bankers. There's a national organization, and he's their man in New York. There's a national conspiracy to take away our civil liberties. Least ways, that's what they tell me."

"Why are they doing that?" I asked, surprised that Gabriel would discuss such issues.

"They want the military to take over the country, you know, like they do down in South America and places like that. One reason is they want to control the blacks. Like they think we're gettin' too powerful what with black mayors and black political power on the left."

"It's really the left wing they want to stop, I guess," I said. Someone must have sent Gabriel to me with this message.

"That's for sure," Gabriel whispered. "But what I want to tell ya is they've got their man on the Liberry Board, name of Tally Leyden."

Wincing at his mispronunciation, I replied cautiously. "The Compumax guy? How do you know that?"

"Look, these rich buggers got to have guys workin' for them." Gabriel looked around him. "These guys mean business and they're makin' headway fast because the general population don't know what's goin' on and can't defend itself."

"And probably wouldn't believe it anyway," I said. "Leyden is single-mindedly bent on computerizing the Library system. He just wants to throw out all the books and put everything on microfiche."

"It's not just money he wants," Gabriel smirked. "He wants control of information. That's where the power is, man. When you got computers, you gotta use them to get at the information in the liberries." Gabriel looked suspiciously at a male reader who sat opposite us. "I'll see ya 'round," he said, and, cat-like, left the reading room before I could respond.

Gabriel, or whoever was behind him, had set off alarm bells in my mind. If all these suppositions were true, I was one of the few people who was privy to the subtle take-over from above. I also knew that I could not trust any of the Board members because they might, like Leyden, be working with the organization to which Gabriel referred. Even Raikes might be working for it. Perhaps his Task Force was just a phony exercise like those government commissions set up to find anything but the truth, I thought. I stood up abruptly and walked in a dream back to my office. A military take-over! Under tight control from the right wing! Then they could save capitalism! and turn the United States into a large Guatemala! I shook my head with the starkness of this frightening scenario which had begun to seem plausible. I leafed through my mail as if half-hoping for an answer there. One letter had a return address with the name Barb Janes. This was significant! Her address was not in the Bronx, but downtown Manhattan near the World Trade Center. I opened the envelope and read: "Dear Rudy: Long time no see, lover-boy. I got a fancy place now. Want to see it? Also, gotta see you like a friend. Call me soon, Rudy baby. I'm serious. Love, Barbie."

She printed her telephone number after her signature. I hesitated to call, wondering if she'd be working at her hospital. The fine look of the note paper and her new address implied she might no longer be nursing. It was lunch time; she might be home. I dialed the number and listened to the phone ring. After the eighth ring, I was about to hang up when Barb breathlessly shouted into the line. "Who is it?"

I identified myself.

"Just came in the door, sweetheart," Barb sang, suddenly cheerful. "No time to talk now. Meet me top of the Twin Towers for drinks about seven, okay?"

"Okay," I said. "Nice to hear your voice."

"It's nice to hear your voice," Barb said seductively. "Bye-bye."

I hung up and my telephone rang immediately. It was Arbie.

"I'm getting the cold shoulder treatment down at the Council," she complained. "Poppin hardly speaks to me as if it's my fault he's suspected by the police."

"Don't worry about him. He just resents having to report on Bratwurst's activities." I tried to think of an excuse for getting home late that evening. "Arbie, sweetheart, I saw Gabriel, the guy I told you about, and I'm following up a lead tonight; don't keep dinner for me."

"What sort of lead?" Arbie asked.

"Can't talk over the phone. Our ruling group is mixed up in it."

"Rudy, why can't you say ruling class? You're so conservative, you're funny. Say, fucking ruling class."

"Some of the library trustees are in on it," I said.

"Who?"

"Tally Leyden for one."

"That asshole! He'd like to see every librarian replaced by a computer. He's got his fingers in the State pie as well. Our union is watching that character. Any others?"

"I don't know yet," I said, "but I think someone wants to get you out as Local president which means he has the sanction of the Board to do it."

"They want me out all right. Bratwurst wants me out. The Democratic Party wants me out. There's an ugly mood of reconciliation in the air. Union and management and their sidekick politicians want a coy relationship so they can screw the worker altogether. Trouble is, I think the worker is laying down to take the screw. And some of the idiots in my Local are too dumb to know what they're doing. Petula Clarkson has announced she's running for President. A children's librarian, some bourgeois feminist, is running with none too subtle assistance from Bratwurst and the Library management, and then there's that little crapper, Bradley Tone, and his thirty-hour work week."

I laughed. "They're really hitting at your base of support. Petula will take away the black vote, the feminist siphons off a lot of the female votes, Tone gets the more radical vote."

"All under false pretenses," Arbie expostulated. "And I'm too worried about the fascist take-over to care about my stupid little election. Oh, Rudy! I'm tired of the whole damn business."

"Never mind. The worker will see through them and re-elect you," I comforted her. "Keep your faith in the worker."

"You're being facetious, Rudy, but you've made me realize I've got to go around to the branches this afternoon to offset some of the rumors spread about me--you know, like I want to bring the Local into the Communist Party."

I laughed. "Stay in there, sweetheart. If I'm not back by midnight, call Buckle."

"You call Buckle," she said. "Take care, Rudy."

"You take care," I warned her. "Remember, you're still a target."

I left my office to check the guard posts on the first floor. It was cooler. The heat wave had been broken. There was the slightest hint of Fall weather waiting to break in upon the city. I saw Ajax watching the computer monitors in the security office. Ajax turned his head and raised his arm in greeting. The big man seemed to care for the Library, seemed to have its safety in his gentle and artistic hands.

"Any action?" I asked.

"No bad action," Ajax said with a smile and returned to his watch.

I stood by the window-door on the left side of the revolving door at the Fifth Avenue entrance and gazed over the steps and parapet at the human traffic. All of us, I thought, are ignorant of the force guiding our lives. We barely have time to read a newspaper, which often is just as ignorant as us. The kidnapping, the disappearances were not just random events but part of a great plan known only to the very few who directed it. I understood the human desire for power. I had encountered it in library management, in supervisors of departments, and watched it in city officials and corporate executives as reported in the newspapers. Why was I not even tempted by it? Was it because I was not in a position to exercise it? Or because I saw it as degrading to the human personality?--an exhibition of the human ego in its ugliest form? When I thought of Arbie I was reminded of the individual's defenselessness. Alone, one was an easy victim. With others, one could begin to fight back. I gritted my teeth with determination. The opposition now seemed immense, amorphous, and enigmatic. It was like a giant squid whose black arms were gradually enveloping the nation. If it were not stopped soon, it would strangle all dissent and hold the citizenry in a paralyzing subjection to its evil designs. I had to stop thinking of Kroneweiss and his bosses, the bankers and billionaires who owned the country. I had to begin at my level, the bottom. For that reason I walked out of the Library and west on Fortieth Street to Seventh Avenue to the office of Benbow and Slidsky. Tom Benbow was at his desk.

"Hello there, Rudyard!" Benbow said and took a large bite of a tuna fish sandwich. "Sit down."

"Sorry to interrupt your lunch," I said, choosing a chair to the side in order to avoid the direct rays of daylight coming from the window behind Benbow's head.

"We're both busy men," Benbow said with his mouth full. "We can't choose our own time. I'm busy making big money. You're busy chasing down kidnapped women. Congratulations! You found our union president."

"Thanks to your partner," I said laconically.

Benbow shook his head with exasperation. "That guy gets in more trouble!"

"Where's Lanzetta?" I asked.

Benbow looked startled, then he smiled cheerfully. "You don't beat around the bush, do you, Rudyard? I don't know where he is."

"But you're carrying on his business."

"Yeah, part of it. But I don't hear from him. Even if I did, I wouldn't tell you, Rudyard. Look, Mr. Lanzetta may be mixed up with criminals, but he brings in an awful lot of money to this office. Without his patronage I'd have to really compete with other realtors. I'm too soft to start doin' that."

"You yourself are mixed up with criminals," I said.

"Hell! We've gotta live. Who in this City doesn't have criminal connections? The City cannot run without lubrication from criminal elements. The Borough Presidents, the Mayor, the Union leaders, everyone's on the take--except for your Arbie Vine. And she's the one in trouble."

"You're in trouble," I said.

Benbow laughed. "Slidsky's out on bail. You're in trouble."

I had not thought of retribution. I had been concerned only with Arbie's safety. "Do you think that he is stupid enough to risk deeper involvement with the law by taking his petty anger out on me?"

Benbow smirked. "Not at all; there's no risk. This City is too enmeshed with organized crime to worry about risks. The courts are well taken care of, Rudyard."

"The City is not as corrupt as you'd like to think," I said. "But I'm not here to argue about the merits of the City." I watched Benbow swig his coffee. "I'm here to talk to you about something more important. I've been warned that some big corporations are using the political right wing to grab control of our country. Now, I know this sounds far-fetched, but I also know that, if it were true, you would not be in favor of it any more than I am. I haven't any details, but, I think you're being used. You're deliberately closing your eyes to what Lanzetta and his bosses are really after because you're getting rich through them. But I warn you that when they get what they want from you, they won't need you. And they'll put Slidsky and you, for that matter, away for life."

"What are you talking about?" Benbow frowned.

"Look, let me explain as it was told to me. A lot of citizens have been disappearing without any reporting of it in the media. A few private groups have been alerted and are trying to monitor what's going on. It seems that a segment of our military establishment with the help of some of our politicians is gradually asserting control over all aspects of our lives. Look, for example, at the gradual militarization of our space program. Star wars would not only control other countries from outer space, it would exert absolute control over us. There isn't a square inch on earth that could not be scrutinized." I leaned forward in my chair and spoke with a passion unusual for me. "What good will your riches be then?"

"Wow!" Benbow looked round-eyed. "You've got it bad! That crazy Leftie has made you as nutty as she is. You don't expect me to take you seriously, do you? Now, beat it, Rudyard. You've wasted enough of my time with all that crazy crap."

I shrugged. "Think about it, Benbow." I stood up, miffed by his refusal to understand but aware that he was no different from the average citizen. "Don't say you weren't warned. There is a far broader and sinister picture than corrupt City politicians in the real estate business. You know I'm right. The pity of it is, I can use your help."

Benbow laughed. "I'm not as brave as you are."

Benbow's intercom buzzed. His secretary told him he had a call from Mr. Leyden. I was alert to the name, and I noticed that Benbow was anxious for me to leave.

"You know where you can reach me," I smiled, and as I went out the door, I stopped it with my fingers from closing completely. I stood listening to Benbow's telephone conversation which sounded subdued, very unlike the ebullient Benbow of a few minutes ago. I overheard the occasional phrase, however, such as, "Slidsky doesn't want any more jobs at the moment.... He's laying low.... At the River Cafe--on the Brooklyn side of the Brooklyn Bridge...." I let the door close noiselessly, and, as I walked past Benbow's secretary with a broad smile, I whispered, "I'll call you for lunch. I haven't forgotten us. Any news?"

The secretary looked alarmed. "Mr. Mack, please be careful. I'm not supposed to talk to our clients outside the office."

"But you were so helpful advising me about Wallenberg and Lanzetta. I need to talk to you again."

"Well, I have no time now," she said, looking away from me.

"I'll call," I said and left as Benbow buzzed her.

I guessed that Tally Leyden was taking over Lanzetta's role as intermediary between the powers-that-be and Slidsky, who did the dirty work--Slidsky and doubtless many other hoodlums who were even now engaged in what I began to think of as the grand conspiracy. I had gathered from Benbow's remarks to Leyden that Slidsky could be reached through the River Cafe. I decided to have a late lunch there and drink a beer while I watched the water of the East River course by under the Brooklyn Bridge. I caught the IRT express subway line and was in the cafe in under half an hour.

I finished my lunch and listened to the pianist playing mood music. A small party was chattering and laughing at the far end of the room. I watched the staff and wondered which of the waiters could lead me to Slidsky. Then, through the glass of the doorway, I saw Tally Leyden, very much the nattily-dressed, young businessman, talking to one of the girls who waited on table on the patio. I shrank down in my chair, fearing that Leyden would enter and see me. But the computer entrepreneur did not look in the restaurant. I signaled the waiter, paid my bill, and left the cafe. I was careful to take advantage of customers who were entering to shield my departure from Leyden on the patio. I walked across a parking space to the music barge--a long building where concerts were held on Sunday afternoons, and, standing by one corner, I could see the patio. Leyden had bared his head to the sun and was sipping a tall drink. The afternoon seemed idyllic. Sailboats and launches passed by. The Circle Line passenger boat moved upriver. I waited a quarter hour. Then I noticed the waitress say something to Leyden, who stood up and looked in the direction she pointed--at the houses in the street behind the cafe. Leyden strode quickly out of the cafe toward the bar-restaurant on the corner. I, following discreetly, began to realize with mounting excitement that Leyden could not only lead me to Slidsky but to the center of the mystery. I had to be careful. Slidsky would take precautions. I stopped by a tree and looked up at the building Leyden was approaching. A curtain moved at a window on the third floor. Someone was watching but could not have seen me as I was still concealed from view by the foliage. I watched Leyden enter the bar and waited. The presence I had sensed behind the curtain was no longer there. I crossed the road, entered the bar, walked through a throng of people, and sauntered through a door at the back onto a stairway, which I ascended, as if I were familiar with the place. Grateful that no one called after me, I climbed to the third floor and walked along to the door of the room which, I assumed, had the window I had observed. I listened and picked up the tones of two men in animated conversation. As I could not hear what they were saying, I moved down the hall to a turning and stood at the corner watching. It was well I did, because a moment later the door was thrown open. An angry Tally Leyden stepped into the hallway and cried back into the room. "Let's get a move on."

Slidsky ambled into the hallway. He was wearing jeans and a sweatshirt. He closed the door and locked it as Leyden walked impatiently ahead. I stayed out of sight until I heard them descending the stairs. Should I follow them or search the room?

Leyden probably had a car, so a room search was in order. I took out my master key, a metal blade that Detective Buckle had given me, and fitted it into the lock of the door. The lock was of the simple kind that turned easily.

Slidsky had left the bed unmade. His socks were strewn on the floor. A shirt lay over the back of a chair. I went to the window and watched Leyden and Slidsky get into a blue Buick. I remembered from my search of Slidsky's apartment that Slidsky kept diary notes. I went directly to the writing desk, and took out a small, leather-bound notebook. For all Slidsky's tough, rough behavior, I thought, there was an inner orderliness that showed itself in the neatly written pages of his diary. I sat in a chair by the window and began to read.

Slidsky wrote with words and dashes, but I was able to interpret his thought. After fifteen minutes I had read all that I needed. Slidsky was involved in several kidnappings and killings. He revered Lanzetta and felt fortunate to be working for the Group to which Lanzetta belonged. Slidsky used letters for names, for instance his "P" might stand for Poppin, I thought. I pocketed the diary and left the room. I had a presentiment that Slidsky was not going to return. I caught the subway back to Manhattan.

TWENTY

When I stepped into the cocktail lounge at the top of the World Trade Center, I found Barb Janes waiting for me. Her hair had been coiffured. She wore a red dress that accentuated her full figure and brown skin. She stood up and held out her arms to me.

"Rudy, come back to me!"

I embraced her and glanced with embarrassed eyes at the other couples in the lounge.

"I been missing you, Rudy," Barb said as we sat at a window table which overlooked the harbor and the Statue of Liberty. "You miss me, huh?"

"I thought of you," I said. "I wondered where you'd got to."

Barb rounded her eyes. "I got to the Land of Oz. Let me tell ya," she grinned. "This sort of good lookin' white guy I met, he goes crazy over me, asks me to live with him. So I find he's got this big apartment overlookin' the river right near here and I sublet my place. The sex is good, the livin' is easy. I got an unlimited expense account. This guy is loaded. He trades on the Stock Exchanges. That's all I know. Oh, and he's in real estate in a big, big way."

We ordered drinks. I looked down at the sun's rays burnish the sea far below. "What's his name?"

"Max Leyden. Ever heard of him?"

"Is his brother Tally Leyden?" I asked in surprise.

"Yeah, a trustee of the Library," she smiled. "He told me. I haven't met his family. I saw snaps of them." She sighed. "But there's a fly in the ointment, Rudy. He's gone somewhere, and I been on my own for a whole week."

"Think it's foul play?"

"Maybe. He sounded like he was goin' to be gone only a night, or mostly two."

"He could have found someone else," I suggested.

"Not him," Barb laughed. "I never saw a guy who was more eager to go to bed. I had him at my beck and call. Oh Rudy, and all that money too."

"Did you report him missing to the police?"

"How could I do that? Suppose he's not really missin'. I might get him into a jam. No, Rudy, only you can help me."

I smiled. "Have you been reading the newspapers? Do you know how busy I've been?"

"I heard about it," she said indifferently. "And Lanzetta's on the run. Max told me."

"There could be a connection," I said. "Our mutual friend, Slidsky, was just taken away by Tally Leyden. There's supposed to be a neo-fascist organization with government connections that's been causing people on the left to disappear."

Barb Janes gave me a quizzical look. "You sure you're all right? You look like you think I can help *you* more than you can help *me*. You think Max is involved?"

I shrugged. "Let's find out where he is first. That ought to tell us something. Let's go to your place."

"Now that's a real nice suggestion," Barb said, swallowing her drink. "It's not far." She led the way to the elevators.

I sensed the sensuality in her movements. She had probably not made love for a week, I thought, which concerned her more than did Max Leyden.

We were alone on the great elevator as it hurtled down one hundred floors. Barb threw an arm about my waist, and we kissed long and hungrily. I could not account for my desire which seemed to flare up from nowhere whenever I was close to Barb Janes. It seemed as if it had been stalking me, and, now, suddenly, it leaped up, making me its victim. At such times Arbie drifted out of my consciousness.

We separated, unlocking our arms from our hold on one another's anatomy, as the elevator coasted to a stop. I wiped the lipstick off my lips with a kleenex as the door opened and a group of tourists stood waiting to board.

"Let's take it easy," I said, "at least until we dig up some clues."

Barb smiled and preceded me through the crowd. She led me out the front door and along the sidewalk southward. A balmy breeze came off the Hudson River.

"What's Max's politics?" I asked.

Barb giggled. "Federally, he's Republican, but in city politics, he's Democrat."

"He's a pragmatist," I smiled.

"Politically," Barb said, "he's a bum. But I can live with that. If he's a neo-fascist, though, that's another question."

She took me across the street into a new apartment complex which appeared to be only for the very, very rich. I found the ostentatiousness of the thick carpets, gold-rimmed wall mirrors, expensive furniture, and large abstract paintings, rather vulgar. There was something false about those who had an excess of money, I thought. Their tastes became grotesque.

Max Leyden's apartment, when we entered it on the fifth floor, was less vulgar than the hallway. The furnishings were modern, but modest, not clamoring for attention. Barb took me to the sitting room whose long window overlooked the Hudson River and the New Jersey shoreline in the distance. The window was tinted to take the strength out of the rays of the sun.

"I've been through every desk in the apartment," Barb said. "I can't find nothing."

"I have a hunch his brother knows where he is," I said. "Trouble is, we can't ask him." I took out Slidsky's diary and began leafing through it. "Where'd you meet Max, anyway?"

"I was havin' lunch with a girlfriend in a little sandwich place off Wall St. She works on the Exchange and knew him sort of, so he started talkin' to us. He was cute, so I took his card. He told me he was in arbitrage."

"He gambles on buying the stock of a Company in the expectation that it will be taken over by a bigger Company which makes its stock more valuable," I said.

"Is that what it means?" Barb said. "He could never explain it to me." Barb sank into an easy chair, opposite me. "What you readin', Rudy baby?"

"I think I know where your Max is," I said calmly. "This entry was written a week ago. 'ML to London (w) La.' He's probably still in England with Lanzetta."

"Doesn't sound right," Barb said. "He was too close to business to take off for England."

"Slidsky is the key to what's going on," I said, continuing to look through the diary.

"Martin Slidsky!" Barb cried. "That's it! Max left a note on his phone pad: 'Slid & Ro at 5.' He must have meant Slidsky."

"Maybe," I said. "And 'Ro' could mean Rockefeller. But I doubt it. Slidsky has the letter 'R' down here a couple of times. And he's got 'contact P' who I think is Harold Poppin."

"That creep!" Barb said. "He thinks he's a Romeo, the slob!"

"How about Hector Bratwurst?"

"He has more success than Poppin. Women think he's powerful so he gets all he wants," Barb said. "But he's another slob. I know what I' m sayin'. I tried him out."

"You know him that well!" I gasped. "Where does he live?"

"In Scarsdale," Barb laughed, pleased at shocking me. "But he's got a pad right in this building."

"Will he be there now?"

"Oh no, Rudy, it's only 8.30, he's out winin' and dinin' with somebody or other. And he only uses it for his women."

"That's it!" I cried, jumping to my feet. "This is the break I've been waiting for. He's got to have information on the great conspiracy."

Barb took me down by elevator to the second floor and along the hallway to a door at the end. I fitted my pass key into the lock, and, after a couple of attempts, I turned it. We entered a small room with a large window looking out on the street. A king-size bed took up half the room. A bathroom was on one side, a kitchenette on the other. I went to vertical files standing along one wall of the room, and, fitting a smaller blade into their locks, opened them.

"Pull the curtains and turn on the light," I said to Barb. "We've got to work fast."

I leafed through the folders of one file while Barb leafed through the folders in another.

"What am I looking for?" Barb asked.

"References to disappearances, correspondence with Kroneweiss or Lanzetta, stuff like that." I paused, pulled out a folder, and said softly, "Actually, stuff like this. It's marked Kroneweiss." I put it on top of the file. "But keep looking."

We had almost finished when Barb held up a thin folder. "This one's called the Z-file. It has lists of names with the words "missing" or "disappeared" or "believed lost," beside each name. And there's letters from Missing Persons Bureaus of various States."

"We'll take it with us," I said, turning to the folder on Kroneweiss and looking through it. "This seems to be on union matters like agency shop for all city unions, Democratic politicians, even family matters. Wait! Here's a letter mentioning Tally Leyden." I handed it to Barb who put it in the Z-file. "I hope we haven't missed anything." I returned the Kroneweiss folder, locked the file, turned off the light, and opened the curtains. "Does Bratwurst know you moved to this building?"

"Nope," Barb shook her head. "Fact is, I haven't been in this room for over a year."

We took the elevator back to the fifth floor and entered Barb's apartment. The sun had set. I turned on the lamp lights in the sitting room, and Barb prepared a snack as I read through the Z-folder. I recognized none of the names on the lists, and there were scores of them. The letters from the State Missing Persons Bureaus merely confirmed that all their efforts to unearth information about the men and women had proved to no avail. There were three pages of a hand-written memorandum, apparently by Bratwurst, conjecturing on the disappearances of Trade Unionists from all over the States and Puerto Rico. I focused on one sentence: "Kroney thinks the Group is using NAM to get information on its targets."

I was startled because I knew the National Association of Manufacturers and the trade associations consolidated with it had had a phenomenal control over American society since World War One. They ran hundreds of organizations compiling information about the workers and the economy. As far as I was concerned, I was prepared to let the big corporations or NAM run the show, co-opt the labor unions, brain-wash the American people, and run the government from the federal to the local level, as long as it was done reasonably. But I was also aware that organized crime had infiltrated legitimate business and had become a powerful influence; moreover, some business leaders, because of the rapid decrease in their profit margin and owing to the nation's extreme economic decline, had reacted sometimes irrationally. I saw from Bratwurst's line of thought that Bratwurst was only concerned with adjusting his position politically to the new threat and to limit any damage to his union. Bratwurst seemed to think that he could "ride out the storm" by agreeing to the demands of the various groups, and merely take note of the disappearances among the opposition left (with which he did not want to be associated). The memorandum left me with a strong distaste for the man. I began reading Kroneweiss's letter to Bratwurst.

"The international banking situation is perilous," Kroneweiss wrote. "There's bound to be a revolt in a big way, so that, if we do not go along with the New Right, the nation will collapse into economic chaos and many of our allies will follow suit. The result will be total revolution. The wolf is at the door!"

Barb entered with scrambled eggs on toast and put the plate on a table beside me. "Found anything?"

"The co-optation of Bratwurst."

"I mean, anything new," Barb said scornfully.

I suddenly whistled. "Listen to this." I began to read. "'Tally Leyden is now the Group's contact in this area and will be in touch with you sometimes. He has a brother on the Exchange who is friendly with us. We're all in this together. Whatever is done is being done for the best.' 'Us' is the bankers supposedly," I said. "By God! I'm overwhelmed by what we're up against. What can we do? Where do we begin?"

"Begin with Bratwurst," Barb said. "We can find Tally Leyden through him and make contact with the group. Alex will get us to Bratwurst. I'll phone him." She went to the phone and dialed. "Hi, honey! Busy? Good. We need you, honey bun. Rudyard and me. We're starting somethin', a counterdrive and you're drivin' the first ways." She smiled and nodded at me. "We'll tell you everything. Come right away. I'm at my Sugar Daddy's." She frowned. "Okay, then, in five." She hung up. "He's meetin' us in the lobby. He's across at the Union. He thinks Bratwurst is getting ready to leave his office. Hector's looking worried, as somethin' might be up."

I swallowed my food and reached the lobby with Barb just as Mackart appeared at the door.

"Come on!" Alex gestured with his long thin arm and rushed ahead of us to his car where Joseph waited at the wheel. "Get in the back." Alex sat in front with Joseph. "Hector will be comin' out of that street," Alex said, looking behind us. "In fact, this is him."

A long black limousine moved onto the avenue and drove by us downtown. Joseph gunned the motor and followed it.

"Any idea where he's going?" I asked.

"He told me the Mayor is havin' a small party," Alex said. "But I happen to know the Mayor's in Washington."

I followed Bratwurst's limousine in silence round by the Battery, the Staten Island ferry station, and up the east side of Manhattan. Then, a block before the Fulton Fish market, the limo turned up a side street. Joseph slowed and made the same turn, but pulled to the side of the street. We watched the limo pass under the glares of street lamps and stop two blocks up. There was no other traffic. We saw the burly form of Bratwurst leave the limousine and go into a small restaurant. The limousine drove off.

"Let's leave the car here," Alex suggested, "and stroll up there for a meal."

"We just ate," Barb said, "but we can pretend."

Joseph stayed in the car while the three of us walked to the restaurant. The modest entrance opened into a large room of small dining tables covered with red cloths and lit by table lamps. The lighting was subdued. The decor and the ambiance of the place strove to give the impression of intimate dining, but there were only three couples in the room. Bratwurst was nowhere to be seen.

"He could have walked through right out the back door," I suggested.

"Let's sit and order," Alex said and led the way to a table. "My union will get the tab."

"You think he's here?" I asked.

"Downstairs. There's a private meeting room," Alex said as we followed the waiter to a table.

"Men's room down there?" I asked.

When Alex nodded, I excused myself, walked into the hall at the back and down the stairs. Two heavies, with bulging stomachs and bulging biceps, stood outside closed doors to a meeting room. Their eyes challenged me.

"Men's room?" I asked timidly.

One of them pointed to a door down the hallway with a sour expression.

A meeting hall to meet fire regulations, I reasoned, must have more than one exit. I waited a few minutes in the men's room, walked out past the heavies, to whom I gave a friendly nod, and returned to Barb and Alex.

"I'm going to find a back way in," I told them.

"Don't bother," Alex said. "You'll only find a big metal door locked from the inside. Wait!" He pulled my sleeve. "Sit down and look up front."

I turned to see Kroneweiss enter with two other middle-aged men. I recognized Kroneweiss from having seen him on television and from photographs in magazines and newspapers. His buck teeth and round marble eyes, exaggerated by cartoonists, gave him instant recognition.

"The other two are bank presidents," Alex whispered. "It must be a meeting of the Muffle men."

The bankers chuckled over a Kroneweiss witticism as they passed through the restaurant to the meeting room below.

"Muffle men?" Barb snorted.

"Municipal Union Financial Leaders Group," Alex smiled.

"I thought they ceased when the fiscal crisis was resolved," I said.

"These things never cease once they all get started," Alex said. "They just get more clandestine."

"All the more reason to try the back entrance," I said with determination.

"Forget it." Alex Mackart waved his hand in tired resignation. "You'll only hear what the unions are going to give back to management and how they're going to fool the workers into doing it. What we want is the group who is doing the dirty work. These phony committees set up allegedly to save the City, but which really dun the citizens--they're being directed from one central authority. It's that authority which is directing the kidnappings and the killings. Believe me, friends, I've heard enough to know that Hector Bratwurst and the bankers are being used to weaken any potential opposition, but they are not the ones responsible for gradually taking away our civil rights. That's being done elsewhere."

"I never thought I'd ever believe in a conspiracy theory," I said.

Alex Mackart's eyes blazed angrily. "Blacks are being pushed into poverty which we thought we were leaving behind. The streets of this nation's cities are home to thousands of people. They defecate in the streets, make love in them, dress and undress in them, sleep in them. You don't think this is a policy?"

"I agree," I said.

"The workers' real wages are half what they were ten years ago." Alex gritted his teeth. "And these stock exchange shits pull in hundreds of millions."

"Careful," Barb warned. "You're speaking of the man I love."

Alex paused and burst into laughter. "I forgot, sweetie, we want to find that cat. Maybe he's got the answer."

At that moment a young businessman entered the restaurant and asked the waiter a question. I recognized him as Tally Leyden and, whispering the name to my companions, I held my napkin to conceal my face should Leyden happen to look at me. But Tally

Leyden, in a hurry, followed the waiter's instructions and went to the meeting room below.

"Obviously, he's never been here," Alex said. "I wonder what instructions he's got."

"He's our man," I said. "He's the messenger. We've got to follow him." I stood up. "Finish up and pay the bill while I get Joseph and the car."

"He might stay for their meeting," Barb suggested, unwilling to leave the veal and pasta she was eating.

"Naw!" Alex said. "Rudy's right. He's got more important interests."

As I left the restaurant, I noted Leyden's limousine at the kerb. The chauffeur was munching a sandwich. I thought that Leyden must be on the move non-stop. I walked a block, stood under a street lamp, and motioned to Joseph to drive up. As Mackart's car pulled away from the kerb, Tally Leyden and Kroneweiss, looking worried, came from the restaurant and got into Leyden's limousine.

Alarmed, I motioned at Joseph to hurry. When the car stopped beside me, I jumped in and shouted for Joseph to follow the limousine just pulling away. Barb and Alex appeared on the sidewalk then. Joseph stopped for them, but Leyden's limo disappeared round a corner.

"I couldn't pay fast enough," Alex explained.

Joseph gunned the motor and sped away in pursuit.

TWENTY-ONE

We spotted Leyden's limousine turning onto the FDR Drive. Joseph stayed close behind it, followed it out the 42nd Street exit through to Broadway and back east along 40th Street.

"They're going into the Library!" I gasped.

"What's new about that?" Barb joked. "Ain't the Library always havin' parties."

"Yeah, but these people are not going to a fund-raiser," I said grimly as we watched the limousine turn into the 40th Street entrance. "Pull to the side and give them time to go under the doors and into the courtyard." I glanced at my watch. "It's after ten. There aren't any events scheduled for tonight."

"Maybe your library president is knocking up some bank presidents for big donations," Alex suggested.

"I don't like it," I said. "Okay, Joseph, they must be in now and the door must be back down. Just drive into the outer yard and wait in the car."

"We're comin' with you, Rudy, aren't we?" Barb cried as Joseph drove the car into an area of pavement inside the stone wall.

"We don't want to miss the fun," Alex smiled.

"Since I think we're going to get closer to the truth, maybe you should come," I admitted. "But, for Heaven's sake, follow me closely."

I led them through the doorway within the great door covering the entrance. Ajax was on duty. I was surprised to see him.

"Why are you working this late?" I asked. "You haven't worked nights in years."

"Special request," Ajax said confidentially as he maneuvered his big frame out of the watchman's booth. "They wanted someone authorized to carry a gun for tonight. Some important folks are upstairs."

"At a public meeting?"

"No," Ajax reared his big head back in feigned surprise. "Very select."

"These two people are friends," I explained. "I'm taking them to my office."

Ajax frowned but replied mildly, "Ain't it a bit late?"

"We're not staying long," I said, leading the way into the building. "We'll climb the stairs to the second floor," I advised Barb and Alex. "I have a hunch they'll be meeting in one of the Executives' offices."

On the second floor we walked quietly down the marble hallway, which was partially lit, to the trustees room. I tried the door but it was locked. I went through the door near it into an anteroom and listened at the door beyond.

"They're in here," I whispered. "This is the President's office."

"How can we hear what they're sayin'?" Barb wondered.

I led them into the office of the President's secretary. The light from the street reflected into the dark room as we huddled by the swing door to Stavoris's office. I very carefully pushed the door open a crack, and we heard men's voices raised in anger.

"I don't care what he's done, he's my brother," Tally Leyden was shouting.

"You had better leave us," warned a voice I had not heard before. It was deep, cutting, and dismissive. "We don't have the time for quarrels. Be gone!"

There was an abrupt silence, followed by the noise of the shutting of the other office door. I let the swing door close.

"Alex, stay and listen. Come on, Barb, we've got to talk to Leyden," I whispered, and, pulling her hand, dashed back through the offices to the hall.

Tally Leyden was standing head down, hands in pockets, in the dim light of the hallway. He did not notice our approach until we were in front of him, when he stepped back in startled amazement.

"Mr. Leyden," I said. "I'm Rudyard Mack, the library detective."

"Oh!" Leyden said, swallowing hard. "I remember you."

"And this is Barb Janes who is living with Max Leyden." Barb stuck out her hand, and Leyden, surprised, shook it. "We've been looking for him. Do you know where he is?" I asked.

Leyden looked at both of us as if stunned by the question.

"Please," Barb said. "I'm so worried about him."

"Well, he's not here!" Leyden said. "I don't see that I can help."

"The men at your meeting know where he is," I said. "They're not as concerned about him as Barb here is."

Leyden paled. "What do you know about the meeting? What did you hear?"

"Never mind about that. Suffice it to know that we overheard your disagreeing with them about what is to be done with Max."

"Then you know he's being held captive," Leyden acknowledged sadly. "Those bastards," he looked back at the president's office, "don't trust him. I think they'll have him killed."

"Oh no!" Barb said in horror. "We've got to save him."

"It's not that easy," Leyden sighed, looking at us as if he were still sizing us up. "If I try, I'm as good as dead," he finally volunteered.

"You're marked for dead already," I said, "from what we gather from that big man's voice."

Leyden looked at me closely. "You are probably very right. Well, I wanted out of the whole business, but...." his voice trailed off as if he were talking to himself.

"Tell us what it's all about. We can help, I'm sure," I said. "Are there library people in there?"

"Oh no! The President, you mean? No, he's ignorant of the whole affair. We're just using his office." Leyden began walking toward the stairs.

"Wait!" Barb cried, "We've got to tell Alex." She dashed into the offices.

"A friend whom we left listening to your meeting," I explained.

Leyden laughed shortly. "And I thought this was the one place that was secure. No bugs. Neutral ground. Difficulty of access."

"Who is inside?" I asked casually.

"Some prominent bankers, industrialists, and the fellow whom you called the big man. Actually, he's from Washington, and he's connected with the National Security Committee. He goes by the name of Colonel Ollie, though I don't know if that's his real name."

"But what's his game?" I asked, fascinated.

"Anti-terrorists, anti-subversives, anti-communists. He thinks we're infested with Socialists, Communists, terrorists and left-wingers, and he wants them all silenced, exterminated if necessary. I must say he puts forward a convincing picture that he knows what he's talking about, and I agree with him, even though I think that sometimes he's going too far."

"Do you mean to tell me that those men in there," I pointed at the offices, "those men on whom our country depends for leadership are plotting the extermination of some of our citizens? Don't they realize that those citizens are patriotic Americans too?"

"I suppose you could say that, but Colonel Ollie and his obsessions are beside the point for most of those men in there.

They're onto bigger things. Big money, power over the universe. They're only humoring Ollie. Through him, they can get the support of the mighty government for their schemes. Max's attitude was the same as theirs. Max even ran the banking operations for the team-- that's what they call it--in Switzerland and Panama, and he ran their offshore operations in the Caribbean by setting up shell companies. I'm sure you know the story."

Barb reappeared and ran excitedly up to us. "Alex wants to stay at his post. He's onto something and he's too involved to leave."

"Okay," I said to Leyden. "Let's act. The first thing is, can you take us to your brother?"

Leyden nodded. "I must warn you, though, that what we're doing is very risky for us all."

"I wonder if Slidsky is being held in the same place?" I said.

Leyden almost jumped as if hit. "You know about Slidsky?"

I nodded.

"Hell. You know more than I give you credit for. Maybe I should quiz you instead, and find out how much you do know."

"Never mind," I said. "Where is Slidsky?

Leyden shook his head. "I'm afraid he's no longer with us."

"Dead?" I asked rhetorically. Silence fell among us.

We continued in silence to the 40th Street entrance where I led them to Alex Mackart's car. Leyden gave an address on East 57th St. near Park. Joseph hesitated to drive off without Alex, but I persuaded him that Alex was perfectly safe.

"Shouldn't we just tell the police?" Barb suggested.

"At the first hint that a rescue was being attempted, Max would be killed," Leyden said. "He's only alive because he's my brother."

"What did he do?"

"He found out too much about the activities of the secret team. He was useful for his talents at laundering money and for raising large sums at a moment's notice. But," Leyden winced, "when he found out about the killings, the disappearances, and their fascist intentions, that was the end of his usefulness. I must say, they made me uneasy too."

We turned off 40th Street onto Madison.

"We thought you was just squeezin' the working man," Joseph said, fascinated by our conversation. "We didn't know you was killing him too."

"Not just the working man," Leyden smiled "Most of the victims have been left-wing and liberal professionals. You'd be surprised at the cooperation we've gotten from politicians and the so-called watchdogs of society. Most of them don't want to know. They close their eyes, turn their heads away, pretend everything's normal. We don't get trouble from them. It's only those who actively object that are eliminated."

We, who couldn't believe our ears at Leyden's confession, goaded him on. "There couldn't have been many," I suggested, "because your secret organization is still practically unknown."

"No longer. There are increasingly more elements in the FBI who are becoming aware, and, I think, even our local police force has been tipped off." Leyden took out a cigarette and lit it. "The fact is, the members of the secret team are in positions of power and authority in the country and can successfully stop any enquiries by the curious."

"Is the White House behind the team?' I asked innocently.

Leyden shook his head. "The White House merely tacitly provides the proper philosophical climate in which whatever the team does is okay. It's not interested in the details of the operations."

"So, what's the game? What is the team aiming for?" Barb asked, her eyes widening in alarm and incredulity.

"The business of power is to stay in power, and the business of the rich is to get very, very rich and stay that way," Leyden laughed. "Now, there's nothing wrong with power or money. What is new in our country now is a sort of vicious mood that is aimed at acquiring absolute power. It's insane--it's like what we've seen in totalitarian countries and alien to our democratic way of thinking. I don't like it, and I think it's harmful to everything our free enterprise system stands for."

"Who killed Martin Slidsky?" I asked abruptly.

Leyden looked blank, as if I had taken him unawares, and then shrugged. "I merely handed him over to a group in Brooklyn. Poor guy, he thought I was taking him to Lanzetta."

"Where is Lanzetta?" I asked, sensing I could find out no more about Slidsky.

"England. He's repairing the damage that Max did to our laundering operations there. Max tried to sabotage us by messing up our accounts," Leyden laughed. "He had them worried for a while."

"57th and Park," Joseph announced.

"Along on the right, that tall white building," Leyden said, peering out the window. "Max is on the second floor at the back."

"Do you know how many are guarding him?" I asked.

"Forget about storming the place. The only way he can be freed is by a ruse. And that's going to take planning."

"But he'll be killed!" Barb cried. "Can't we do something now?"

"Max will survive until the banking mess is straightened out," Leyden calmed her. "They need his expertise still, but he wont tell them how he mucked it up--unless the pain becomes too great."

"Do you mean, he's being tortured?" Barb cried in alarm.

"Even if we do rescue him," Joseph interrupted, "how we goin' to hide him? These cats is one powerful group."

"We'll need Detective Buckle," I said.

"You'd better warn him that he'll be running up against personnel in his own force," Leyden warned. "It just might be possible to save Max, but Buckle had better leave the organization alone."

"No!" I said angrily. "The organization must be destroyed, exterminated off the face of the earth!"

"Right!" Barb cried.

"I'm trying to be realistic," Leyden smiled. He was surprised and pleased at our vehemence. "You, together with the New York Police Force, cannot destroy it. It's too integrated in society, and, besides, it involves a large number of people who find it very profitable. And you can't eliminate greed as easily as you think." Leyden threw his cigarette end out of the car window. "But I'll tell you what. Someone, and I mean one individual, can infiltrate the organization, and I suggest that person be you, Mack."

I was taken aback. "Me? I wouldn't know how to go about it."

"I'll introduce you," Leyden said.

"But ain't you under suspicion yourself?" Barb asked.

"I'm doing this because I want to help Max, no other reason," Leyden said with a frown. "Rudyard could never become one of the top members--you have to have a couple of hundred millions for that--but he can be suggested as one of our security force."

"I might accept just to spring Max Leyden free," I said quietly, as I watched a homeless family find shelter against a building.

"Good! That's settled!" Leyden cried. "I'll put in a word with Kroneweiss tonight and call you tomorrow. Let's get back to the Library."

Joseph started the car and turned down Park.

"I can't leave my library job," I said. "I've got too many years toward my pension."

"Don't worry, Rudyard. It'll be only part-time. And you won't have to exterminate anyone. We have special personnel for that."

When we turned into the Library yard, Alex Mackart stepped out of the shadows. He took Tally Leyden's place in the car. Tally waved at us as we turned back onto the street.

"What did you find out, Alex?" I asked.

"This group's into everything--drugs, weapons, prostitution, and what's crazy is that they see themselves as conservatives upholding the values of the nation." Alex shook his head in disbelief. "They're probably still talking about deals with the Middle East and Latin America--all with heads of nations. It's incredible!"

"Rudy baby is goin' to join 'em tomorrow," Barb said. "He's goin' to join 'em and defeat 'em."

"Uh huh," Alex said. "We'll drop you off at your place, Rudy. You'll be needing a good night's sleep."

TWENTY-TWO

Arbuthnott Vine was sound asleep when I crept into bed. In the morning I heard from her.

"I'm going back to my own pad," Arbie said angrily. "This living together is ruining my health. I worry when you don't come home. I think you've been shot or stabbed."

"Have it your way," I said. "I'll miss your breakfasts, though!"

"You won't miss my dinners," she retorted. "You're never here to eat them."

"You want me to solve your kidnapping, don't you?"

"Yeah," she grimaced. "That union is bothering me. I went round to some of the branches yesterday, and the librarians looked at me strangely. Someone's been spreading stories."

"You got enough enemies," I said. "Management is helping that smart-aleck kid, Bradley Tone. Then Petula Clarkson is wooing the black vote, and you got that children's librarian who's got Bratwurst and the resources of the Union behind her."

"Don't remind me!" Arbie groaned. "Harold Poppin is already looking at me as if I were defeated. He's been talking to my executive board, pushing for the ballots to be sent out."

"You'd better hire an independent agency to run the election, sweetheart."

"Not on your life. If Bratwurst has to cheat to defeat me, then I want him to cheat. I'll get a lot of satisfaction from that!"

"You sound as if you don't want to be re-elected Local president," I said concernedly.

"Well," she sighed, looking ruefully at me. "I'm beginning to think it's not worth it. What good is just me fighting management, union bureaucrats, city bankers, and politicians. I'm tired of doing all the fighting, Rudy. I think I've been screwed enough!"

I felt a compassion for her, and went to her, and put my arms about her. "Maybe you should take a rest. You've earned it, sweetheart."

"I'm not quitting," Arbie said fiercely. "I'll fight this election, and if I lose, no one can say I didn't damn well try."

"It's a bad time for the democratic left." I went back to my coffee. "I'm joining the fascists--the type that kidnapped you."

"You're what?" Arbie cried in alarm.

I raised my arms placatingly. "As undercover. I'm going to bore from within."

"But, Rudy," she said, running to me and throwing her arms about me, "You'll be killed! You mustn't do it!"

"It has to be done, sweetheart. If we let those bastards take over the country, we'll never see another union leader like Arbuthnott Vine."

Arbie laughed and kissed me. "I've always wanted a man who would sacrifice himself for me."

"Very funny," I said. "The truth is, I am nervous. If I'm found out, I'm dead."

"Who knows about it?"

"Tally Leyden, who suggested the idea, Alex Mackart, his girlfriend, and his chauffeur. I'm counting on you to tell Detective Buckle. By the way, warn him that there are people in the police force working for the other side. He'll have to keep it to himself."

"What about your library job?" Arbie demanded.

"Leyden suggested my taking a week's leave," I said. "He thinks I can finish my undercover work in that time."

The phone rang. I answered it. It was Buckle. The State Police found Slidsky's body in Lake Nyack. Although it had been weighted down, it was washed ashore by a violent storm. "And about our friend, Arbie Vine," Buckle added, "Poppin tells us she doesn't have to worry about being killed. The powers-that-be have decided she's going to lose the election."

"You can discuss it with her," I said. "She wants to meet you today. I'll put her on." I held the receiver for Arbie to take and went to my bedroom to finish dressing.

I decided that I had to both rescue Max Leyden and expose the conspiracy--both momentous and impossible. The fact that the organization comprised an international network of sophisticated financiers daunted me.

Arbie was still talking to Buckle when I left. I kissed her on the cheek, which she acknowledged with a smile and then, clapping her hand over the receiver, she cried after me, "Be home by eight o'clock, Rudy. That's when we'll eat the last dinner I'm cooking in your apartment."

"Okay, sweetheart," I said with a sense of guilt because it was probable that I would have to disappoint her again.

I had no time to reflect on our relationship because when I reached the street door, Tally Leyden's limousine pulled up exactly to the minute. I got into the back seat with Tally.

"It'll take us an hour and a half," Tally said. His black hair was neatly combed. He looked freshly washed--a typical Wall Street yuppie, I thought.

"Max is your older brother?" I asked.

"By ten years," Tally smiled. "He taught me about the Exchange, how to turn a quick buck, you might say."

"So your secret group expects you to forget him?"

"They do, but as you remarked last night, I don't think they trust me. I guess I spoke out of turn."

"To whom?"

"To a guy called Everyman. I'm taking you to see him. He's a very, very important man, Mack. He heads our operations in North America. A brilliant guy."'

"If he's such a big shot, what would he want with me?" I asked.

"I suggested you as his security guard," Leyden replied.

"You want me to be his security?" I asked, astounded. "Surely, he's not going to hire an unknown just like that."

"He's funny that way," Tally said. "He tends to lose trust in men who have worked for him for a while. He's always looking for someone new. I've got bodyguards for him before, and, whereas he was satisfied with them for awhile, he got rid of them on the slightest of pretexts."

"What happens to them then?"

"Oh, they're usually transferred off to operations in Latin America or Europe or somewhere else. He can't fire them or downgrade them because they know too much. The last guy he got rid of landed a good job with the P-2 in Rome."

"You mean the Masonic lodge?" I asked. "I thought it was finished."

Tally laughed. "Everyman will like your naiveté."

"What's his real name?" I asked.

Tally shrugged. "I think he's Maltese. He told me once that he was descended from one of the Grand Masters of the Knights of Malta, but he could have meant it figuratively."

I felt suddenly apprehensive. Leyden could be leading me into a trap and further, to the bottom of some lake in upper New York State. But I dismissed that thought as I felt that Leyden really had put the safety of his brother before every other consideration.

While driving to Everyman's, Leyden filled me in with some background. He told me about the weapons and drug smuggling from Venezuela into Florida and Colorado, which netted the group five million dollars a day, a part of which went to support the right wing forces in Latin America, which in turn encouraged the weapons and drug smuggling. Leyden told me how most of the profits were laundered through Panamanian banks.

"Panama is the key point of transshipment for Asia and Europe, as most people in this game know," Tally said.

"Why Panama?" I asked, fascinated by the details Tally was giving me.

"First, its national currency is in dollars, which makes it easy for Panamanian banks to ship and deposit enormous amounts of cash into the American Federal Reserve System," Leyden explained. "It goes something like this: a Panamanian lawyer sets up a shell company which deposits cash into a secret account," Leyden said. "No one has access to that account, not even the Panamanian authorities, except when forced by a court order. But first, someone's got to prove criminality." Leyden smiled. "It's a piece of cake. Panama has no exchange controls, no form of registration requirements or restrictions on currency shipments in or out of the country. Our Spanish-speaking couriers there ship our weapons to the right dumps in various Latin American countries."

I noted that Leyden took a kind of ecstatic delight talking about the group's operations in Europe, Latin America, and the Near East, and particularly in the part he had played. He talked non-stop so much that I rarely found an opportunity to ask questions. But I found that when I was able to direct the conversation to other matters, such as the Irish Republican Army, Julius Savimbe of Mozambique, the attempted assassination of the Pope, I would get an earful of information in each case. Leyden's knowledge was extensive. I suspected that Tally Leyden may have been willing to divulge these confidences because he thought that I would never be able to use them.

On the other hand, Leyden was very proud of the remarkable exploits he and his group had accomplished, and he could not resist the opportunity of boasting about them. The way he talked of vast sums of money sloshing around the world at the behest of the group astonished me.

As Leyden turned along a side road leading to a country hotel on the north shore of Long Island, I could not help but ask one more question.

"What if this whole operation of laundered money, bonds and everything brings about one big global financial collapse?"

"What if it does?" Leyden smiled. "The whole world will be in the same boat, won't it? But the group is smart. We've got gold. Lots and lots of gold to fall back on. Come on, Rudyard, our resident genius is waiting."

We stopped in front of the hotel and walked across a lawn to a white porticoed entrance. There was a lone doorman who accompanied us over Persian carpets, up a winding staircase to the first room on the second floor, the door of which opened automatically as we approached.

I sensed that cameras operated from every corner, and I saw occasionally a tell-tale, red, pin-point glimmer.

The doorman crossed the outer room and opened a tall white door. Leyden motioned for me to precede him. The office I stepped into was a riot of color. Purple rugs, orange and mauve coverings on the furniture, colored lights, and dozens of paintings by the French Impressionists, the French Fauvistes, some Surrealists. Then from behind a partition near a wall of window overlooking a ravine, stepped a tall, heavy man in clerical garb and carrying a glass of whisky and ice.

"Hello, Rudyard," the man said as he stepped in long strides across the room and held out his hand. "I'm Everyman."

I did not realize how truly big Everyman was until I stood confronting him--seven feet tall, at least, and, maybe three hundred pounds. He had a huge, portly face, and the cleverest eyes I had ever seen. I felt my hand slipping like an envelope into a mail box when I extended it, but Everyman squeezed it gently and smiled slightly, reassuringly.

"You're small for a bodyguard," Everyman said. "But you might see down there what I can't see from up here." His eyes twinkled at Leyden. "Your brother likes captivity, Tally; he's not giving us what we want. Go down and see the tapes we made. You might decipher more than we did."

Leyden winced. "I don't want to see him in pain."

Everyman frowned, and the atmosphere in the room changed to a dark mood.

"But I'll see what I can do," Leyden added quickly and, walking to the distant side of the room, disappeared behind a partition.

Everyman motioned for me to sit on a couch while he sprawled at the other end of it. The furniture was large, as if custom-made for the colossal Everyman.

"Tally's briefed you on what I want, right? Do you understand who we are?"

"You're a secret political organization pursuing right-wing goals," I said.

"Forthright and a pragmatist! I like that!" Everyman said, his deep voice cracking with humor. "Pursuing right-wing goals," he repeated.

"Profit, I should say," I said.

"You are right both times. You see, the hard core right pursues goals whereas the soft core right, whom I call Waverers, pursue profit, which we allow them to do to keep them loyal." His eyes studied me, as if he were talking on one plane and thinking on another.

I nodded. "So your soft-core element is always ready to oblige progress so long as they get enriched along the way. But knowing how to go about it, they have to have a leader with Lord Wharncliff's desire for power."

"Sh! So you know English history," Everyman said, standing suddenly and with surprising agility, considering his great bulk. He was impressed that I knew what every student of English history learned about Wharncliffe's role when the House of Lords revoked the Corn Laws. "I look for intelligence in bodyguards. You'll do, Rudyard. Now, go down with Tally while I get on with my business." He took a swig from his glass, which he still held in his hand, and, dismissing me with a wave of his hand, he walked across to a communications panel.

I walked to the far side of the room with a feeling of great relief, as if I had just passed a bar examination. I noted a Bonnard painting, the soft color of girls' dresses, and flowers catching in the light from the room's wide window, before I passed behind the partition and descended a stairwell.

On the floor below, as I suspected, there were banks of computers and telectronic equipment that looked like the control room of the national space headquarters. A few men and women tended these machines with utter concentration. I walked among them unnoticed. There was no sight of Tally. I proceeded into a room marked with the sign 'Video.' Tally sat with two other men in shirt sleeves in half-light watching a monitor. I pulled up a chair behind them.

A slim, good-looking man with silvery sideburns shuddered in contortions on the screen as electric shots were administered to the tenderest parts of his body--his testicles, his armpits, his ears, the soles of his feet. Every so often the camera would move to a close-up on his red and blotted face crying with pain and rage. I thought of man's implacable hatred for man and of the thousands upon thousands upon thousands of people who had gone through unspeakable tortures in the past few years, as if they had borne the brunt for all humanity. How different were the hopes of the world into which I was born. After World War Two, man was supposed to care for his fellow men. I thought of the epigraph of Hemingway's novel, *For Whom the Bell Tolls*. It was a quotation from John Donne's "Meditation." I remembered how deeply moved I was when I read those lines, and how I had committed them to memory, "...any man's death/ diminishes me, because I am involved in mankind; And therefore never send to know for whom the bell/ tolls. It tolls for thee." Who in the twentieth century had not felt as Donne? Who had not recognized his wisdom after witnessing the catastrophes of World War I and II? And who today could not feel insufferable shame for the human race at the generation after generation of mindless tortures and cruelty inflicted on man by man in all parts of the world? Had it always been thus? Then, what hope is there for man against himself?

I came out of my reverie and saw Tally Leyden sitting rigidly, his fists clenched tightly by his sides. I sensed his fury and his fear as he listened to the mutterings, lispings, and groanings of his brother over the sound system. When his brother fainted, Tally stood up and said with great control to the two men on either side of him, "He has admitted nothing. None of this makes any sense."

"We've got lots more tape," one of them said.

"Not now," Tally said mildly with utmost control. "Mr. Mack has to be shown around the place. He's going to be the boss's new man."

The two men, in their twenties, still fresh-faced but with hard expressions, looked curiously at me. I felt their hostility, and I nodded a friendly greeting.

"Let's go, Rudyard," Tally said, taking me by the arm.

Tally led me back to the large main room and stood before the screen of a videotex. "This tells us what's happening as it's happening. Every operation of ours is monitored and reported back to this center. We get reports from across the world. You see here?" Tally pointed to a particular screen. "There's our latest drug deal completed and the amount made. It's stored on tape and indexed automatically by subject, place, persons involved and date. That way we can pinpoint any action within seconds."

"Aren't you afraid of government investigators?" I asked, surprised that they would record their crimes in such detail.

Tally looked at me patronizingly. "You still don't understand that part of the government is with us, and we are part of the government, do you?"

I swallowed to conceal my surprise. "You are a faction of the government?"

Tally nodded. "Covert, of course. Capital has been international for many years. Nowadays, governments have to accommodate the transnational corporations, and, because these corporations are bigger and more powerful than governments, they have to do their bidding. There may be laws within a nation, but they are inapplicable outside of it. This is where we come in. It's for operations within a nation that governments use us. We do, in democracies like ours, what governments cannot do legally themselves."

"You can't mean that the drug and weapon smuggling, killings, terrorist activity, and all these criminal acts on the international scene are actually aided and abetted by governments, even ours?" I frowned.

Tally laughed at my astonishment. "That's the way it is. We aid the governments by supplying them with intelligence they cannot obtain legitimately, and we can make it easy for them to invade certain nations by covertly weakening, or, as you'd say, corrupting the centers of resistance. Corruption is easy--the good life is irresistible bait for people all over the world. The profits from just one drug deal can finance one covert operation in a small country."

The deep voice of Everyman thundered through the room. "Mack!"

"He wants you," Tally whispered. "First chance you get, please help Max."

"But how do you know this guy trusts me?" I asked, incredulous at what I had just heard and what was happening to me.

"We've checked you out. You're conservative. No political involvement. You're with the public library. Everyman likes books. You're okay. You'd better hurry!" Tally gave me a tap on the shoulder.

When I climbed back to Everyman's office, Everyman introduced me to two trusted gunmen, who immediately ducked out of sight behind the partition from where Everyman appeared to get his drinks.

"You sit with me and listen," Everyman instructed me. "The man who's coming up the stairs," he pointed to a video screen suspended near the ceiling on which his visitor could be seen walking behind the hotel clerk, "is an emissary from Her Majesty's Government. He's also very close to the United States Government. He is a military man. He is a man of action. He is not a thinker. But listen to what he says and we'll discuss it later. You are armed, of course."

I nodded.

"There'll be no trouble with Major Boyle. Ah! Major!" Everyman said, holding out his huge hand as a short, thin officer in uniform strode across the room to shake hands. Everyman introduced me to the major, a sandy-haired man in his thirties, with eager blue eyes. We sat down in easy chairs pulled together for the purpose.

"I have been instructed by the Minister to thank you for your good offices in the Sudan. The grain has reached the people it was intended for," said Major Boyle in a cultivated English accent. "And he asked me to assure you that the American TOW's and heavy artillery are available for shipment within two weeks. No later, please."

"Sorry, it has to be later," Everyman grumbled. "We can get a Danish ship to Newcastle in three weeks, no sooner." Everyman stared at him with hooded eyes.

"Well, sir, it costs a good deal for the extra storage time and makes concealment all that riskier."

"I'll make it worth your while," Everyman smiled, and, taking a piece of paper from his pocket, he scribbled a figure on it and handed it to the major. "It'll be in your Swiss account in ten days."

The major's face broke into a big smile, and he pocketed the paper. "Splendid!"

"Are you going to Washington this trip, Major?" Everyman asked.

"My first wife and my two daughters live there," the Major said. "I always pay them a visit."

"To be sure," Everyman chuckled, beginning to get up.

"One moment, sir," said Major Boyle. "I have a special request from Mr. Lanzetta who is anxious to return to the United States and resume his real estate business."

Everyman made a sour face. "Tell him there's a price for all things. He knows what the deal is. Either he turns over to me his three largest buildings in Manhattan or he won't kiss his native soil again. He'll know which buildings I mean, Major."

"I'll convey that message to him," Major Boyle said smartly. "Good luck, sir, and good-bye, Mr. Mack."

When the major had gone, Everyman remarked to me that Lanzetta was not a trustworthy man, that he found the organized criminal by and large too greedy and too inclined to ignore the safety rules. "Those buildings run themselves, and they're worth a fortune and make a fortune. There's no reason why Lanzetta should be allowed to destroy them by neglect." He took a swig of whiskey from the glass he kept on the table beside him. "Want to know how it all works? The major will transmit my message to England as soon as he gets in his car. Lanzetta will be contacted, and he'll send me a message of agreement by this afternoon. He has no choice. It's an offer he cannot refuse. Our London lawyers will then prepare the papers for signing tomorrow, and Lanzetta will get his cherished wish and fly back to his native soil at the end of the week, after I have touched all the required bases." Everyman looked at me with a twinkle in his eye. "Now, here's where you come in and when we test your character. On Sunday when he arrives, you will be waiting in his home, and you will put him out of his misery."

I gulped. My heart began to pound. But I maintained a calm exterior. "That's a cruel homecoming," I managed to say.

"This is a cruel business," Everyman retorted. "But don't think this is going to be simple. You'll be dealing with a man who has been in this game a long time. Lanzetta can wipe you out, first. He'll be expecting a rub out."

"He's not without foresight, then?" I said.

For some reason Everyman found this very amusing. He roared with laughter and clapped his big heavy hand on my shoulder. "You're not needed for the rest of the day, so why don't you take a look at what we're doing."

"By the way, sir, Tally asked me to ask you whether I can see his brother," I said. "I saw Max Leyden under torture on the video a little while ago. He's not talking," I explained.

"Sure!" Everyman grunted, glowering at me. "Go to the lobby and a car will take you there. That will be your first test of character," he smiled.

I felt an immense relief as soon as I left Everyman's presence. The sense of menace was gone. When with him, I was compelled to think of his schemes, of his goals, and of his powerful personality which seemed to have global influence. When I reached the hall desk, the hotel clerk informed me that my car was waiting. I stepped into the private limousine provided. The driver, a sharp-featured man with a peaked chauffeur's hat, said nothing and drove expressionlessly.

The secret organization was too overwhelmingly extensive to be overthrown by a people's revolution let alone by one man. Moreover, I had been asked to kill a man, which, I knew in my guts, I could not do. I would fail the test as surely as my name was Mack, and, consequently, I would be extinguished like a little mouse that wandered by mistake into a furnace. But the magnitude of the evil that Everyman represented appalled me. Everyman was like an octopus with tentacles clasping the whole world. The thought of Mr. Mouse versus Mr. Octopus amused me despite my fear. The fight of the century, I mused. Yet how vital it was that the likes of me triumph over the likes of Everyman. But as I gazed at the back of the head of my impassive chauffeur, I realized sadly that much of the world was content to be controlled regardless of whether justice was done, whether indiscriminate use of force was administered, and whether irrationality ruled the roost. I believed that opposition from some quarter should be a permanent state, if only to keep the ordinary people thinking, let alone to keep them sane. At the moment, I felt that I alone was the opposition. Even though I had no idea of the true size and complexity of the secret force confronting me, I knew, at least, that it was transnational, inter-governmental, and involved a maze of legitimate and illegitimate bodies all working for the control of the world.

We were now in Manhattan and on 57th Street cruising toward the building that held Max Leyden. The hidden cameras and microphones around Max Leyden would make my visit useless, I thought. I could not really communicate with him. I passed a drug store whose pharmacist I knew was from Haiti, and I remembered the man telling me about Papa Doc Duvalier's trick for winning the whole-hearted devotion of the Haitian people. Duvalier would play the role of miracle man. Duvalier's doctors would feed to the members of families a drug which lowered the blood pressure to zero and made the victims appear dead for twenty-four hours, after which the drug would wear out, and Duvalier would arrive at the right moment and resurrect them.

"Stop here, driver," I said. "I'd like some cigarettes." The driver reacted quickly and swung the limousine to a stop at the kerb. I went into the drugstore and, with a sigh of relief, caught sight of the Haitian alone at the pharmaceutical counter.

"Mr. Mercier," I said hurriedly as he approached. "I'm on special police assignment." I lowered my voice and leaned over the counter. "Do you have Papa Doc's special prescription?"

Mr. Mercier raised his eyebrows slightly, and, wiping his hands over the front of his white coat, he disappeared into an area behind the counter. He knew me well and trusted me. I walked to the front of the store, bought cigarettes from the cashier, and returned to the pharmaceutical counter just as Mr. Mercier returned with a small bottle, which he was about to put in a bag.

"I'll take it without a bag," I said, reaching for it.

"Take care," Mr. Mercier warned. "Use it in the right proportions." He pronounced "proportions" in the French manner. He brushed aside the money that I offered him, and, looking round to make sure no one was watching us, he wagged a finger at me furtively, and went back to the concealed area behind the counter.

"All set," I said to the driver as I got back into the car. "Want a cigarette?"

"No, sir," the chauffeur said.

I fingered the bottle in my pocket as I left the limousine and approached the entrance to the house. A young, good looking woman opened the door and smiled as she stepped aside to let me enter. She led me without a word up a flight of stairs and along a hallway to the back of the house where she left me at an open doorway. I looked in and saw three untidy-looking men sitting in front of a television. They turned expectantly to watch me enter. One of them, shuffling to his feet, held out his arm to shake my hand.

"We've been expecting you," he said.

His two companions grunted. None of them volunteered their names. They looked bored beyond redemption. These were the torturers of the day-shift, I suspected.

"Want to see him now?" the leader asked. He seemed impatient to get my visit over with.

"I'd like to see notes on what's he confessed so far," I said in a business-like manner.

"We don't keep that stuff here," the leader said, anger and suspicion creeping into his eyes. "We feed it indirectly into the center."

"All right," I said. "Let's see the bastard."

Sighing, the leader, a pudgy-looking man of middle height with a shock of black hair, seized a key ring from a hook on the wall, and walked to a door across the hallway, which he opened with a key.

"He's not gonna be awake," the leader warned. "We just gave him a work-over for four hours."

I walked along a hall to a room in which the window was blanketed over. The guard turned on the overhead light. I saw the thin body of a man lying on his back on a small couch. The man's naked feet jutted over the edge of the bed. A torn shirt and slacks were all he wore. From his face in repose, I recognized the Max Leyden I had seen under torture on the video screen.

"Why can't you make him talk?" I asked as I looked for tell-tale signs of cameras in the ceiling and walls.

The leader shrugged. "He's got a high tolerance. What can I tell you? We do our jobs."

"Let's have a glass of water. I'm waking him up," I said.

"No water!" the leader admonished me. "He gets a drop or two just to keep him alive."

"Water," I repeated firmly. "He's got to talk to me."

The leader saw the grimness in my face, and, shrugging his shoulders, retreated to a nearby bathroom where I heard him running the water. I went to the bed and touched Max Leyden's arm. Leyden's eyes flew open in terror. His body seemed to go rigid in expectation of pain. I smelt decay in the air. I looked kindly at Leyden, but the eyes staring back at me showed only fear and hatred.

"Here's your water," the leader said as he shuffled back into the room and held out a glass to me.

Leyden focused on the leader as if he awaited some sudden abuse from him, a cuff, a slap, a kick, a karate chop. I gave him the glass of water, which Leyden grabbed in both hands and drank feverishly, slurping some water onto the bed.

"Another glass," I said to the leader when Leyden had drained it. "And a glass for me."

The leader looked askance at me, swiped the empty glass from Leyden's hands, and went back to the bathroom.

"Your brother thinks you should tell them what they want to know," I said looking down at him. "I'm his friend and your friend."

Leyden stared back at me, the horror still in his eyes.

"We'll get you safely out of this place," I smiled. "Just say what bank accounts there are--where's all that money."

The leader shuffled back carrying two glasses of water.

I took the two glasses, looked at them, and said, "Second thoughts, maybe we should have some beer. Got any beer?" I asked.

The leader's pudgy face fell in amazement. "Beer! For him!" he exclaimed with disgust.

I nodded and winked.

The leader frowned, and sighing, walked along the hall to his quarters where his companions were watching television. I gave a glass of water to Leyden and watched him drink it greedily. At the same time I felt for the small bottle of Papa Doc's drug in my pocket, unscrewed the top without taking my eyes off Leyden, drew my hand out of my pocket, and surreptitiously poured the drug into my glass of water. When Leyden finished drinking, I took back the empty glass and handed him my glass. Leyden drank it down as quickly as he did the other glasses. The intense hatred in Leyden's eyes diminished somewhat as he handed the empty glass to me.

"Can you say anything?" I asked.

"I'm not talking," Leyden said hoarsely between his teeth.

"Good!" I cried as I pocketed the bottle. "Want a cigarette?" I opened my package and offered it to Leyden, who gingerly took a cigarette. I struck a match and lit it.

The leader came into the room, a beer in each hand. He looked at Leyden smoking as if he was prepared to accept anything.

I took one of the cans, opened it, and poured myself a beer, which I proceeded to drink. "You can have the other if you tell our friend here what he wants to know."

The leader looked at us skeptically. Leyden stared from me to the leader and back to me. His eyelids flickered. His head sank back onto the bed. His eyes closed.

The leader started forward, a curse on his lips and his arm raised to smash Leyden.

"Hold it!" I caught his arm. "He's passed out. I guess the quantity of water and the cigarette has shocked his system. Let him sleep. He'll come to in a couple of hours."

"I don't get it!" the leader said, genuinely puzzled. "What the hell do you think you're doin'?"

"Trust me," I said. "Everyman does."

At the mention of Everyman, the leader became immediately calm. He shrugged one shoulder and walked with me through the house to the front door.

"Let him sleep. Let him dream of that beer," I said. "I'll be back." I watched the leader sullenly close the door behind me.

The weather was cooler, a sign that summer nights were coming to an end. I suppressed an urge to call Arbie Vine. I got on a downtown bus, got off at 42nd Street, and walked to the Library. I felt I could understand the connection between the criminal profiteers, the bankers, and the trade unions. I could understand the logic of politicians wanting to push Arbie out of union affairs, but I could not fathom the Library's involvement with an operation like Everyman's. That Tally Leyden could use the Library President's office for clandestine meetings proved that someone connected with the Library, whoever it might be, allowed it. Arbie claimed that all of the universities and cultural institutions in the country were controlled by one group or another of the capitalists such as the Rockefellers, and I had seen the countless books she had on the subject. But even granting she was right, it seemed improbable that the capitalist groups could be involved in criminal international, right-wing, terrorist organizations. Could their paranoid fear of communism or progressivism or liberalism have driven them to such evil alliances? I could not figure it out. I shook my head in dismay as I walked into my office where I was confronted by my secretary crying my name with astonishment.

"We didn't think you worked here any more," she said archly.

I smiled weakly, took a pile of messages from her desk, and leafed through them. "Everything under control?"

"Barely," she said. "A mental patient, just released, tried to strangle a woman in the hallway this morning. He thought she was his wife."

"Did they catch him?" I frowned at being reminded that, even in this mundane library, insanity was rife, and not confined to the secret halls of government.

"Ajax brought him in," she said, the fear of the experience entering her voice as she spoke of it. "The man wasn't sorry. I think he was looking for a substitute for his wife."

"He *must* have been mad," I said in humor, but my secretary continued to look serious and concerned.

"We need better security," she said. "We need you back with us." She handed me a green memorandum. "From Mr. Raikes. He wants to see you." I took it and went into my office. The memo simply granted me a week's leave, and congratulated me on my diligent work leading to the safe return of the library union president.

I wrote a note to him expressing my thanks. I was in no mood to talk over library security with Joshua Raikes. My main concern was to see Annie who had left the cryptic telephone message: "See me."

"Don't tell anyone I was in," I instructed my secretary as I left.

"Not even Mr. Raikes?" She rounded her eyes with a naughty look.

"No," I smiled. "I mean from outside."

"Oh," she nodded. "Outsiders like Miss Vine."

"Right," I said.

My secretary had the strangest sense of humor, I thought as I passed through the Library to the 42nd Street exit. At a break in traffic I cut across the street, through the hallway of a building into 43rd Street, and up the stairs leading to Arbie's Local headquarters. At the first level I stepped into the massage parlor and asked the young man, with the athletic build and business-like expression, for Annie.

"She's just finishing with a customer," he answered politely. "Would you care to wait?"

I gave the young man my card and told him I would wait for Annie in the restaurant on the ground floor. I had time to drink a coffee when Annie came to my table in the restaurant. She looked pert and pretty and gave no hint that she had just been through the sexual orgy that I had been imagining as I waited.

"We can't stop here," Annie said. "It belongs to the mob." And when I was walking out with her, she gave my card back to me. "Look: this says, 'detective,' and it got me into trouble in the parlor. Thank God, it said 'library detective,' and I could tell them it had to do with books I borrowed."

"Sorry," I said.

We walked west on 43rd Street.

"Poppin was running off at the mouth again," she said. "They've got a way of marking the ballots that are out for the librarians' election. They expect Arbie Vine is going to win the election by a little bit. Then, since she has to have 51%, she'll be made to lose the run-off."

"Who's running off with her?" I asked.

"A librarian name of Isabelle."

"Anything else?"

"Naw, he was just pretty happy about the whole thing. He thinks with Vine gone, Bratwurst can put the union in wrappers for the bankers. He jumps around like a small boy every time he talks about it."

I smiled. "Want a drink?"

"No, baby, I got an appointment. Big spender uptown." She waved at a taxi moving up 6th Avenue. "Next time."

I opened the cab door and helped her in.

"I'll keep you informed. I hate that old bugger."

I watched the taxi speed away as I decided not to inform Arbie. The real cheating would happen in the run-off election, but I wondered if it were not better for Arbie to lose. She was a target now. If she won re-election she would probably be found dead within months. Better to let the sharks thrash about among themselves. Then she could step back in when the carnage was over. Yes, I thought, Arbie should take a rest from union work.

"Hey, Rudy!" Alf Landy stepped out of the crowd with a hand raised in greeting and a smile on his broad Irish face. "What cha' doin' here?"

"Going uptown," I said. "Where you been?"

"Grievance meeting at the Central Building. A guy's bein' denied permanent appointment 'cause he's on the left."

"What's the charge?"

"No charge," Alf cried angrily. "They don't have to give a reason. That's one of Hector Bratwurst's gifts to us."

I felt someone brush against me and stepped aside. "What's it look like for Arbie in the branches?"

Alf turned his lips down. "They're blamin' her for the layoff threats. The word's out that we need a conciliatory leader."

"They're swallowing that?" I looked incredulous.

"Sure," Alf said. "That's been a sub-theme with librarians long as I can remember." Alf moved away. "I'll tell her I saw ya."

I caught a bus to 57th Street, transferred to the cross-town, and got off opposite the house holding Max Leyden hostage.

I thought of the irony of thousands of sedate town houses right around the world, the very epitome of respectability, in which grisly acts of torture were taking place. In Argentina and Ecuador and maybe half a dozen other countries, torture was being carried out in schools, infirmaries, big estates,--the respectable right wing at work. But in New York City, it was done on the corner of Park Avenue and 57th Street.

This time the leader opened the door. His face registered alarm as if something had gone wrong inside him.

"I thought you was the doctor," he said, peering out the door and looking agitatedly up and down the street.

I stepped inside and waited for the pudgy little man to lock the door.

"What's wrong?" I asked immediately.

"That crazy guy. I think he croaked!" the leader cried.

"You weren't supposed to disturb him until I returned," I said angrily.

"I didn't! I just looked in on him, you know, just to keep an eye on him. He's white as a sheet."

I raced up the stairs to the back of the house with the leader behind me. The two other torturers were still watching television, but they looked guiltily at me as I passed their room. Max Leyden looked rigid in death. His skin color was ashen. I put my ear to Leyden's chest, but I could detect no heart beat. I suddenly feared that I really had killed him--poisoned him. Maybe the drug was too strong for him in his weakened condition. I held his pulse.

"There's no life!" I shouted. "This guy's had it!"

I glared at the leader whose shock of black hair seemed to stand even straighter.

"We didn't touch him!" the leader expostulated.

"Get your friends to wrap him in a sheet and carry him out the back. You got a car?"

"Yeah, in the garage. But what about the doctor?" the leader asked hesitantly, his fat face reflecting his worry.

"He's dead!" I said simply. "We need a mortician, not a doctor."

"But the doctor's one of us," the leader insisted.

"But he's too late, you fool!" I cried angrily. "Now get moving!"

I wrapped a sheet around Leyden's body and pulled it loosely over his head so as to allow him to breathe, should he still be alive.

The leader returned with the two torturers from the other room. They towered over the leader and me. They picked up Leyden's body, one on each end, as if it were a sack.

"To the garage?" one of them asked indifferently.

"Into the back seat of the car--on the floor," the leader said as he rushed ahead of them.

I pulled the curtain partially away from the window. The room looked onto the back of another building through the windows of which I saw a nursery and small children playing. I quickly followed the others and took the opportunity to look into the rooms I passed in order to see if there were other prisoners. The rooms were vacant, but some seemed to have been detention cells. I descended to the basement and entered the garage which harbored three cars. The men had put Leyden in the back of one of them and waited for instructions. Their leader, holding the car keys in one hand, stood stricken with indecision. I took the keys and sat in the driver's seat.

"Don't say a word of this to anyone until you hear from me," I instructed him.

"It's all recorded on tape," the leader said dejectedly. "They'll know about it when they look at it."

"Don't worry," I smiled. "You can't be blamed." I started the motor, moved the car forward, and the garage door rolled up automatically. I did not look back, except, once I was in the street, I glanced into the back seat to see Leyden wrapped in a sheet and lying on the floor.

I drove to Leyden's apartment house on the Hudson River, parked outside the front door, and, finding Barb Janes's telephone number in my wallet, I called her from a phone booth. She answered, delighted to hear my voice and beside herself with excitement that Max Leyden was with me. I had to insist that she come down before I explained Leyden's death-like condition.

"Is he gonna pull out of it?" she asked, concern and doubt in her voice.

"Yes," I said reassuringly, "but we've got to hide him somewhere."

"Why not here?" Barb said. "Who's gonna look for a dead man in his own apartment?"

We arranged for Barb to come down, drive the car into the garage of the apartment complex, and park it beside the elevator leading to the wing where Leyden's apartment was located. The maneuver went well. No one saw us roll the body out of the back of the car and into the elevator. We laid the body at the back of the elevator and stood in front of it. Barb kept her finger on the fourth floor button and instructed the elevator not to stop at any floors in between. When it passed the main floor, we began to relax, but it stopped, inexplicably, on the third. As the doors opened, Barb stepped forward to confront a tall lady carrying a fruit bowl.

"No passengers!" Barb waved her away and put her other hand on the close door button. "Movin' furniture."

Perturbed, the tall lady looked curiously at the extra room in the elevator and opened her mouth to protest when the doors closed. Barb laughed with satisfaction. On the fourth floor the hallway was clear. We dragged Leyden to the apartment door. Barb had her key at the ready and opened the door in an instant. We dragged the body over the threshold.

"Where do we hide him?" I asked.

"Put him in his own bed in his own bedroom," Barb said, closing the door and grabbing Max Leyden by the legs. "When he wakes up, he'll recognize where he is."

We dragged him into the bedroom and with extra effort laid him between the sheets on his bed. Barb rolled up the sheet that had been covering him. "This smells like it's never been washed," she said. "This is one time where we're goin' to burn the evidence, detective."

"He doesn't smell good either," I said.

"Go in, help yourself to a drink and relax," Barb said, beginning to tear off Leyden's clothes. "I'm cleaning him."

I went into the sitting room and poured myself a whisky. I began to think of what I would tell Everyman. I could say that I weighted the body and dumped it into the East River, a favorite solution for disposing of bodies because its strong currents carried refuse out into the Atlantic. It was not original but it was believable. I felt uneasy, however, because Everyman gave me the feeling that he could see through me, could see every devious move I made. But then, why should Everyman mistrust me? I asked myself. I had done nothing to make him suspicious.

Barb came into the room. She was almost dancing with joy. Her black eyes shone with gratitude and her hands fluttered through the air. "Come on, Rudyard," she said, taking me by my coat lapels. "I'm goin' to give you a treat you'll always remember."

"What's that?" I said, amused. I put down my drink as she led me away. "Where are we going?"

Barb opened the door to a large bedroom with a king size bed. It was her room. The rows of perfume bottles and powder boxes on the dresser attested to that. She pulled off my coat.

"Get them off," she said. "I am just so happy I could cry."

I stood indecisively watching her strip off her sweater, brassiere, skirt, underpants. Her full rounded body with pointed tits, soft brown skin, long legs, and cute rump stood, arms outstretched, to receive me. "Well," she said. "Don't I look familiar to you?"

I smiled and nodded at the bed to where Barb went to stretch out while I threw off the rest of my clothes. In a moment I was beside her, kissing her tits, and feeling the warm wet cunt that became suddenly a home to me.

TWENTY-THREE

Three hours later, having celebrated Max Leyden's return with Barb Janes, I left Leyden's apartment. My head felt light, my body glowed, I had no fear of Everyman, no fear of anyone. The world was my oyster.

I adopted the car I had taken from the 57th St. house of torture as my own and drove it back to the secluded hotel on Long Island which served as Everyman's world headquarters. It was dark when I arrived.

Tally Leyden, who was drinking at the bar situated just off the lobby, hailed out to me as I entered. Except for two men at the other end of the bar and the barman who was talking with them, we were alone.

"Did you see Max?" Tally asked in a low voice.

I nodded. "He was in bad shape, but we got him out of there."

"You did?" Tally looked incredulous.

"They think he's dead," I winked, "so play the game."

Tally bent forward to ask me more, but I touched his arm and motioned to a tall man approaching us.

"He wishes you to join him?" the man announced to Leyden and withdrew.

"Everyman is meeting with Bratwurst," Tally said. "Want to listen in on it?"

"Without being seen?" I asked, following Leyden.

"Of course! What do you think?" Tally smiled. "Everyman tapes everything." He pointed to a small room beside the room he was about to enter. "Just turn on the monitor and you'll see and hear it all."

I found the light switch which activated the air conditioner as well as the light. I turned on the monitor and sank into an armchair to watch. That Hector Bratwurst would be meeting personally with Everyman seemed extraordinary to me, because I had assumed that Kroneweiss was the intermediary through whom even labor union leaders had to deal. Bratwurst's large face with its customary hangdog expression came onto the screen. I pushed a button and the view moved from close-up to the whole scene.

Tally was just taking a chair beside Everyman who sat at a table across from Bratwurst and another man.

"We want to be made whole," Bratwurst was saying. "Just get the Governor to give the public employees in New York City agency shop."

"How many dues-paying members have you lost in layoffs?" Everyman asked.

Bratwurst looked at the ceiling. "About forty thousand. If we go on like this we won't have enough revenue to run the union."

"Agency shop compels all city employees who are not union members to pay union dues. Am I right?" Everyman asked. "Then you'll fill up the union coffers," Everyman said with amusement. "God! you fighting tigers of the work force would be unemployed yourselves if it weren't for the kind-hearted politicians who run our State. Well, Tally, shall we give him what he wants?"

"Unions keep control of the city workers," Leyden reasoned. "They regulate salaries and working conditions. They're cheaper than managers, who don't mind paying higher wages for the workers if it means more for themselves. Moreover, I don't see how the City could have laid off thousands of workers without a riot, had Bratwurst and his friends not talked them into accepting it."

"You've got a supporter," Everyman winked at Bratwurst.

"Best of all," Leyden continued. "The workers pay the salary of Bratwurst and all the union officials through their dues. Think of the money the City saves by not having to create another bureaucracy to control the work force."

"All right, Hector," Everyman said. "The Governor will alter a clause in the Taylor Law to give you agency shop. But remember, the next time your members go to the polls, this Governor's a Democrat."

Bratwurst laughed and his companion laughed too. It was with a shock, then, that I recognized Hector's companion as Alf Landy. The young radical, the Trotskyite, was in league with Everyman? The idea seemed preposterous.

"Look!" Bratwurst frowned suddenly. "Leyden can run on at the mouth about us keeping salaries down and collecting dues, as if we were pullin' a fast one on our own workers. But they know what we're doin'. The workers don't want to fight," Bratwurst protested. "They want us to fight for them. I look after them."

"I didn't mean anything by that," Leyden said quickly. "I think you do a great job, Hector."

"He does do a great job," Alf Landy broke in. "Hector's nullified all the Local presidents. He's got to the point where only he negotiates for all the Locals. Absolute control! The guy is a genius!"

Hector laughed sheepishly. "Shut up, Landy."

"Has he got control over your Local president?" Everyman asked, his eyes alive with sarcasm.

"Vine?" Alf affected nonchalance. "She's finished. She's got no more support. I mean, can she take on City Hall, Hector Bratwurst, Library management, the military-industrial complex, the bankers and everyone else?" he laughed. "Naw! Arbie Vine's out on a limb, and we demonstrated that when we marched on City Hall."

Everyman nodded. "Go see our friend in the control room. We need clarification on the recent changes in the Workers' Party. Tally will take you."

"Now?" Alf looked disappointed, as if he thought he was being dismissed just when they were getting down to real business. But, seeing Bratwurst's displeasure, he grimaced and followed Leyden out of the room.

"He's a punk! Half the time I think he's spying on me," Bratwurst said. "But he's useful."

"Aren't we all?" Everyman said. He took a sheaf of papers from a briefcase. His big hands spread the papers in front of him. "You know the code word "Trinity," don't you, Hector? It's our operation against the liberal churches. Kroneweiss and you must begin to attack the Church's involvement in Latin America whenever you're on television. You must target the priests and ministers. Bring the subject up at every rally, at every meeting of the union delegates--whenever you can. We'll give you the names of the Churchmen in New York and Connecticut and some dope on each of them. But don't call them commies!"

"You want us to call them names?" Hector asked with a frown.

"Use innuendo," Everyman said. "At this level, we just want to see if we can scare them."

"I don't know," Bratwurst looked pained, as if he were upset in the stomach. "I've got a lot of religious people in my union."

"Just keep the focus on Latin America and support only the Bishops we tell you to support," Everyman replied impatiently.

"But," Bratwurst shook his large shaggy head, "you don't understand. My union supports democratic causes. I've got lots of Hispanics and blacks. I've got to be careful."

"Be careful, by all means," Everyman growled, "but do as I say." The anger in Everyman's eyes persuaded Bratwurst to nod eagerly in agreement. "Now, you'll go to Latin America a few times--after you visit with unions there, you will report back on their general dislike for socialism and atheism, etc. While you're in Latin America, we'll give you some assignments, which, considering your record with the Agency," he smiled slightly, "you will be able to handle."

Bratwurst nodded uneasily, as if he wished that his CIA past had not condemned him to a lifelong flirtation with danger.

"The job I have in mind will take you a couple of weeks," Everyman said, taking papers from his briefcase.

"I never see you but you got a job for me," Bratwurst said in mock complaint.

"We're working against the tide of history," Everyman smiled. "We've got no time to waste. This job, by the way, will involve your friend Kroneweiss. Our turncoat, Max Leyden, just died of natural causes, but he told us that his substantial Cayman Island account can be accessed through a Panamanian bank to New York and into the U. S. Reserve System with no questions asked."

"I take it you want Kroneweiss to find a home for it here," Bratwurst surmised correctly, "but where do I come in?"

"You're going to appear to have suddenly made a pile from an international financial deal," Everyman said. "You bring back the money, and we use it in domestic operations against the left."

"What do I get out of it?" Bratwurst asked, his face clouding with suspicion.

"You get what you always have been getting--your union," Everyman stirred impatiently. "And a commission for working for us."

"Does that mean you'll support a decent wage raise in negotiations?" Bratwurst asked. "My people are restless. It's been three straight years and no increases."

"You'll probably get it," Everyman said sourly. He handed Bratwurst some papers. "Your instructions. Get rid of those sheets after the operation is completed."

Bratwurst folded the papers and put them into his breast pocket. "We'll get you the money, but, remember, I want a say in how it's used. You guys too often confuse liberals with the left wing. It's the liberals who keep my union going. Don't forget that."

Everyman looked annoyed. He stood up and, from his seven-foot height, glared down at Bratwurst sprawled in the chair across from him. "Ideology bores me," Everyman snapped. "Landy will be waiting for you in the lobby. We'll be wanting some provocateur work from him soon. Be nice to him."

Bratwurst smiled as he departed. "He's eatin' out of my hand."

I watched Everyman sit and scribble on a yellow pad. I could not get over the vast area of operations that this giant seemed to control and of the immense detailed work he must engage in every day. Everyman seemed to me to be an invention of the times, a sort of symbol of the present universal political climate, which had no past and no real identity, except to be called the far right. After all, no one knew or seemed to care from whence Everyman came. It was an extraordinary fact when I examined it. Everyone acknowledged Everyman's authority. But from where did it derive? Who instructs him, and to whom does he report? Or did he simply evolve as the supreme authority over the select group of capitalists who had gradually in the past two or three decades been consolidating their power over a large part of the world. Perhaps, I thought, Everyman was the human equivalent of the giant computer center he controlled. He seemed to run the world like the machinery. I turned off the monitor and went into the lobby in time to see Tally Leyden bid good-bye to Hector Bratwurst and Alf Landy at the door.

Tally, his smiling face falling into a scowl, came up to me. "I hate types like that. They're opportunists."

"I thought that was an epithet only the left wing used against the right," I said.

Tally stared at me. "Whoever coined it, it's an apt description. But, tell me, where are you hiding Max?"

I raised my hand. "Now, now. I have a feeling I should report to Everyman." I turned round and saw Everyman standing at the door to the conference room and watching us. I sensed at that moment that Everyman knew that I was an impostor. The sensation soon passed and, gathering my confidence, I approached Everyman as his willing servant.

"Had a busy day, haven't you?" Everyman said, his deep voice rumbling like a purr. "You're going to be busier tomorrow. We fly to Washington where the bad boys are." He smiled impishly. "I'll need your protection. Breakfast at five-thirty, Rudyard." He waved to Tally

Leyden, who had remained where I had left him, and went back into the conference room. I watched the tall boulder of a man shuffle away and wondered what government officials this mysterious personage would meet.

"He means the bad boys of the capitol, I bet," Tally said directly behind me. "You'll see how he plays the political side of the street. He's a master!"

"But he can communicate with anyone anywhere without leaving this place," I said.

Tally nodded. "He's on a new initiative. He needs to squeeze some flesh, as President Johnson used to say."

"What's it going to be this time? Arms dealing, drug trafficking, white slavery, child stealing, trade in human organs?"

Tally eyed me warningly. "Careful. Don't display such sarcasm in his hearing. Those things bring in large sums routinely. No! His business in Washington is purely political. You just have to make sure he comes back alive."

I retired to my bedroom on the second floor. I found an envelope on my bureau. It was a contract for two months at five thousand dollars a day. I whistled softly in disbelief. I was making more in a week than I did in a year as a library detective. I wondered what would happen at the end of the two months other than the loss of my riches. I took out my revolver and put it on the table beside my bed. I began to question if all the money in the world was worth the anxiety that I was beginning to feel.

TWENTY- FOUR

A wake-up call, the company of Everyman at a large breakfast of porridge, steak and eggs, which Everyman gobbled up as if he were famished, and the take-off in Everyman's DC-8 from a private airstrip close to his hotel, brought me to a state of preparedness. I sat with six blue-suited, serious types in the office compartment of Everyman's jet as we flew to Washington. Digital computers showed the altitude and weather conditions. A long coffee table revealed the earth in detail below us on a color monitor running the length of the table. The furniture was all king-size. The skins of leopards, tigers, polar bears, moose, and lesser animals decorating the walls seemed to boast of Everyman's extensive hunting capabilities. Everyman came bursting out from the pilot's cabin and paced with enthusiasm as he appeared to be inspired by one idea after another. He called for two of the blue-suited men to go with him into another room where there were maps on display monitors, microcomputers, the latest electronic gadgetry, and, surprisingly, in one corner, a set of traps where Everyman went to sit and beat out rhythms while he pondered.

I tried to follow them into the room, but Everyman waved me away with the words, "This is private, Rudyard."

The four blue-suited men left behind were just as "private." They spoke quietly among themselves and hardly glanced at me. Perhaps, I thought, the importance of the upcoming meeting had sobered them to the point where they could think of nothing else. I wandered to the pilot's cabin.

The pilot and co-pilot in blue shirts and peak-caps sat before rows of dials, lights, and buttons, and a stewardess sat behind them reading a magazine. The stewardess glanced up at me and returned to her reading. The pilot looked back over his shoulder. He was young and good-looking.

"Well, well, who do we have here?" he gibed and swung his chair round to face me. "A new bodyguard? Another sacrificial lamb to the Big Man's ego?"

"Correct," I said. "I'm his bodyguard but not his lamb."

"Not yet," the pilot laughed, and the co-pilot smiled as he continued to watch the panel of indicators. "But you don't look tougher than the guys before you."

"What happened to them?" I asked.

"Killed," said the stewardess dead-pan. "All in the line of duty," she volunteered sarcastically. Their light banter made me think they were joking.

"I'm not a dedicated man," I said, imitating their badinage.

"By the time he's finished with you, you'll be so devoted to him you won't know who you are," the pilot said. "The process is so subtle you won't notice it."

"At the same time he becomes mistrustful of absolute loyalty," the stewardess informed me. "As soon as you lose your sense of objectivity and become his lap dog, he gets rid of you."

"Like the Queen Bee," said the co-pilot still staring at the instrument panel.

"This is ridiculous!" I laughed. "You're kidding, of course."

"Don't say we didn't warn you," said the pilot, amused at me.

"But what about you?" I shot back. "How long have you been with him?"

"Over ten years," said the pilot. "This is our third plane. But we're not bodyguards. We are more indispensable."

"We're just enslaved for a longer time," said the co-pilot.

"That's right," laughed the pilot. "The pay and the job make us unfit to work elsewhere. But the Big Man demands a lot and makes sure we earn every penny he pays us."

I realized that under their light-hearted chatter they were trying to warn me. But why?

As if in answer, the stewardess suddenly said, "We're sorry for you. We thought you ought to know some facts." She was pretty with soft eyes.

"Heh," said the co-pilot. "Maybe, if you don't like your job, you can escape in place of us."

"Oh, shut up!" the stewardess cried. She looked sadly at me. "Just remember what we told you."

The pilot turned back to look at the panel, and said, "We're nearing the Washington airport. You'd better return to your seat." I sensed a tone of resentment in the pilot's voice. Perhaps it was against himself rather than me.

"Do you know why we're going to Washington?" I asked.

"We don't," said the stewardess shaking her head. "We don't ask questions and we don't want to know."

"We're not interested in politics," said the co-pilot, turning to look at me for the first time. He had a dark mustache and a sarcastic twist to his mouth. "But that doesn't mean we're not shot at." He nodded at a spot on the roof of the cabin which had been repaired.

"You'd better get back to your seat," warned the pilot. "And take care of the Big Man. We like our big salaries."

I smiled at the stewardess and left the cabin. All organizations, I reflected, depended not upon dreamers and fanatics but upon the thousands of people who do dead-end jobs like these pilots. After I sat down and buckled my seat belt, Everyman bounded up to me, threw his huge bulk into the chair beside me, and put his long arm around my shoulders to hold me in a python-like grip. Everyman was exuberant.

"All's well, Rudyard!" he cried. "God is in heaven, and all's well with the world! Browning, right?" he laughed. "Our ambassador to the Vatican will be with us today. Do you know why we're going to Washington, Rudyard? You are going to witness one of the greatest gatherings the world has ever seen. All the Christian and Islamic fundamentalist leaders will be present. They are part of our family, Rudyard. We'll control the big 'ole world, yet. We'll put God back in his heaven and keep Him there." He jumped to his feet and strode back to the other cabin. The altitude, I thought, appeared to infect Everyman with unbounded enthusiasm. The plane dipped and began to descend. I watched the digital computers register the fall.

As we descended, I felt I was literally as well as metaphorically coming down to earth from a flight of fancy. I could scarcely believe that Everyman would trust me just on the word of Tally Leyden, who had admitted that even he was suspect because of his brother's betrayal of the cause. Perhaps, as the pilot of the plane indicated, this was Everyman's method of transforming an uncommitted nonentity like me into a fanatically loyal servant. Maybe all this confidential information was part of the process of turning me into a lap dog. But there was something else which I could not define. I touched my gun under my armpit as the plane touched the ground. I had to remember that I was Everyman's bodyguard and must protect him against his enemies. Already, a sense of loyalty was overtaking me. The thought made me smile to myself. It occurred to me then that it was not Everyman I had intended to destroy but the cruel and intolerant organization of which he was a part. In fact, I was beginning to admire Everyman.

I walked off the plane beside Everyman like a Lilliputian beside the giant Gulliver and looked sharply about me. Within a minute, I was sitting in the back seat of a limousine with Everyman and waiting for the six blue-suited men to seat themselves in front of us. Everyman resumed his phlegmatic personality. He seemed to have left his exuberance behind in the plane.

"You don't have to worry about attacks in public places," Everyman said to me as the limousine began to gather speed. "I'm not known. It's when we are in private places that you have to be on the watch out. You must keep an eye on the government agents--ours as well as foreign governments."

"Why would they want you dead?" I asked innocently.

"The world's like a swamp," Everyman sighed. "Frogs lick up bugs, snakes swallow frogs, you know how it is."

"Is life a swamp then?"

"It's a question of survival of the fittest. Whoever is the fittest controls the lot." Everyman gritted his teeth. "It had to take a scientist like Darwin to discover this truth. Philosophers, on the other hand, write fairy tales. They've never had to deal with the real world. It's men like me who create a safe environment in which they can indulge themselves in their ivory towers." He watched the land fly by from his limousine window and lapsed into silence.

As we entered the inner city, Everyman said: "By the way, these six men are armed. They will back you if you need help. But if you try any hanky panky," he regarded me with humor in his eyes, "they will not hesitate to put an end to you."

"I thought they were accountants," I said, rather unnerved.

"You could call them that," Everyman agreed. "They furnish me with details."

We drove up Pennsylvania Avenue and watched the great marble buildings of the Capitol dazzlingly white in the early morning sun. We stopped at the Rayburn Building. Everyman charged from the limousine like a huge linebacker. I followed rushing with eyes darting in every direction. The respectable-looking six "accountants" followed me. We met a senator in the lobby--gray-haired Southerner of mild demeanor, who led us onto an elevator, up a score of flights, and into spacious offices where already about one hundred men were gathered, drinking coffee and eating bagels and Danish Pastry. The mood was jovial. All eyes swung to Everyman as he entered and towered over them all. The senator led him to the middle of a long table. Everyman's six assistants took up chairs behind him. All the other men began to take seats at the table and at the two tables which ran at right angles from it. I helped myself to coffee and sat near the door from where I could see all the participants. They seemed to be of various nationalities, some in clerical robes of different religious denominations, the majority in conservative business suits. They represented leaders from all walks of life:

politicians, businessmen, scientists, academicians, religious leaders, and so on. What a coup for a zealot to destroy them all at one go, I thought.

The senator brought a laugh from the assembled dignitaries as he introduced Everyman in an amusing way. I was concentrating on the faces of the listeners. I watched for tell-tale signs as Everyman rose to address them. All seemed well. Every face appeared to regard the massive man, whom they only knew as Everyman, with admiration. I listened closely to Everyman's argument. According to him, the world did not look bright in the twenty-first century. Population explosion, godless and ruthless men leading the masses, all threatened the world with chaos and anarchy, unless controlled by rational men. Technology was advancing faster than man can cope with it. Computers were freeing men from heavy toil, the number of unemployed was rising every year, threatening property and privilege. A two-tiered world society was the solution. We must go back to the system of oligarchy. Two-thirds of the population must be contained. They must be taught the traditional values of civilization, and be ruled by the one third whose cultivated intellect gave them the right. To make the world an enlightened planet, people must be made to return to religious faith, but it must be a universal faith. The globe was now too small to tolerate religious wars. To preserve this universal faith, an alliance with the military was absolutely necessary. But the military, too, must be a universal power. A world army, as it were.

As Everyman talked on enthusiastically painting his view of the world's future, the delegates sat spellbound. They seemed to relish his view that the pleasures of life in a shrinking world should be the privilege of a few, and that that privilege must be maintained by the ruthless exercise of force.

Everyman proposed plans, scenarios, plots, and hypotheses by which his view of the world could become a reality. The unrestrained development of more powerful weapons was essential for them to reach this objective. If the world was to be prevented from remaining a swamp, then men of foresight and character such as those present in the room must build the weapons to make sure order is kept.

I had to go to the bathroom. I remembered that Lincoln had been assassinated when his guard answered the call of nature. But I saw the six "accountants" and thought Everyman had sufficient protection while I would be out of the room. I asked directions of one of the secret service men in the hallway, and walked to the right, then to the left, along corridors until I spotted a "Gentlemen" sign on a door. I entered and addressed a urinal with relief. I thought I was alone until I heard the click of a lock from one of the booths and the flush of a toilet. I did not try to look at the man but listened to his footfalls approach from behind me and turn away to the sink area. I finished, went to a sink, squeezed soap into my hand, and glanced in the mirror at the other man at the same time he glanced at me. The surprise of the man reflected my own.

"Father Ian!" I cried. "What are you doing here?"

"What are you doing here?" Father Ian cried, taking a step backward and looking at me as if he had seen a ghost. "There's a convention of the radical right in this building. You're not part of it, are you?"

"Are you?" I countercharged.

"Of course I'm not!" Ian said angrily. "They won't let me near the meeting room. What are you doing?"

I smiled. "They let me in. I'm Everyman's bodyguard."

Father Ian stood stunned.

"You weren't intending any violence, I hope?" I continued.

"Of course not!" Ian cried. "But, my word, I thought you were one of us."

I put a finger to my lips and looked round as if fearing to be overheard. "I'll explain when I see you in New York," I whispered. "Call me."

"Wait!" Father Ian seized my arm. "They're going to discuss some plan called the "Trinity." I've got to find out what it is."

"I'll listen," I reassured him and moved toward the door just as it opened. A secret service man walked in and held the door for me.

Fearing that the secret service man intended to eject Father Ian, I paused in the hallway uncertain whether I should help the priest. But Father Ian came out and waved as he walked in the opposite direction. "I'm all right," he called softly. "Thank you for your concern."

When I re-entered the meeting room, Everyman was still speaking. He had the concentrated attention of all in the room. I, who was basically conservative, found myself responding to Everyman's intensity and evident sincerity. His deep clear voice, his animated manner, and his stories of his individual suffering and achievement made him all the more attractive, I thought. These touching personal details subtly led his listeners to sympathize with his proposals. At the moment, his main purpose was to emphasize the importance of closing down the liberal movement in Churches. "Jesus Christ was a conservative," he said, "because he believed in individual salvation. He opposed the radicalism of the zealots."

I smiled to myself because every person present must recognize the irony of that statement. They knew that the Zealots were the radical right and Christ was the communist. By the time the meeting broke up for mid-morning coffee, every listener was fired with enthusiasm. I observed the glow in the eyes about me, and would have been in the same state had I not known the murderous truth about Everyman.

I followed the long-striding Everyman to a small room where ten other delegates gathered. Everyman's six helpers dispersed to other rooms to guide other discussions. Everyman chaired his group in a genial and familiar manner. His broad face beamed approval. His long arms reached out to pat backs and punch arms. His colleagues, powerful men from whence they came, paled before the dominating presence of Everyman.

"Trinity," the plan that had concerned Father Ian, as expressed by Everyman, provided for the transport of heroin and cocaine from Colombia and Venezuela to airfields in Colorado with the help of agents from the Central Intelligence Agency. The millions raised from this heroin traffic would be deposited in Panamanian banks and transferred legally into accounts controlled by Everyman in North America and Europe. All of the money would be used to combat liberal churchmen and Marxist clergy in third world countries. The argument that it is immoral to profit from the drug trade, that it was illegal, and that it undermined the fabric of American society was dismissed by Everyman, whose pragmatic attitude was that the drug trade existed from time immemorial and was a fact of life. Until someone found an effective way to stop it, the capitalists should profit from it, otherwise it would fall into undesirable hands. Moreover, the profits were being used for a noble cause. I noted that the group seemed easily convinced and readily amenable to Everyman's suggestion that their regional banks receive the deposits. As they discussed the operation in more detail, I lost interest. I felt depressed. All along I had thought that members of organized crime were the scum of the earth. What shocked me was my seeing that the highest government officials, business and community leaders, whose sympathies were on the right, were part and parcel of organized crime. Actually, I thought, the right was destroying itself from within by its blind, immoral pursuit of greed and power as its goals. But since it controlled society, the danger was the corruption and decay of society. What they were doing, then, was to achieve goals that were the direct opposite of what they desired. My depression was induced by what I saw as the willful criminality of these powerful men. What deeply disturbed me was the grief I felt for my own conservative views, which had been expropriated and distorted out of all recognition by these ruthless rascals. Although I loved Arbie and understood and often applauded her socialist views, I had never been able to accept her liberal philosophy. Now I saw how important it was for the individual to maintain his own distinctive feelings, ideas and spirit. The liberals always seemed like bleeding hearts to me, but up against these ruthless right-wing bastards, I saw the sense of the liberal view. Man was an incredible creature, diverse in his talents to create beauty and to destroy it at the same time. He must be allowed the freedom to nurture his native talents. The individual counts. That's why the liberals like my spunky Arbie were so endearing in their seemingly hopeless crusade for the freedom of the individual. But then, I smiled, for I recognized that I was a prisoner of my own conservatism, and just as unable to free myself from it as were Everyman and his colleagues. My sadness, however, derived from the realization that my brand of conservatism was no longer a force, indeed, it was outdated and no longer recognizable in the face of Everyman's criminal usurpation of conservative thinking and his deliberate, malevolent re-interpretation of it to suit his evil purpose.

Everyman did not stay for lunch. He shook hands with his hosts, his towering figure giving the impression of strength and wisdom. The senator walked with him while the six aides and I trailed behind. When we reached the lobby, I sprang up beside Everyman and strode beside him to the waiting limousine. Everyman instructed me to sit up front while he sat in the back with his six aides. As we drove to the airport, I listened to them excitedly discuss the success of Everyman's speech and the various points he raised. On the flight back to New York, Everyman remained closeted with his aides. I ate the lunch, which the stewardess brought me, alone. The time had come, I decided, for me to upset this grand conspiracy.

TWENTY-FIVE

Back at the hotel headquarters, Everyman went immediately to his computer room to check the many activities that his organization pursued about the globe. Watching him stoop over monitors as he read the ticker tapes, his long fingers stopping it now and then, then slipping it along to the next place of interest, I sensed that Everyman did not like to be away from this control center. It was what gave him the energy and meaning of his life. From this center, Everyman could speak to whomsoever he wished by telephone, and he could communicate with video to any part of the world. For secret business he would send emissaries or use codes by telegraphs. The forces at his command were so powerful, he could match any sovereign government. So independent was he, that unlike any other men of notoriety such as the infamous Gelli of the P-2 lodge, he did not have to depend on personal contact to influence governments. But there were occasions where he had to be seen by large groups of people. I was thankful that those occasions were rare and that Everyman discouraged visitors. The grounds around the hotel were guarded by a dedicated security force which was independent of my authority. Because of it, I was free to leave Everyman safely in his cocoon of mechanical playthings while I borrowed one of the cars and drove to Manhattan

I parked near Max Leyden's apartment building and was soon in the presence of Barb Janes and a refreshed-looking Max Leyden, who was still in bed. Max was effusive in his thanks, but I quickly turned the subject to "Trinity." Max was alarmed. His sharp eyes lit up excitedly as I recounted all I knew.

"Tell you what," he said. "I know those accounts from which Kroneweiss and Bratwurst are collecting, but we must wait until all the money is deposited in the Panama account; then I'll arrange, through my contact, for the money to be disbursed before they can put their hands on it."

"Disbursed to whom?" Barb cried. "Where you gonna hide all those millions?"

"That's easy," I chipped in and wrote out a telephone number which I gave to Barb. "Call Father Ian and ask him for a list of needy organizations, especially those ones helping Third World countries get and keep their independence."

Max laughed. "Anything to make those bastards squirm."

Barb put her arm about my neck. "You're sweet. Do you know that it means screwing up their Swiss bank accounts and making some of their Italian banks crash?"

I was alarmed.

"Don't worry, my friend," said Max, seeing my fear. "They won't know what really happened for weeks," he smiled. "They'll be too busy suspecting one another."

"But when they finally find out it's you, and they come to know you're alive, then I'm a dead man," I said.

"Don't worry, Rudy." Barb looked at me sympathetically. "No one called; he's never left this bedroom, and I haven't let anyone into the apartment. So our secret is still safe."

"And my contacts in Europe have always acted with the greatest discretion. Moreover, for most Swiss accounts, I use a number or an alias," Max added. "I wouldn't let down the man who saved my life."

I nodded with embarrassment . "Your brother Tally wants to see you."

"Not yet," Max warned. "I'm not sure of him."

"He' s persuaded Everyman that you've been disposed of," I said.

"But I still don't trust him, and don't you do so either, please," Max looked plaintively at me. "He's very ambitious. He might very well want me alive only because I have access to the money. You watch out for him," Max reiterated.

I acknowledged the advice and left them with the suggestion that only Barb, not Max, should speak to Father Ian and disclose as little of the plan as possible for prudence sake.

I drove to the Library and left my car in the outer courtyard. My secretary looked surprised to see me. She was her same sweet sexy self, I thought, as I watched her approach with a message marked "urgent."

"It's our union president," she said, arching her eyebrows. "She's in trouble--again."

I glanced at the word "sabotaged" and, frowning, reached for my telephone. I called her headquarters.

"Rudy!" Arbie cried. "Where have you been? There's been a disaster here."

"What happened?" I asked calmly.

"Somebody blew up my headquarters last night," she said angrily. "The bomb was set on our floor, but our door is heavy metal and bomb-proof so it deflected the blast upwards, and it took the roof off."

"What!" I shouted.

"They spilt gasoline all the way down the stairs and that spread the fire to all floors. If there weren't a fire station next door, we'd have had a roaring inferno."

"Anyone hurt?"

"No, it was in the early hours of the morning, I think," she said. "The fire captain got trapped on the second floor and almost lost his life."

"I'll be right there," I said and hung up. "I'll be back," I cried to my secretary who was waving other messages at me.

This time, I thought, the order did not come from Lanzetta who was still in London preparing to return. It must have been Bratwurst or Poppin. The glass front door of the building, in which Arbie's headquarters was located, was smashed and wrenched off its hinges. The hallway was burnt and stained with wet. The stairs looked unsafe. The railing was burnt away, and the steps were charred. The massage parlor on the second floor opened onto a deserted room of cubicles. On the third floor, the messenger service manager, the same blond-haired, thin fellow who had taken the stabbing intended for Arbie and was now recovered, collected the furniture from his office, among which were folding chairs which I recognized as belonging to the Guild. On the fourth floor, I found the union's iron door blown off its hinges and flat on the floor of the outer room. The headquarters, untouched by the fire, looked a mess. The furniture was tossed about, and the shutters and the glass windows of the room office were smashed through. Arbie, kneeling by a vertical file, looked up in alarm.

"Rudy!" She ran to me and threw her arms about me. "I thought you were a murderer."

"Poor sweetheart," I comforted her. "How long have you been here?"

"Since about ten." She hugged me for more sympathy. "I found it like this after a grievance hearing at the Central Building. The firemen broke in through here. But our files are okay. Nothing missing."

"What are you going to do with them?" I looked at the desks, chairs, and refrigerator.

"The library maintenance has agreed to put it in storage, and I've been waiting hours for movers to take them all out," she said, pacing the floor. "Half an hour ago, these fancy Dan movers I was waiting for told me they wouldn't carry anything down those stairs."

"So you can't get your files out?"

"I called movers from the Bowery. They'll move it. Christ! I never thought I'd be depending on winos to serve our Local. Meanwhile, I've been scared stiff expecting looters to come through here any minute." She paused and raised her hand in caution. "Listen!"

There was a noise in the courtyard, that space of cement between the walls of buildings, and I noticed the fire escape tremble.

Arbie looked out the window and drew back. "There's a guy climbing up here!"

I looked out to see a burly fellow in a brown sweater and carrying a hammer. The man was hammering boards over the window below.

"Who are you?" I shouted.

Pausing only a split second from his work, the intruder shouted, "Insurance," and continued hammering.

"Maybe that's the motive--arson," I said to Arbie. "Maybe Benbow wants to get the insurance money to renovate."

"And get rid of us at the same time," Arbie added.

"It's just as well you have to give up this dump," I said.

"It means the end of the Local's independence. We can't afford to rent another room around here." She looked glumly at him. "Now we'll be forced to move down to the Council building and come under Bratwurst's control and his bloody spies."

I put my arm about her shoulders. "Cheer up, sweetheart. How's the election going?"

"Who knows and who cares?"

The insurance engineer clambered into the room and began hammering away to seal the window in a barrage of noise. They moved into the next room.

"I'm suspicious, Rudy," Arbie said. "I've got to tell you something. You know, when I met in the Library this morning, the grievant and I were on time, but the directors were not. They had to be called together hastily as if they had not expected us to turn up. That never happened before. I've taken hundreds of grievance cases, and those guys were always ready and waiting. You know, Rudy, they knew about the fire-bombing, and they didn't say a word about it."

I looked at the floor. "You may be right," I said. "But you couldn't prove it."

"No, I'm sure I can't," Arbie said. "I don't know whether I want to go on being union president. I can't stand to look at them anymore."

"I'd be happier if you weren't," I said.

"Hell!" Arbie stamped her foot. "That's defeatism. Here!" She took the framed charter of the Local off the wall. "Take care of this for us, please, Rudy."

"Okay, sweetheart," I took it and kissed her. "But if I were management, I wouldn't want you to win the election."

"Most of my executive board feel the same way," she pouted. "They've got one attitude: accommodation. They want to kiss the bosses' asses and follow Bratwurst into the banker's pockets."

"Isn't anyone campaigning for you?" I asked.

"Alf Landy was, but he's gone on vacation," she laughed. "What a great leftist he turned out to be!"

I heard men coming up the stairs and turned to see a crew of movers from the Bowery. With faces red with drink, their clothes spotted and torn, they introduced themselves with forced cheerfulness.

I left Arbie as she directed the men in moving the files. I picked my way down the blackened stairs and thought that the Bowery movers, who knew how to survive, would be able to negotiate these stairs more easily. As I passed the massage parlor, I pictured the buxom ladies in bathing suits standing at the door. I suspected Benbow had set the fire, but on whose orders? I hitched the Local's charter under my arm and hurried back to my office where I put it behind a filing cabinet. I was angered by the destruction of the Library Guild. I guessed that Arbie would be defeated in the union election. The workers had to be beaten down and every vestige of independent spirit had to be crushed. I gritted my teeth and rang Detective Buckle.

Buckle's laconic voice answered. He seemed surprised that I was still alive.

"I can't tell you anything yet," I said. "But I want you to do me a favor. Pick up Benbow and charge him with firebombing Arbie Vine's Local."

Buckle chuckled. "You'd better come up with some proof."

"I want to know who was behind it," I said.

"We'll pressure him," Buckle promised. "By the way, we just got word at the station that Lanzetta died of a massive heart attack on a flight back from London."

"My God!" I said.

"It looks suspicious," Buckle added. "He was traveling with an international agent by the name of Major Boyle."

"Really!" I cried. A rush of relief and joy suddenly filled me. "Are you sure about this?"

"Of course. Why do you ask me?" Buckle said, annoyed.

"Because I was assigned for the job."

"Then you're in trouble," Buckle said quickly. "Because that means they've lost faith in you."

"Thanks for the good news," I said and hung up.

Obviously Everyman had changed his mind, or forgotten that he had asked me to finish off Lanzetta. Maybe Everyman had already taken over Lanzetta's real estate properties. Was he joking when he suggested that I shoot Lanzetta? Was it some diabolical humor of his? Was he setting me up for something else? One could never be sure of what Everyman was thinking. Suddenly, I remembered something. I had observed when Major Boyle and Everyman met that I had the distinct impression that they were equal in stature and acted independently of one another. Boyle could have been taking orders from someone else when he killed Lanzetta. I began to look methodically through my messages when my telephone rang. My secretary had gone on a break. I answered reluctantly.

"Thank heavens I found you!" It was Tally Leyden. "I've been looking all over. Everyman is furious. Something's happening to our flow of funds. Our Panama source has dried up suddenly, and our European accounts are in a mess. Something is drastically wrong. Someone's tampering with the funds, and only Max had access to them. Consequently, he's been giving me suspicious looks and wonders whether Max is really dead!"

"Is the organization in trouble then?" I asked innocently.

"It will be if we don't straighten out this mess. Where is Max?"

"In hiding," I said firmly.

"Rudyard, I can be killed!" Leyden's voice rose an octave.

"So can I," I replied with a chuckle. "Lanzetta's dead, so it appears that Everyman has decided not to put me to the test of killing him."

"If he finds that Max is still alive," Leyden said, "you're as good as dead. And so am I."

"Well, then, we'll have to work together to save our mutual skins, won't we?" I said. "We must find a way to put the organization out of commission somehow, and that's just what your brother is doing."

"That's impossible. The organization is too huge and too powerful. Beyond anyone's reach. What Max is doing would be a temporary setback," Leyden scoffed. "They can repair the damage in a week."

"Who is 'they'?" I asked. "Who's behind Everyman?"

"A score of really powerful people," Leyden said dejectedly. "They can't be touched."

"We'll have to try, whatever the odds. Think of something and meet me at eight tonight at Hector Bratwurst's union office."

"Bratwurst's!"

"He's due back from Panama tonight, and he'll go right to his office, or so I overheard Everyman say," I said. "I think your brother has put Bratwurst into a lot of trouble."

"I'll be there!" Tally said.

As I hung up, I caught a glimpse of a black man looking into my office and pulling himself quickly back out again. I stared at the door and nervously took my gun from its holster. The face seemed familiar, but the motion had been so quick I wasn't sure. Then Gabriel appeared smiling and striding jauntily into the office.

"Don't be alarmed, Rudy," he said. "Just makin' sure you were alone."

I relaxed and put my gun back into its holster. "You know, you're getting more mysterious every time I see you."

Gabriel came up to the desk and, still smiling, pulled out his pistol, and pointed it at my forehead. "I'm supposed to kill you, but I won't if you come peaceful-like." He put his gun in his pocket with his finger still on the trigger.

I gulped down my surprise and, standing up, said quickly: "And I thought you were my friend."

"I am, Rudy," Gabriel said taking my gun. "That's why I'm not killing you right now." He motioned for me to walk ahead of him. "We'll take your car at the 40th Street entrance."

"Won't they get mad when they see that you're taking me prisoner instead of finishing me off?" I asked.

"It's my option," Gabriel said.

My secretary came down the hallway toward us. I pretended I didn't know her.

Her smile of greeting froze on her face as she realized I was snubbing her. She looked after us and, shrugging, continued to the office.

The guard at the 40th Street entrance barely looked up from the paper he was reading in his wooden booth as we passed by. Gabriel made me unlock the passenger door, get in, and slide over to the wheel. He took his gun out of his pocket and rested it in his lap as we drove into the street.

"You know that house on 57th and Park?" Gabriel said.

"Thanks a lot," I said as I thought of the torturers and the cell-like rooms I had expected never to see again.

TWENTY-SIX

"How do you know that I know about that house of torture?" I asked. "Are you with Everyman's organization?"

"Not directly," Gabriel smirked. "I worked for Kroneweiss. I've never met Everyman."

"Worked?" I asked. "Past tense?"

"He was blown up on a flight out of Miami this afternoon," Gabriel said indifferently. "All passengers dead."

I slowed the car. "And Hector Bratwurst?"

"He was with him."

"Phew! Who did it?" I asked with amazement.

"Never mind who did it. Everyman is suspected," Gabriel said. "You're Everyman's bodyguard so I'm to put you out of commission."

"But how come you work for those thieving bankers?" I cried incredulously.

"'Cause I need to eat and sleep like everybody else," Gabriel said. "The Kroneweiss crowd didn't get on with Lanzetta and his mob, so I found a place where I was useful for the stuff I knew."

"What are you going to do about me, Gabriel?"

"I won't kill ya unless I have to," Gabriel said seriously. "I want to see which way the wind's blowin'."

"So Everyman thought that Kroneweiss and Bratwurst had diverted the millions from Panama to their own use," I surmised uneasily. "Poor Hector! and all those other passengers--completely innocent!"

Gabriel seemed to pick up his ears. "Who said anything about money," Gabriel said, his suspicion of me increasing. Then, cunningly, as if he were in the know, he asked. "Do you know where the money went?"

"I might," I smiled cunningly, in turn. I suddenly realized I might be able to persuade Gabriel to keep me alive by pretending I would give him this vital piece of information.

"Look, Rudy," Gabriel spoke seriously, his black eyes probing my face. "I'll make a deal with you. If we can get that money for ourselves, we can kiss these white asses good-bye."

"How do I know I can trust you and you won't betray me?" I asked.

"I hate the buggers!" Gabriel cried. "They're racists. They got me to do things to my own kind that I can never forgive them for!"

"Then why threaten your friends?" I asked.

"If I let you go, Rudy, I'd be dead within a day. And they'd get you anyway," Gabriel explained sadly. "I'm trapped and I been this way all my damned life."

"I'm fighting them," I said pulling the car to a stop outside the house on 57th Street. "And I'm just one of hundreds. Think of all those prosecutors, judges, investigators, and so on in Italy and Argentina and dozens of other countries who've been exterminated because they felt as you and I do. The risk I'm taking is like nothing when you think of them."

"Yeah," Gabriel said, "but you're white middle-class. You've got somethin' to gain if you win. But what have I got?"

"The same as me," I argued. "We're working for ideals, for the common good. That's what every battle is about, Gabriel. Everyone of us who fights, if he survives, is a contributor to that kind of world."

Gabriel looked at me for a moment, then he put his gun away, and gave my gun back to me. I heaved a sigh of relief.

"You'd better get us to do somethin' smart fast," Gabriel said angrily, "Or I'm goin' to regret this."

I laughed. "Only thing I can think of is to go to the center of the storm." I pulled the car into the traffic. "I'm still Everyman's bodyguard, and you're going to help me do my duty."

"Everyman's safe so long as he stays home," Gabriel said. "The crowd I'm with won't invade his fortress."

I stopped at the toll booth before the bridge leading to Long Island. "Who gave you the order to kill me?"

"A guy from Bratwurst's union, Harold Poppin."

"Poppin!" I started the car with a jerk.

"He was ravin' mad about Bratwurst's bein' killed," Gabriel continued. "He even broke down. I almost felt sorry."

"But Poppin's taking orders from someone," I insisted.

"Oh yeah, yeah," Gabriel nodded, "but I don't know who it is."

"Whoever blew up that plane was a cold-blooded monster," I said. "I don't think Everyman did it."

"Why not?"

"He's a thinker. He'd use Kroneweiss and Bratwurst to find out about where the funds are that were supposed to have been stolen by them," I said. "Everyman's not the kind to act rashly by jumping to conclusions."

"That's hard to follow," Gabriel said. "Why would they want Everyman killed, then, if they knew he didn't kill Bratwurst?"

"Whoever the mysterious power is, he could suspect Everyman of being in league with Kroneweiss and Bratwurst," I argued. "Remember, we're not talking about peanuts. We're talking about billions of dollars. That's enough to cause a falling out among thieves."

We talked in this vein, each adding what he knew of the secret organization of which he had recently become a part, until I reached Everyman's hotel headquarters. The security was heavy. I was stopped three times before I could park by the building.

"These guys have come out of the grass," I said. "I had no idea they were around."

When we ascended the stairway to Everyman's office, we found no one. I led the way to the stairwell on the far side of the room and descended to the computer room. The scene was of barely controlled hysteria. Men and women were dashing about among the machines, paper was strewn about the floor, buzzings and alarm systems sounded here and there that sent the accountants into panic. Everyman towered over a group of men, to whom he was giving orders, and punctuated his words with thrusts of his long arms.

I followed by Gabriel, who regarded the confusion with apprehension, stood behind Everyman and confronted him as he turned round to rush off in another direction. Everyman almost knocked me down.

"What the damned...!" Everyman shouted. "The last thing I need now is a bodyguard."

"Wrong!" I cried. "You've been targeted for assassination by someone in the organization."

"So what else is new," Everyman said angrily. "Our whole financial operation is all screwed up. We're losing billions! There'll be bank failures right across the world."

"My job is to look after you," I said. "So I'm warning you that someone you know could kill you."

Everyman looked at me suddenly with amusement. "Who's your friend?" he nodded at Gabriel.

"He's part of us and you can trust him," I said.

"Like I can trust you?" Everyman asked. "I smell the dead hand of Max Leyden in all my troubles. I hope, for your sake, that I am mistaken."

"I hope so," I said, uneasy under Everyman's stare.

"I'm too busy now," Everyman said. "Get on with your job and we'll talk this evening."

There was something final about his last word, as if "evening" were equivalent to "good bye" or "sweet dreams."

Everyman brushed past us, his great body moving like a huge locomotive on a twisting track. Gabriel and I went back to Everyman's office where I poured two glasses of beer from the bar. We raised our glasses and I caught sight in a nearby monitor of Harold Poppin approaching the front door of the hotel.

"Our friend from the Council is paying his respects," I said to Gabriel and pointed to the video. I took out my pistol and held it behind my back.

"I'd better get out of sight," Gabriel said and moved behind the bar.

I took my beer and stood in the center of the room to await my visitor. Poppin approached puffing slightly from the stairs. Surprise transfigured his face when he saw me, but, recovering quickly, he adopted his usual jaunty sarcastic manner.

"I didn't expect to see you here, my man," Poppin said with a sneering smile.

"I protect the Big Man from unwelcome visitors," I said. "What's your business?"

"So you've been one of us all along," Poppin said with admiration. "You had me fooled."

"What's your business?" I asked patiently.

"Well," Poppin shuffled on his feet as if his large stomach was getting too heavy to carry. "Now that Hector's passed away, there's a vacuum at the head of the Union. I want Everyman's help in getting the Executive Directorship."

"The Delegates vote for whom they want," I said.

Poppin laughed as if he thought me naive. "Elections can be fixed just like we're arranging one against your girlfriend," he smiled. "But the way things are going against her, she would have lost anyway."

"The count's in?" I asked with interest.

"Being counted," Poppin said. "That's one cat we'll be glad to see the last of. Man, was she a pain!"

I thought of the problems Arbie had given this union bureaucrat over the years as he tried to keep her actions to a minimum. "She'll be back," I said. "Were you in on the bombing of her headquarters?"

"Who me?" Poppin raised his eyebrows in mock surprise. "Would I do such a thing?" His demeanor changed, however.

"Like ordering my assassination?" I said.

Poppin looked worried. "What do you mean? Why did you say that?" he cried. "Why would I do a thing like that?" He became suddenly agitated as if he could no longer control his violent feelings.

"Not you, buster, you're too insignificant," I said. "You just take orders."

Poppin drew his gun and pointed it at me. "This conversation has gone on long enough. Where's Everyman?"

I stepped to the side and motioned for Poppin to follow me to the far end of the room. At that instant a gunshot sounded, and, Poppin, gripping his arm, let his gun fall to the carpet. I returned my gun to its holster as Gabriel, holding his pistol, stepped out from behind the bar. Poppin, thinking that Gabriel had shot him, gaped in disbelief.

"You sure are one stupid guy," Gabriel said, shaking his head. "Try and force your way in here. Man! Unbelievable!" He picked up Poppin's gun and pocketed it.

Poppin stared at him with a hurt look. "I should have known I couldn't trust you."

We heard someone rushing up the stairs and turned to see two uniformed guards enter the room. I explained that Poppin was trying to kill Everyman, and watched as they took him away. Poppin shouted angrily back over his shoulder, "You fucking bastard, I'll get you!"

"What I know of this place," Gabriel mused, "he won't get out of here alive."

"Rudyard!"

I turned to see Tally Leyden enter the room.

"I heard the shot, but I'm truly surprised to see you here. You know, I'm in the same position as that madman who was just hustled out of here. I'm under house arrest."

"Because of the financial mess?" I asked, amused at Tally's predicament.

"Don't laugh. You can't leave here either."

Alarmed, I glanced at Gabriel who seemed resigned. "Okay," I said to Leyden. "What do we do?"

Tally shrugged. "Wait. Just wait. You wanted to bring down this organization? It might just happen."

I shook my head. "It's too huge, too deeply entrenched, too many people involved who profit from every operation of the organization."

"You are correct," Everyman's clear, deep voice said. The big man appeared suddenly, as if from nowhere, at the top of the stairs. He had just left the control room below and, after pausing, as if to catch his breath, he walked toward us. "It is the activity that transcends the players. Remove the players and other players will take their place. As long as guns, babies, women and drugs are in demand, there will be willing players to run the operation for profit."

"And what if that profit turns into loss?" Leyden asked.

Everyman frowned, his eyes glowing angrily at him. "Your brother seems to succeed in that endeavor, but he can't destroy us." Everyman turned and glowered at me. "So you knew Max Leyden was alive. You helped him and allowed him to hurt us. And all along you lied to me."

I expected to be shot on the spot.

"Will you get me a scotch and whisky?" Everyman called to Gabriel and sank into a chair. He seemed exhausted. For the first time I saw Everyman down. Everyman motioned at the chairs near him, signaling that the others should sit. "To be truthful, I don't mind if this part of the organization goes kaput," he said softly. "I need a rest. Your brother is actually doing me a favor, Leyden."

"But our whole international business is threatened," Leyden said. "There's bound to be government investigators looking into the bank crashes, and they are bound to find out about our billions, and the whole cat will be out of the bag."

"They'll have a devil of a time!" Everyman shouted. "Thanks to your brother; he has mixed things up so thoroughly, it will take months, maybe years, to unravel the mess. I wish them luck!"

Gabriel brought him his scotch and sat with us. Everyman looked at Gabriel curiously with a slight hint of suspicion in his eyes.

Everyman took a long drink and smacked his lips. "So, I am to be assassinated on the orders of an unknown, eh, Rudyard?" he said. "Now listen, all of you. Let us not concern ourselves with the motive for wanting me out of the way. Frankly, I can think of a dozen motives. Now, personally, I don't want to be deprived of some years on a sunny island where I have my nest egg, which answers your question as to why I put you all under house arrest. Not that I think any of you would murder me, or you wouldn't be here in the first place. I choose my men carefully. You are all loyal, and the way you dealt with this Poppin character deserves my sincere thanks." He nodded at me and Gabriel. We nodded back. He took another long drink. "Fact is, you have been a good and loyal bodyguard," he continued looking at me, "which leads me to the conclusion that you don't believe that I gave the order to blow up Bratwurst's plane."

I nodded.

"Which brings me to the point I'm going to make." Everyman looked directly at me. "Your next and last job for me is to find out who my would-be killer is and settle his hash so that I can enjoy my declining years in peace."

"I myself would like to know and do that anyway," I said.

"In return," Everyman continued, "the three of you will earn your liberty." He smiled. "I give you the present of your life in return for mine. Fair deal?"

"Sounds fair," Gabriel said.

"On one condition, though; no recriminations against Max!" Tally interposed.

"None!" Everyman said, "at least, not from me. His treacherous secret is safe with me." He finished his scotch and stood up. "Give me another day of fooling around with this mess. That's all the time I need before I disappear."

"Agreed," I said.

Everyman strode across the room to the stairwell, and, with a final wave of his big hand, he descended into the control room now so thoroughly out of control.

I went to the telephone by the bar, which was deserted and therefore safe to use, and called Detective Buckle. Buckle told me that after three hours of questioning, Benbow admitted that the order to firebomb Arbie Vine's headquarters came through Harold Poppin from someone in the Public Library.

"Incredible!" I gasped. "You know, Arbie was right all along. She always claimed that the library management wanted her out of the way more than Bratwurst did, and I always thought it far-fetched."

"Whoever it is," Buckle warned, "has your number now. By the way, there is a Father Ian who wants to get in touch with you. He can be reached at Barb Janes's residence."

I checked Barb Janes's number in my address book and dialed it. "Max and the good Father must be dispensing the ill-gotten millions to many good causes," I said to Tally while I waited for Barb to answer. Barb passed the phone immediately to Ian. I recognized the youthful idealism in his voice.

"Rudyard, we need you here. We've been receiving death threats, and the police can't really help us."

"Is Max there?"

"He's in his office on Wall Street where he has the means to divert funds as planned. I've supplied him with a long list of worthy recipients."

"Okay, listen carefully. I want you and Barb to go to the Union Council right away. It's across from you. Go to Alex Mackart's office and tell him what's happening. Barb knows him," I said.

Barb was on the line. "Petula Clarkson's been callin' us. Wants to see me about some Democratic Party business. I keep puttin' her off, but she's comin' anyway."

"Get over to the Council right away!" I cried. "Petula Clarkson is the last person you want to see."

"You suspect her?" Barb laughed in surprise.

"Play it smart and safe, please," I said urgently. "Tell Alex we'll be in touch!" I hung up and, turning to Gabriel, handed him the keys to the car in the yard below. "See if Everyman's men are making Poppin talk. When you find out who was directing him, meet us at the Council HQ in Manhattan." I turned to Tally. "Let's leave in your car. I think I know who is behind it all, but it would be nice if Gabriel can confirm it."

TWENTY-SEVEN

Until the last minute, I was not sure that Everyman really intended to let us leave so that it was with great relief when Tally Leyden and I passed out the main gate away from that mad center of world "intelligence." The sun was bright in the late afternoon as we sped into Manhattan

"I can't figure you out," I said. "You're on the far right, you work hand-in-glove with an organization that thinks nothing of blowing up innocent people, and you're ready to junk the whole business to save your brother's life."

"Well," Tally said defensively, "Max's life is worth something. Besides, I wasn't getting much out of the organization, anyway. The big money was going to other people. My lack of dedication was beginning to show, and it was becoming dangerous." He laughed abruptly. "That's when I got you in so you could get me out."

"Either you took a great risk in putting such blind confidence in me," I said as I regarded the handsome features and slicked-down hair of this ruthless young entrepreneur behind the wheel of his car, "or you were desperate."

"I was desperate," Tally admitted. "I still am because the most we've done is to shut down one of the branch offices. Everyman may keep his word to say nothing about Max, but word will somehow leak out to the others, and our lives will be worthless."

"Does that include me?" I wondered.

Tally laughed. "You were Everyman's responsibility. They won't bother with you. But Max and I are different. We are part of the group. We can't run and hide anywhere. That is why it's essential that we change our identities completely. We can start again somewhere in the Caribbean or in the South Pacific, and, knowing Max, I bet he's already arranged for a nest egg, as Everyman put it, to be forwarded to wherever we're going."

"I have a hunch you'd better get us to Max's office soon or he won't be going anywhere," I warned.

Tally frowned as he weaved in and out of the traffic on the F.D.R. Drive with intense determination. He brought us into the Wall Street area and to a stop before a tall glass building.

"I'll stay in the car," Tally said. "He's in 1019."

I felt uncomfortably out of place in modern rich buildings. They seemed designed for people from another planet. I took a crowded elevator to the tenth floor and rushed down the hall to Max's office. A plump woman with a dour face confronted me when I pushed through the door.

"He just left," she said, "with another gentleman." She was surprised by the urgency of my plea for a description of the man and answered, rather apologetically, "He was short, balding, with a broad forehead, spoke in a clipped voice. Why? Is anything wrong?"

I ran back to the elevator and leaped into one of them as its doors were closing. "The worst has happened," I told Tally as I got into the car. "They've taken him."

"What do we do?" Tally looked frightened.

I threw up my hands. "Drive to the Library."

Tally looked at me quizzically and was presently driving in pace with the green traffic lights up 6th Avenue.

I instructed him to drive into the inner courtyard of the Library. We paused at the guard's station long enough for Ajax to identify me. When we walked from the courtyard to the door of the building, I asked Ajax about the shiny new Plymouth parked in the yard.

"That's Mr. Raikes's car," Ajax said. "Just drove in with another gentleman."

"Was the other gentleman red faced with graying sideburns?" Tally asked.

"Yes sir," Ajax said, looking askance at Tally.

As Tally followed me up the stairs to my office, he argued, "But Raikes can't be doing Max in. Raikes is with the Central Intelligence Agency."

"Still?" I asked doubtfully. "I know he was once."

"Remember that night when you overheard our meeting in the President's office upstairs?" Tally said excitedly. "Raikes had called it to put pressure on Bratwurst to come down hard on his union members, and also to tell us members of the organization to cool it for a bit. He warned us that certain people in the government felt that some of our activities had gone too far and that some Congressmen and reporters were getting suspicious."

"So that means Raikes is a good guy?" I asked, sorting through the messages that my secretary had left on my desk.

"Everyman called him a 'Waverer'--a conservative who had to be persuaded to vote liberal for his self-interest. He has influence over the Kroneweisses and the Bratwursts."

"Here it is!" I said, pulling out a paper on which my secretary had scribbled, "Call Annie," and a number in Yonkers.

Annie answered her phone and complained about being limited to only one massage parlor now that the place on 43rd Street burned out. "But last time I was working, I heard Poppin with a buddy of his talkin' about you, Rudy. They were plannin' to use you to get at all the men, or something like that. I thought I'd warn you."

"They didn't say 'Everyman' did they?" I asked.

"Everyman! That was it! Does this good deed earn me another drink at the Plaza? This housewife bullshit is boring me stiff."

"Anytime," I promised. "I'll call you. Was Poppin's buddy short and bald?" I asked.

"Sure was," Annie said, "but easier to handle than Poppin."

I asked Tally to follow me as I led the way up a narrow stairway leading off the first floor hallway and into a small paneled room where the telephone operator was settling down for the night shift.

She was pleased to see me and agreed to let me listen into the next call from Raikes's office.

"He's getting a call now, Mr. Mack. Just put that thing in your ear and listen in, honey."

I winked at Tally. "Like the CIA," I said, putting an earphone to my ear.

It was the hoarse, excited voice of Gabriel that disappointed me at the same time as it pleased me to have Gabriel confirm my suspicions. "They had Poppin on the verge of spillin' the beans," Gabriel was saying, "so I had to spring him loose. But they got him before he got to Everyman."

"And what about Everyman?" Raikes demanded.

"He was hit. I don't know if he was killed. I had to get the hell out of there."

"Just get lost," Raikes said. "The operation's over, and I don't want to hear from you unless I call you. Poppin really screwed up and so did you for not taking care of Rudyard Mack."

"He doesn't know from nothin'," Gabriel said sarcastically. "And you won't hear from me unless the payments stop comin'." He hung up.

I signaled to the operator to shut the key. I raised my finger to keep Tally from speaking and, after a moment, signaled the operator to open the key again. "Who's he calling?" I asked.

"I think someone in Washington, D.C.," she said.

A gruff hello sounded over the line. Raikes spoke quickly, "Everyman's finished, I've got Max Leyden with me. Do we need him, or shall I dispose of him?"

There was a pause and then the word came in a voice of tired indifference. "Dispose."

I did not wait to hear more. "Let's go, Tally," I said as I put down the earphone and dashed ahead to the stairwell and up to the second floor hallway.

We paused in the deserted hall, for it was long past the closing time, and caught our breath. I took out my pistol and pushed into Raikes's office. Raikes, sitting behind his desk, reached in alarm inside his coat when he saw us, but I cried, "Freeze!" as I had seen detectives do in the movies. Raikes brought his hand out of his coat empty, and I went behind his chair, and took the gun out from under his coat. Max Leyden, happy incredulity spreading over his face, sat on his hands on the floor before the desk.

"Tally!" Max Leyden shouted in disbelief and, springing to his feet, embraced his brother who ran to him. "Are you all right?"

"What do you mean, all right?" Tally laughed, tears in his eyes.

"He told me they'd kill you if I didn't go with him," Max explained happily, pointing to Raikes.

"That's one kidnap victim they didn't have," I said. Then, turning to Raikes, I said, "Now Joshua T. Raikes, we could turn you in and have your dirty deeds and your government connection exposed in a long court trial."

Raikes, his clever eyes narrowing, replied slowly, "You could, but you won't. Because if I'm exposed so would be the Leydens and people more important than you would dream possible, and it would be worse for them than for me."

"He's right," Max said. "The organization will take care of him for it will continue to function despite the damage done to the American operation. It is still a very powerful operation with memberships of the highest influence in every part of the world."

"But I can testify against him in the courts of this nation," I said sternly, "and maybe we can demand a full-scale congressional investigation."

"Maybe," Raikes admitted, "and maybe not."

I loathed the smugness of the man, but realized that Raikes was an important member of the organization and that nothing, not even America's highest courts would touch him. The organization was too powerful for me to take on alone. I gestured to the library note paper on Raikes's desk. "At least, I can make you write your resignation to the Library President owing to ill health," I suggested, refusing to be beaten by Raikes.

Raikes smiled grimly and with a shrug began to write. I moved to watch over Raikes's shoulder as Tally and Max chatted animatedly.

"That's good," I said as Raikes signed his statement. "Now, write a note to Miss Arbuthnott Vine and apologize for contributing to her defeat."

"That's a silly request to ask, Rudyard," Raikes said. "What good will it do her?"

"It'll be a nice souvenir," I said. "Go on." Raikes at first refused, but when I jabbed him with the pistol, he complied reluctantly.

After he signed it, I picked up both letters. "A rather brief apology," I said and, folding the papers, put them in my pocket. "By the way, how did your candidate Bradley Tone make out?"

"Good!" Raikes cried. "They bought him a bookstore where he'll make a good living." He grinned smugly.

I swallowed my irritation. "And Petula Clarkson? How did you reward her for taking away the black vote?"

"The Democratic Party will reward her with something," Raikes said jauntily. "You're a hard-working man, Rudyard, but this time you're way over your head."

"I'm a patient man, Mr. Raikes. I can wait you out. For, after all, the pendulum swings," I said. "Let's get out of here," I said to the Leydens. Then, turning to Raikes, I announced, "From now on, Joshua T. Raikes, the security of the public library is my turf. I consider you a threat. So make sure you never come back."

Raikes, swaggering, got to his feet, and walked ahead of the others out the door and down the hallway to the cars in the courtyard. Tally and Max were chatting and laughing over their experiences. They barely noticed Raikes drive away in his car. I got into the back seat and thought of Arbie as Tally and his brother chatted away in the front seat.

"Oh, I'm taking you to the Union Council building, aren't I, Rudy?" Tally asked suddenly.

I nodded. "I wonder who blew up Bratwurst's plane."

"That was the work of Colombian drug dealers," Max explained. "They didn't want the competition."

I fell silent as the brothers continued talking. I watched the buildings on Fifth Avenue pass by the window. Now that the strain that I was under began to dissipate, I sympathized with Arbie's loss of the Local presidency. She had put so much effort into it for so long, it seemed terribly unfair that she had to return to her librarian job. I knew the library management would isolate her from library activities in an effort to keep her from ever being a force in the organization again. So her library career, too, was ruined.

"Here we are!" Tally cried, pulling to a stop at the Council building. "Thanks for all you've done, Rudyard. I'll inform the right people about Raikes. He's finished, don't worry. And they'll find Gabriel, too."

"I'll remember you in my prayers," Max said, stretching his arm over the seat back to shake my hand. "Tell Barbie we're waiting for her."

I left them with a wave and plunged through the swing doors. Tally's promise of retribution for Raikes and Gabriel consoled me because I knew Tally, despite his bantering tone, was deadly serious. Loud music sounded from a meeting room on the ground floor.

"You looking for Arbie Vine's party?" asked the building super, giving a hitch to his pants and pointing to the sound of the music.

I walked into a party in full swing and encountered Barb Janes who threw an arm around me and gave me a big kiss on the cheek.

"Max is waiting for you outside," I told her. "You're probably going to Hawaii or parts west."

Barb's eyes rounded with joy. "Rudy, you always bring me the best presents." She turned to wave to Alex Mackart and dashed away.

Alex approached with a drink of scotch for me. "Congratulate me," he smiled impishly. "I've just been appointed to take Hector Bratwurst's job."

"Yeah," said Joseph standing somewhat tipsy beside him. "That means my salary goes way up."

I toasted Alex. "Maybe you can give Arbie a job in the Council," I suggested.

Alex raised his hand defensively and backed away with a smile as if to say, "No radicals."

I spotted Arbie who was talking to a willowy girl who, someone told me, was Isabelle, the children's librarian, the new Local president. Arbie looked suddenly sad when she saw me approach.

"We can always get married," I quipped.

"Oh, Rudy," she laughed. "You took the words right out of my mouth." She grimaced suddenly. "Isabelle is just a tool of the Council and management. The membership will find out soon enough and want me back."

I was less optimistic about the good sense of the working man who was going to be deluged with propaganda from all sides for a long time, but I smiled reassuringly. I saw Detective Buckle move away from the buffet table and approach us with a huge grin on his round fat face. "We heard you really did a job on Long Island. We can't find Everyman, though."

"In a way, that's good. It's as if he was a mirage," I said. I took out Raikes's letter of resignation and handed it to him. "Will you kindly make copies and send it off. We'll discuss it later."

"Surprise," Arbie said to Buckle while he was reading Raikes's letter. "Rudy just proposed to me. But I think I still love the Union."

Buckle looked quizzically from her to me.

Beaming, I gave her Raikes's other letter in which he confessed to influencing the vote. "We'll frame this," I said and watched her tenderly as she read it.

"If I weren't looking forward to my new career as wife and mother," Arbie joked, "I'd use this confession to call for a new election." She put her arm about my waist. "But I'll wait for the next one and spend the interval with you, my sweet."

"That's a conspiracy I approve of," Buckle said.

finis

NOTES AND QUERIES

What are examples of conspiracies from our recent political experience? The P-2 Lodge in Italy, led by Gelli, operated for the extreme right in many parts of the world and was involved in assassinations and terrorist bombings, especially in the terrible destruction of life at the Bologna railway station. It controlled much of the international finance, only partly revealed by the scandals of the Vatican Bank and the Banco Ambrosiano. The ongoing investigations into the Italian Mafia's control over Italian political life is revealing a part of this global criminal activity. The Israeli-U.S. secret services connection which made millions for politicians and sacrificed hundreds of thousands of civilians in Third World countries to Ronald Reagan's right-wing agenda is well described in all its labyrinthine splendor in Ari Ben-Menashe's *Profits of War; Inside the Secret U.S.-Israeli Arms Network* (1992). Of the many examples, quite a few fit together as products from one plant of manufacture.

Who were the Waverers to whom Everyman and Rudyard Mack refer at one point and what significance does Everyman give to them in pursuing his goals? The Waverers were a group of Tories in England's House of Lords led by Lord Wharncliffe when the Lords controlled 19th Century England. Wharncliffe, who owned coal fields and was the primary pusher of Railway Bills through parliament in support of the Lancashire capitalists against the landed interests, persuaded these conservative large landholders to vote for the first Reform Bill on the second reading and secured its passage, thus beginning the shift in power away from the landed interests to the industrialists and financial classes. Today the clever Everyman sees that present-day conservatives, although somewhat concerned about the loss of civil liberties, are attracted to the global control which he promotes because of the large profits they can secure. He thinks they need only his persuasive pressure to commit themselves just as the Waverers of the 1830s committed themselves to changing the power structure in England, the consequences of which they did not foresee.

How is it that the conservative Rudy and the socialist Arbie are attracted to one another? They are essentially honest and possibly recognize the unexpressed half of themselves in the other.

REPRODUCE AND SEND TO DAVUS PUBLISHING, 150 NORFOLK ST. S., SIMCOE, ON. N3Y2W2 CANADA or P O BOX 1101, BUFFALO, N.Y. 14213-7101 UNITED STATES or ASK YOUR BOOKSTORE. [Libraries call Coutts 800-263-1686] PLEASE INCLUDE $3 FOR POSTAGE AND HANDLING FOR ORDERS FROM 1-3; $4 FOR 4-7; $6 FOR 8-10. FOR LARGER ORDERS CALL DAVUS 519 426 2077.

PLEASE SEND ME _____ COPIES OF THE GRAND CONSPIRACY; A NEW YORK LIBRARY MYSTERY FOR $10.95 (U.S.). & 14.95 (Cdn.)

..........COPIES OF WHO REALLY INVENTED THE AUTOMOBILE $17.95 Cdn., 13.95 U.S. "Excellent."

.... COPIES OF THE JENNY; A NEW YORK LIBRARY DETECTIVE NOVEL AT $7.95(U.S.).& $9.95 (Cdn) Library detective solves case of biggest stamp theft in U.S. history. "Held me rivetted"--*ROTARY ON STAMPS*; "a fascinating tale,"--*STONEY CREEK NEWS*. "fun reading,"--*GLOBAL STAMP NEWS*. "The solution is as surprising as it is ingenious."--*THE SIMCOE REFORMER*. "It gets Gold for the "whodunnit" plot and the exciting, don't-put-me-down read that it is."--*CANADIAN STAMP NEWS*. "The writing is fast paced, ... a pleasant diversion on a hot summer afternoon."--*THE CANADIAN PHILATELIST*.

.... COPIES OF HAMILTON ROMANCE; a Hamilton-Toronto Nexus $19.95 Cdn., $14.95 U.S. (Roamnce and society after World War II. A sesquicentennial edition.) "A good read... funny and sad, just like life itself, as it traces the tale of young love... when everything seemed so different, yet things weren't really so different."--STONEY CREEK NEWS.: "thoughtful and often humorous... an enjoyable, rebellious, anti-establishment rant,...deserves a wide audience" *VIEW*

..........COPIES OF CHOCOLATE FOR THE POOR; a story of rape in 1805 $13.95 Cdn. $11.95 U.S.. (Berkshires in 1805; a father accused of raping his daughter) "Held me spellbound," Angela Ariss, Children's Rights Advocate. "Gripping story...interesting cast of colourful characters...well written novel...Beasley paints pictures with short phrases."VIEW. "The political intrigues are brought to life vividly....Beasley allows us to see, and more importantly to feel, some of the forces that enmesh a man only too easily and drive him to acts otherwise incomprehensible." HAMILTON SPECTATOR.

.... COPIES OF THAT OTHER GOD, A NOVEL $18.95 (Am. and Cdn) American mystic brings people through telepathic communion into the universal subconscious to a realization of the God of humanity. "Compelling, really interesting, exciting...a cry for peace at a time of anarchy," *BRANTFORD EXPOSITOR*; "Absorbing....Gripping style, detailed observation, poetic images. Vital, entertaining, apocalyptic," Peter Rankin, NYC. "Compelling story [of] the saving values deep within the human spirit," *HUMAN QUEST*.

.... COPIES OF THROUGH PAPHLAGONIA WITH A DONKEY; A JOURNEY THROUGH THE TURKISH ISFENDYARS [illus.] $9.95 U.S. $11.95 Cdn. "Charmingly written,"--*EXPLORERS JOURNAL*; "Now that I have concluded my fourth re-reading, I have become...a thorough-going dweller in Paphlagonia and an ardent partisan of Bobby, the donkey"--*LOCAL 1930 NEWSLETTER*; "Insightful for students of cross-cultural communication."--*INTERNATIONAL JOURNAL OF INTERNATIONAL RELATIONS*.

.... .COPIES OF THE CANADIAN DON QUIXOTE; THE LIFE AND WORKS OF MAJOR JOHN RICHARDSON, CANADA'S FIRST NOVELIST $6.95 Cdn.; $5.50 U.S. "Definitive "; "Not only a good read but the fulfillment of 'an aching void'." *BRICK*; "Very useful... mass of new information," *TORONTO GLOBE & MAIL*. "A roaring good adventure yarn about a highly eccentric dreamer," *LIBRARY JOURNAL*. "Brings to life the early history of this country," *KINGSTON WHIG STANDARD*;

NAME:
ADDRESS:

ENCLOSED PLEASE FIND A CHEQUE TO DAVUS PUBLISHING FOR $................

ARBUTHNOTT VINE AND RUDYARD MACK OF **THE GRAND CONSPIRACY** FIRST APPEARED IN

THE JENNY; A NEW YORK LIBRARY DETECTIVE NOVEL (110 pages, ISBN: 0-915317-04-4 $7.95 Am. or $9.95 Cdn) Published Fall 1994] A fascinating tale based on a true story--the largest recovery of rare postage stamps in U. S. history. It's clever and keeps you guessing.--*Stoney Creek News*; The nearly insoluble twists and turns of changing suspects held me riveted. Beasley has detailed knowledge of the inner workings of the great library in New York which, together with his apparent excellent philatelic knowledge, make the story come to life with believable realism.--*Rotary on Stamps Bulletin;* An entertaining book based on the famous 24 cent U S airmail invert. One you would enjoy on a rainy afternoon.--*Global Stamp News;* An unexpected romance, in a nice little subplot. But the unraveling of a master plot is still the main focus and the solution is as surprising as it is ingenious--*The Simcoe Reformer;* The writing is fast paced, and for this reviewer the novel offered a pleasant diversion on a hot summer afternoon.--*The Canadian Philatelist.* It gets Gold for the "whodunnit" plot and the exciting, don't-put-me-down read that it is.--*Canadian Stamp News.* Available from Davus Publishing (150 Norfolk St. S., Simcoe, On N3Y 2W2, 519-426-2077)or through Christie and Christie at 1-800-263-1991